Thwarting her attackers . . .

They tried to pull me into the alley, but a hard stomp on a foot and a bite on a hand let me escape to dash toward the street, holding up the fabric of my ripped skirt. A carriage pulled up, the horses reined in before I collided with them. The Duke of Blackford jumped out. My savior, or reinforcements for my attackers?

I started to dash down the sidewalk, but strong arms grabbed me around the middle, wrapping my cloak tightly around me. I kicked out and hit my pursuer by driving the back of my head into his nose. He let go and I ran. Behind me, I heard grunts and thuds, wood against metal, wood against bone.

I glanced back to see the duke thrash one figure with his cane. As my other attacker rose from the ground, he was pummeled down again. I'd have to pass the fight to return to the safety of Lady Westover's. Too dangerous. I rushed away from the fracas.

Horses whinnied and coach wheels creaked, but no footsteps pursued me. I slowed my pace to a brisk walk, staying as far from the street as I could as I approached the corner. Looking over my shoulder, I saw two figures prone on the ground behind me and a large carriage with four horses nearly at my side.

"Miss Fenchurch."

I picked up speed. So did the horses, pulling past me.

The duke's familiar baritone came from the coach. "Wait, Miss Fenchurch. I'm trying to rescue you."

THE
VANISHING
THIEF

KATE PARKER

BERKLEY PRIME CRIME, NEW YORK

THE BERKLEY PUBLISHING GROUP
Published by the Penguin Group
Penguin Group (USA) LLC
375 Hudson Street, New York, New York 10014

USA • Canada • UK • Ireland • Australia • New Zealand • India • South Africa • China

penguin.com

A Penguin Random House Company

This book is an original publication of The Berkley Publishing Group.

Berkley Prime Crime Books are published by The Berkley Publishing Group.
BERKLEY® PRIME CRIME and the PRIME CRIME logo are a registered trademark of
Penguin Group (USA) LLC.

Library of Congress Cataloging-in-Publication Data

Parker, Kate, 1949–
The vanishing thief / Kate Parker.—Berkley Prime Crime trade paperback edition.
pages cm
ISBN 978-0-425-26660-1 (pbk.)
1. Booksellers and bookselling—Fiction.   2. Women private investigators—Fiction.
3. Kidnapping—Investigation—Fiction.   4. Parents—Death—Fiction.   5. Cold cases
(Criminal investigation)—Fiction.   6. London (England)—Fiction.   I. Title.
PS3616.A74525V36 2013
813'.6—dc23
2013027648

PUBLISHING HISTORY
Berkley Prime Crime trade paperback edition / December 2013

PRINTED IN THE UNITED STATES OF AMERICA

10 9 8 7 6 5 4 3 2 1

Cover illustration by Teresa Fasolino.
Cover design by George Long.
Interior text design by Kristin del Rosario.

*This book is dedicated to my mother
because she said I had to.*

Mothers are frequently right.

ACKNOWLEDGMENTS

No one creates a story that reaches publication without a great deal of help, and I've been blessed with wonderfully talented, supportive people on this journey. Lara Otis, a librarian at the University of Maryland Libraries, provided me with excellent Victorian-era sources on antiquarian books and their preservation. My daughter, Jennifer, who's always up for a research trip, introduced me to the Linley Sambourne house and other wonders of Victorian London.

Critique partners Hannah Meredith, Nancy Bacon, Gail Hart, and Peggy Parsons have spent years helping me hone the craft of writing. My agent, Jill Marsal of Marsal-Lyons Literary Agency, found the spark in this novel and helped me create a work worthy to be published. My editor, Faith Black, and the unknown artists and copyeditors at Berkley Prime Crime have taken my work a step further to create a book I am so proud to share with the world.

I thank them all. But most of all, I have to thank my husband. Even as he kept telling me to try something different in my writing and to add more bodies, he always believed the day would come when I'd be published and readers would discover my stories.

While the rest of the story is based on solid late-Victorian sources, I willfully threw out everything learned in seven semesters of college chemistry to create amylnitrohydrated sulfate and the fictitious Royal Society. These were created to honor the spirit of Victorian scientific research and the single-minded quests of so many now-famous Victorians. Any other errors, technical or otherwise, are my own.

CHAPTER ONE

EARLY spring rain drenched London in a cold damp that either kept customers away or drove them into the bookshop. Today the rain was in our favor. We had three browsers searching the shelves when a woman barreled in, flinging droplets in the musty air and onto the wooden floor. "The Duke of Blackford kidnapped Nicholas Drake and you must save him."

My assistant, Emma, looked up from the recent arrivals she was discussing with a female customer and said, "Is that a new novel?"

The woman planted thin fists on her hips, shoving back her cloak and displaying a green dress faded to the shade of mushy peas. "No. I'm demanding the Archivist Society do something to free Nicholas Drake from the Duke of Blackford."

All three customers stared at her, mouths agape. The Archivist Society unfortunately appeared in the penny press occasionally, earning us a notoriety we didn't desire.

I didn't want my customers to learn Emma and I worked

for the Archivist Society. Respectable women didn't court notoriety. Even the old queen kept her activities private. And our work required secrecy.

I had to silence this woman. Now.

Stepping forward from the gardening section, I said, "I'm Georgia Fenchurch, owner of Fenchurch's Books. You've come to the right place. We should be able to find answers to your questions about the Archivist Society and the Duke of Blackford as we do for all our customers. Everyone comes here for the most up-to-date sources of information in print." I swung my arms out to encompass our stock. "Perhaps you'd like to join me in my office. But first, let's do something about your outerwear."

She put her umbrella in the rack by the door and carried her soggy cloak into the back hall, where I hung it up. We entered my office and she looked around with a little sniff.

The room was a trifle crowded. Truthfully, the tiny space was stuffed, with two chairs, a desk, record storage cabinets, piles of books, and very little room to walk. But it was my office and I was happy with it. I moved the books off both chairs and, at my gesture, she sat in one chair and I on the other.

I was determined not to waste time. We might have more customers come into the shop, even in this rainstorm, and I make it a practice never to miss a sale. I can't afford to. "Who are you? And why have you come to me?"

"I'm Edith Carter. My next-door neighbor, Nicholas Drake, was abducted from his home by the Duke of Blackford in the duke's carriage last Thursday at eleven in the evening." The words spilled out in one quick gush as if she were afraid I'd stop her. If she'd gone into a long explanation, I would have.

"Have you been to the police?" I really hoped she hadn't so I could throw her out. I had paying customers to wait on.

"Yes. They spoke to his housekeeper, who said he'd gone to Brighton to visit a friend. They believed her."

"Perhaps he did."

"I saw him dragged out to the duke's high, antique carriage and tossed inside. Besides, would you go to Brighton in this weather?"

As if in answer, rain mixed with ice beat on the windowpanes looking out over the back alley, and the wind howled through every crevice. "Perhaps it's nicer in Brighton."

"Not until summer." She was snapping her answers at me.

I wasn't going to be dragged into a discussion about weather. I wanted her gone. "I repeat, why come to me?"

She smoothed her skirt, ignoring the mud splatter on the hem as she dug into her bag. "I saved this article from a recent newspaper. It contains the symbol of the Archivist Society, the same as you have in your front window. It also contains a picture of an unnamed young woman member of the Archivist Society. That member is you."

I don't know how the reporter learned I was a member. I don't advertise my membership. And the black-and-white portrait didn't show my better features, a pair of violet eyes and a long, graceful neck. However, if Edith Carter could recognize me that easily, perhaps my better features weren't that impressive.

"You don't need anyone's help to ask the Duke of Blackford if he knows where Mr. Drake is. You said the duke's carriage was involved. You should talk to him."

"I did ask him. He threw me out. He was frightfully rude. He—he threatened me."

Interesting. "Threatened you how, Miss Carter?"

"He said if I didn't leave his house immediately and stop asking questions about Mr. Drake, he would have me arrested and thrown into prison." The woman whispered the last word with terror in her eyes.

"Those were his exact words? Stop asking questions about Mr. Drake?"

"Yes. I've tried to be as accurate as possible."

"What do you hope the Archivist Society can accomplish?"

"Talk to the Duke of Blackford. Ask him to release Mr. Drake. I can't afford a ransom, but I doubt a man as rich as the duke would need one." The woman reached across the space between us and clutched my hand with a surprisingly firm grip. "You must help me. I've nowhere else to go. The police won't listen to me. And Nicholas is such a fine person."

Nicholas? I recognized the glow in the woman's eyes and the blush on her cheeks. Nothing could compel me to help her more than to see his importance in her heart. "You're in love with him."

Miss Carter jerked back as if I'd slapped her. Casting her eyes down, she said, "No. No, of course not."

I counted slowly in my head until the woman revealed all. I'd reached nine when Edith Carter turned her head to the side. "He's unobtainable. I don't wish to discuss this."

"He's married?"

Miss Carter gasped. "No. Not at all. Why would you say such a thing?"

"It's the most logical explanation as to why he's unobtainable."

The woman looked everywhere but at me. "It's a private matter. That's all I'll say on the subject."

Miss Carter was lying to me. I was willing to bet Nicholas Drake was married. Edith Carter wasn't prepared to reveal the truth, and that made her a terrible client. In spite of my doubts, I began the usual list of questions. "How long have you been Mr. Drake's next-door neighbor?"

"Since I moved in a year ago."

"Who moved in with you?"

"I—my parents."

"And you hope that if you organize Mr. Drake's rescue, he will feel what? Indebted to you?"

Edith Carter looked me straight in the eye. "I prefer his high regard, his love, to a debt of friendship."

"Do your parents approve of him?"

"They are not your concern. Mr. Drake is."

Miss Carter showed every sign of already being in a relationship with Mr. Drake. Since she appeared to be near thirty, perhaps her parents were not as worried about chaperoning her as they ought to be. Maybe she would get the happy ending I never could. A home and family with the man she loved.

I kept searching for a hole in her story. "You said you looked out last Thursday night at eleven and saw the Duke of Blackford's coach."

"Yes. I told you."

"You're completely certain the coach belonged to the Duke of Blackford. You couldn't have made a mistake about that?"

"I'm absolutely certain. The fog hadn't yet come in. The coach was stopped near a street lamp. It was the ancient, tall carriage with the matching black horses he always uses. I could see the crest clearly from my bedroom window. It was the Blackford crest. Two men, thugs in his employ no doubt, although they didn't wear livery, carried a third man out of the house. Mr. Drake."

"You saw his face?"

"Who else could it have been?"

Georgia suggested, "The duke visited and was taken ill."

Miss Carter dabbed at her eyes with her handkerchief. "The duke would never make a call in my neighborhood. I have no doubt it was Mr. Drake who was carried out."

"What is Mr. Drake's occupation?"

"He's a broker, arranging sales of artworks and jewelry between buyers and sellers."

"Perhaps the duke was there as either a buyer or seller and was taken ill during the negotiations. Perhaps this or another business arrangement required Mr. Drake to travel to Brighton." I spread my hands in a gesture of defeat.

"He would have told me if he needed to travel to Brighton or had a duke calling. You have to help us. Please. No one else can or will help. I haven't much money to pay for your services, but . . ."

This was a woman deeply in love. Despite my misgivings about her honesty, I knew I couldn't turn her down. She could lie about the facts, but her emotions were genuine. I knew. I'd had the same desperation in my voice when I'd cornered Sir Broderick a dozen years before, begging for his help in rescuing my parents. The mixture of grief and fear choking off the ability to speak can't be faked. My heart still ached over my failure to save my parents, and every time I heard that anguish in someone's voice, I was driven to ease my pain by helping a fellow sufferer.

Even as I called myself a fool, I said, "I'll speak to the duke. Then we'll see if we have enough to begin a search."

Miss Carter stood and nodded. "Thank you for seeing me on such short notice. Life without Nicholas is unbearable. And when I saw the blood on the floor—"

"What?" I sprang from my chair.

"When Mrs. Cummings, his housekeeper, arrived that morning, she found a pool of blood in the front hall. She cleaned it up, but it stained the wood."

"Did either of you tell the police this?"

"I did, but she denied it. It was just a stain when they arrived and could have been anything."

People didn't bleed profusely from business discussions. Not real blood. But people did kill for money, and I still knew nothing about Nicholas Drake or his finances. "Do you know anything of the items he was brokering currently?"

"No. But the Duke of Blackford is a terrible man. Mr. Drake was afraid of him." She reached out and grabbed my hands. Her grip hurt.

"Did he say why?"

"He said the duke's sister killed a friend of his. He's afraid his life's in danger, since he knows what really happened."

"What happened? When was this?"

Her voice dropped to a whisper. "Before I moved next door, so it was over a year ago. I won't say exactly what happened, but it had to do with the death of the duke's intended bride."

"You need to tell me what happened."

"I was sworn to secrecy. But I will say the duke and his fiancée had a terrible row over his sister. The next day, the sister and the fiancée met, and the fiancée was dead within the hour. Mr. Drake's life was threatened if he ever spoke of those events to anyone."

"Do you know where we can find a photograph of Mr. Drake? It would be very helpful if we could recognize him."

She let go of my hands and reached into a pocket. Gently she smoothed the back of the thick paper then handed the photo to me. It was postcard size, taken in a photography studio in Durham, showing a fair-haired young man with a pleasant face trying very hard to look serious and failing.

"May I keep this, please, for copying? I'll return it to you unharmed."

After a moment, she nodded.

I wrote down a few details and ushered Miss Carter into her cloak. As we walked to the front door of the shop, I saw all three customers had wandered into travel, the section closest to the office. All three were closely examining books, their faces averted. Emma stood with them, her business smile in place.

Miss Carter bid me good day and left, holding her umbrella at an angle to block the wind and rain. Then I turned and faced our customers. "Does anyone need help?"

With the excitement over, all three paid for their purchases and left, leaving Emma and me in an empty shop.

"Do we have a case, Georgia?"

"Possibly. I don't trust her, but the story is so amazing it may be true. Can you handle the shop by yourself?"

Emma glanced around the vacant shop and gave me a dry stare. I've seen strong men grovel at her feet after such a look, probably because of her blond beauty. After working with her for years, I hardly noticed anymore that men looked around me to stare at her.

That didn't mean that her youth, good looks, and self-assurance didn't annoy me on occasion. Not bothering to hide my sarcasm, I said, "Since you have no objections, I'll be absent for a few hours. More if I float down the Thames. Don't leave until I return."

She picked up a novel and sat on the stool behind the counter. The new electric chandelier above her gave perfect light for reading, even on a day when gray, waterlogged light came in the large front windows of the shop. "I have everything I need."

I checked the omnibus schedule and found the one I needed to take me into the new suburbs northwest of town. The vehicle was jammed but dry, and I managed to get a seat where I could look through the window at the activity outside. Pedestrians hurried along the sidewalk bundled in drab wool, pale faces peering out from under umbrellas and hats.

We were riding along Hyde Park Place just past Marble Arch, and I was staring at the crowded sidewalk. Moving smartly in the opposite direction, a book tucked under one arm, was my parents' killer.

As we approached, I could see most of his face above his ornately tied cravat, and then as we passed, I studied his profile under his top hat until a carriage blocked my view. I pressed my face to the glass, wishing the carriage away. It moved, and I was able to glimpse the murderer again from behind.

For a moment I stared openmouthed. He was dressed similarly to the other businessmen on the street, but I was certain.

It was him.

And I wasn't going to lose him a second time. Every muscle tensed as I leaped up. My heart pounded as I ran to the back of the bus, ready to jump off if the driver didn't stop the horses immediately.

"Wait, miss," the conductor said, blocking my path as he signaled the driver to stop.

After a dozen years, I'd finally seen the monster again. I pushed the conductor aside and was off before the horses came to a halt. Heavy traffic flowed around me, blocking my way to the sidewalk. Knowing the man I sought must have a minute's head start on me, I was braver than usual, dodging behind a brewer's cart and a hansom cab. After close misses with a carriage and horse waste in the road, I was on the sidewalk, pushing past people in my hurry.

There were top hats in front of me as far as I could see. Which one was his?

As I strode down the sidewalk, looking each man in the face as I passed, being shoved aside by taller, heavier bodies, I was once more a powerless seventeen-year-old. My parents were newly dead. I suddenly had no one in this world to care about me. Tears again welled up with the grief and the terror. That horrible day was never far from my mind.

I had been helping my mother dust the shelves, since we'd just opened for the morning, and this immaculately well-tailored man was our first customer.

My father came forward to greet the man when he entered our bookshop. The man took off his top hat as he entered but left his newspaper under his arm. His hair was a white blond or silver and his stance proclaimed him a man of power and status. The man talked in a low voice to my father, who took a step back and said, "We don't have anything like that."

The man grabbed him by the collar with his free hand and said, "I know better. Don't lie to me."

Then he threw my father to the side and forced his way behind the counter. My father's mouth opened and shut twice without any sound emerging, as he grabbed at the man's sleeve. The man began to search through the antiquarian volumes but didn't find what he wanted. In his fury, he knocked books and papers off the counter, which my father kept trying to catch.

Then the man removed a gun from inside the newspaper and pointed the barrel at my father. My father raised his hands as an antiquarian volume he'd caught slid from his grip and fell to the floor in a cascade of pages.

My mother gasped. The man said, "If you want to see your husband alive at the end of the day, do as I say, Mrs. Fenchurch. You, too, Miss Fenchurch."

His gaze on me made my skin feel like I'd fallen in a coal furnace, stabbing hot and falling away from my bones. How could I forget the wide brow, the long nose, the thin lips, the cruel eyes?

Unable to find what he was looking for, he forced us all outside into his well-kept black carriage. We left civilized London for the emptiness of the small farms just north of town. And all the time we huddled together, he kept his pistol aimed at us.

My father tried to talk to him, to bargain with him. "We don't have a Gutenberg Bible. We don't have anything that expensive. Why don't you let my wife and daughter go? You can have anything you want—"

"I want your Gutenberg Bible."

"I don't have one," my father wailed.

The look the man gave us—cold, ruthless, unyielding, indifferent—stopped all further talk.

I couldn't find a chance to unlock the door and jump from the carriage, so I spent my time memorizing his details. His boots were polished. His linen was sparkling white and not frayed. He wore a cravat tied in a high, elegant flourish.

When the vehicle paused and we climbed down, he sent the unmarked carriage off with just a gesture and marched us into an isolated cottage. Work was being done to the building and some of the interior walls were gone. Construction debris was everywhere. But there was no one around, inside or out, whom we could call to for help.

Several steps in, my father turned on the man, although he was taller and heavier than my father. My mother shoved me toward the door as I saw the fiend hit my father in the face with the butt of the pistol.

I ran.

Dear Lord, how I ran, sides aching, legs wobbling by the time I reached the suburbs and an omnibus line. I was lost, and it took three buses before I found an area I recognized. All that time, I knew that monster had my parents. What would he do to them?

It was midafternoon by the time I arrived, weary and tearstained, at the home of my father's partner in the business, Sir Broderick duVene. He was in his thirties then, an Oxford graduate, fencing enthusiast, and antiquarian collector. Since I thought I could lead him to the farmhouse, he secreted two knives on his person and hired a carriage to follow my directions. They were jumbled directions, and twice I got lost.

On the way there, I told him every detail I could think of. The man's expensive tailoring. The unusually pale shade of his hair and side whiskers. His fearsome glare.

We arrived at sunset. The cottage appeared deserted. Sir Broderick sent the driver to the nearest village to request the help of the local bobby and then return to us.

Just as we entered, the building exploded into fire. Sir Broderick pushed his way through the flames and debris. I followed and saw my parents tied up at the far side of the cottage. The evil man was gone.

Smoke made me gasp and stung my eyes. I screamed my parents' names over the fire's roar. We'd made our way about halfway across the inferno, pieces of plaster and roof raining around us, when a roof beam crashed down, striking Sir Broderick.

My parents were on the far side of the beam and Sir Broderick was directly in front of me, pinned under the beam. I could hear my parents screaming to me. I could see them struggling against their bonds through the smoke. Sir Broderick was groaning, trapped, right in front of me. If I could get him out, then I could get past the beam somehow and save my parents.

Coughing and sniffling, I rushed to save them. I managed to wedge wooden boards from the construction debris under the beam enough to free Sir Broderick. He couldn't move his legs. As I dragged him out of the house, the carriage driver returned and jumped down to help when I stumbled out the door.

As we pulled Sir Broderick to safety, I saw my parents' abductor standing nearby. He waved and then walked away.

I didn't have time to chase him. I grabbed one of Sir Broderick's knives and turned to run back in to free my parents, when the roof crashed down. I screamed, running toward the door. Strong arms stopped me as I struggled against the carriage driver, who held me back from running into the wall of flame. I shouted my parents' names, I cried, I wished I could stop the flames, but I knew I had failed.

There was nothing but an empty lake of flame where a cottage, and my parents, had been.

Blinking away the tears those memories always brought, I kept hurrying down the sidewalk, looking into the face of every top-hatted man I passed. For the first time since that day, I'd seen him. I had a chance to find the murderer and learn his name. To get justice for my parents.

Walking for blocks, I peered at the faces of a hundred men,

but none of them resembled my parents' killer in the least. I passed upscale homes that overlooked Hyde Park. Had he turned into one of these elegant brick buildings or walked off onto a side street? Did he live in one of these houses, even now looking down on me as I rushed by in search of him?

No. I would have felt his presence. His evil.

I was frustrated I hadn't caught him today, but at least now I knew he was in London. There was a chance I might finally find my parents' killer, but today's opportunity was gone. I released my fists and took a deep breath. It was time to go in search of Nicholas Drake.

In the dozen years since my parents' death, I'd eased the pain of not seeing justice done for my parents by helping to rescue others. When there was no hope of rescue, I helped their loved ones find closure. And many of the people we assisted went on to aid the Archivist Society.

I glanced along the sidewalk once more, knowing I'd return here soon. This was the place to begin to solve my own investigation.

CHAPTER TWO

RETURNING to the omnibus stop, I caught the next, equally crowded vehicle to take me into the suburbs to learn what I could to help Nicholas Drake.

Drake's house was one in a redbrick row a few chilly minutes' walk from the omnibus stop, above working class in attitude but not in cash. There was no rubbish lying around, but mildew had already appeared on some of the wood trim and the sidewalks were starting to crumble.

I checked the address again. Not what anyone would expect for a man who traveled in society's upper strata. As I walked to the door, I passed by a tiny front garden holding only a single, scraggly bush. When I rapped on the door, a wrinkled woman with a mop of white hair stuffed under her cap opened the door a few inches.

"I'm looking for Mr. Drake. Are you his housekeeper?"

"Aye. Mrs. Cummings." She crossed her bare forearms over her ample chest and blocked the doorway.

"I'm Miss Fenchurch. Miss Carter has me looking into

the whereabouts of Mr. Drake. Could you spare me a moment of your time?"

"I told that woman—" She looked me over and glanced at the rain. "Well, never mind, come in and I'll tell you, too." She stepped aside and I walked into the front hall.

In the dim illumination coming from the fanlight, I saw a closed door on one side of the hall before a flight of stairs that rose steeply upward. Next to the stairs, the hall leading to the back of the house was barely wide enough for one person to walk. The walls were painted, not papered, and the coat tree held one short garment. Mrs. Cummings's, I guessed.

"I believe you told Miss Carter that Mr. Drake has gone to visit friends in Brighton."

"That's right." The housekeeper smelled of cabbage and bread dough, but the hallway smelled of polish.

"Could you give me their name and direction, so I can verify his safe arrival?"

"Why would I do that?"

Wonderful. She was as obstinate as Miss Carter. "So I may put Miss Carter's fears to rest."

"Her? An impossible task."

"You find Miss Carter to be excitable?"

"Aye, and a busybody, too. Mr. Drake didn't mind living next door to her, but I can tell you, she's a difficult sort of neighbor."

I'd had quite enough of hearing about Miss Carter. "Did you do Mr. Drake's packing for him?"

"No, he took care of that the very evening he received a message from his friend. After he returned from dinner with some lord."

"Did you see the message from this friend?"

"No. He must have taken it with him."

"Why would he do that?" I gave her such a look of concern she must have forgotten I'd never met Nicholas Drake.

"I don't know. And there was such a mess." She glanced up the stairs. "There were plenty of things out of place, but I'm certain that was just from Mr. Drake packing in a hurry for his trip. He's like most gentlemen. He expects you to pick up after him." She made a move to open the front door to show me out.

"And the pool of blood in the front hall? Is that part of the normal packing process for most gentlemen?"

She stopped, her shoulders slumped. "Miss Carter told you about that?"

I pointed at a dark stain on the floorboards. "What if the disorder was caused by his abductors?"

She shook her head. "It couldn't have been. Mr. Drake must be all right."

I tried another line of inquiry. "When did Mr. Drake tell you he was traveling to Brighton?"

"The same morning Miss Carter came over in a state, saying Mr. Drake had been abducted. She had a nightmare, silly woman."

If she saw him that morning, the blood in the hall wasn't Drake's, and Edith Carter had lied. I was furious at the dishonesty of my client, and my fury came out in my tone. "You saw him that morning?"

Mrs. Cummings shuffled back in surprise. "No. He left me a note. He often did when he'd be gone before I arrived."

"Only Mr. Drake was in the house that night?"

"Any night."

"Are you the only one who looks after Mr. Drake?"

"Any help I need, he's given me permission to hire from the neighborhood." She put her hands on her hips and gave a sharp nod.

"If Mr. Drake were in any danger, is there any family or friends that he would go to?"

"He's alone in the world as far as family goes. He has two

friends, Mr. Harry and Mr. Tom, he's worked with on occasion."

"What are their last names?"

"Mr. Drake only used their Christian names. I've never heard last names."

"What line of work are they in?"

"I don't rightly know. From what I overheard, they did some of this and that."

They didn't sound like a law-abiding trio. "There was no sign of a disturbance at any of the outside doors?"

"Not that I saw."

I put sympathy in my voice. "He must have fallen on hard times if he lives here and dines with lords."

"It's only right he eat with lords, since he's descended from French royalty." The housekeeper nodded to herself at the rightness of it. "Then, when he returned home, he had a message from a sick friend and off he went to Brighton."

"Please tell me this friend's name and address."

"He told me the name of his friend and he told me Brighton. More than that I didn't need to know. And I don't see where it's any business of yours."

"There's blood in the front hall, the house was left a mess, and no one's heard from Mr. Drake in days. Someone needs to make sure Mr. Drake is in good health."

The puzzled look on her face told me she now doubted Drake had left under his own steam. I pressed my advantage. "What is his friend's name?"

"All right. Just don't tell her next door. He went to visit Mr. Dombey."

"Paul Dombey?"

"Yes. You know him?" The housekeeper looked relieved.

"Oh, yes." Dickens was popular with my customers. In *Dombey and Son*, Paul Dombey, the son, goes to Brighton. Was Drake forced to lie to his housekeeper? Or had he written that note before his intruders arrived?

* * *

"**THE DUKE HAS** no wish to discuss Nicholas Drake again." The gray-haired man, presumably the butler, spoke in a hush that didn't echo in the marble-tiled front hall.

I restrained my desire to stare at the ornately carved balustrade, the delicately painted ceiling with its pastoral settings, and the exquisite oil paintings. The duke wasn't short of a pound if the entrance hall was anything to go by.

"I only need two minutes of his time and then I won't bother him again." I tried to fill my words with quiet authority, since my appearance wouldn't garner respect. Wind had forced rain under my umbrella while I'd walked from the omnibus stop. Then, as the rain continued to pour down, I'd spent time arguing that my business was with the duke and I would not use the tradesmen's entrance. Thank goodness there was no mirror in the hall. I must have looked like a drowned pup.

"He doesn't wish to be bothered at this time."

I'd seen the door the butler had left and returned by. One quick dodge around the older man and I'd be through that doorway. "That is most unfortunate."

I turned as if leaving, and when the butler moved around me to help me on with the cloak I'd previously shed, I dashed down the hall.

Skidding on the polished floor in my wet shoes, I grabbed for the door handle. I threw open the door and entered a warm, paneled study filled with enough books and maps to make me feel at home. My shoes squished as I hurried across the thick Oriental carpet.

"Your Grace," the butler said from behind me.

The Duke of Blackford remained seated at his massive desk studying the papers in his hand. "I'll handle it, Stevens." His voice was a weary growl. I could imagine this man, wide shouldered, craggy faced, immaculately tailored, throwing the unimposing Edith Carter out of his house. He hadn't risen or even looked up when I entered the room. Philistine.

And then he set his papers on the pristine desktop and stared at me with eyes that challenged my right to breathe the air in his study.

I could play my role better than he could. I curtsied. The door clicked softly behind me as the butler left, followed by an icy raindrop skittering down my cheek. I didn't like being left alone with this man. For once I wasn't worried about my reputation; I was worried for my life. His dark eyes bore into me, proclaiming he ate more important people for breakfast. And there was the small matter of the blood on Drake's floor.

"Well?" he demanded in a deep voice. "Why are you here?"

"Your carriage was seen at the site of an abduction." My voice didn't tremble, but my knees did.

"Whose abduction?"

"Mr. Nicholas Drake."

A cruel smile slashed across his sharp-angled face. "Another of his lovers? The middle class grows more interesting."

Heat rose on my cheeks. "I've never met the man."

"Then why do you care?"

"Friendship."

"For that drab little mouse Miss . . . ?" He made a graceful, sweeping motion with the long, tapered fingers of one hand. Then his gaze returned to the papers on his desk.

If he thought he could convince me to leave by ignoring me, he was most certainly wrong. I stalked toward the smooth mahogany desk and glared at the seated man. "Her name is Miss Carter. Are you familiar with friendship, Your Grace?"

He rose and looked down on me. I'm of insignificant stature, and he had the advantage of height as well as the bearing of a duke. His black hair was ruthlessly slicked back and his dark-eyed gaze burned inside me. "You're dripping on my desk, Miss"—he glanced at the card I'd sent in with the butler—"Fenchurch."

I hopped back a step and gazed down. Two drops shimmered on the polished wood. I wished I'd sent in one of my cards with a false name. This man knew how to intimidate his inferiors without even mentioning his title. I decided not to ask about the death of his fiancée. I'd already made the mistake of letting him know my true identity.

He pulled out his handkerchief and wiped off the rain, then looked from the cloth to me as if he didn't know how to proceed with propriety. He held out the large white square. "You might want to pat yourself off. You appear to have spent too long outdoors."

For an instant, I saw concern in his eyes, but was it for me or his desk? Then all expression vanished. I took the handkerchief and wiped my face and hat brim. "You haven't answered my question."

His voice was dry with annoyance when he said, "I am familiar with friendship."

"Then you understand why I've taken on this commission for her." I handed back the handkerchief.

"No." He tossed the cloth on the floor as he came out from behind his desk. "And if you're going to continue this ridiculous debate, you need to stand close to the fire. Otherwise, you'll soak my carpet."

The infuriating man was making this as difficult as possible. Debate, indeed. All he had to do was answer my questions. But the grip on my elbow was gentle as he led me close to the comforting blaze.

For a moment, I shut my eyes in bliss. The welcome warmth made my fingers and toes tingle with renewed sensation. When I opened my eyes, my gaze fell on a seventeenth-century terrestrial globe in pristine condition. "Oh, how beautiful," slipped out before I thought.

Blackford strolled over to the sphere and ran one forefinger along the Atlantic. "It is magnificent, isn't it? The third duke brought it back from Italy."

I stared at the globe in wonder for a moment before I gave him a grateful smile and said, "Perhaps you'll save both of us time by telling me where your coach was on the night of March fourteenth?"

"Which coach?"

He was a duke. He probably had more carriages than I had dresses. "A tall, ancient one, all black, pulled by black horses."

"The Wellington coach. Why? Was that the night Drake disappeared?"

I shook out my damp skirts before the fire, reveling in the heat. Perhaps that was what made me less cautious. "Yes. If your coach was otherwise engaged, then it couldn't have been involved, and I needn't bother you any longer."

The duke returned to his desk and opened a slender volume. As he flipped through the pages, a curly lock of black hair slid over his stiff white collar. I was certain he'd have the errant strand chopped off for unruliness. "Last Thursday, I attended the theater and then had a late supper at the home of the Duke of Merville, where my carriage waited for me. My coachman was unaware of when I would next require him. We returned here at two o'clock on the fifteenth."

"The theater let out about eleven?"

"Yes. The duke and duchess rode to the theater and back in my carriage."

Eleven was the time Edith Carter saw Drake tossed into the duke's carriage. "I will, of course, verify this with the Duke of Merville."

A smile, a genuinely amused smile, crossed the duke's face. "Merville will enjoy providing my carriage with an alibi."

"Then the task will prove an easy one."

The smile broadened. "He won't see you. He's less tolerant of young women breaking into his study than I am. You'll have to take my word."

"Why?"

His smile vanished. In its place, his eyes narrowed and his lips thinned. Hadn't anyone given this haughty man a taste of his own insufferable attitude before? "He doesn't see anyone without an appointment. Neither do I, but when you burst in I made a bet with myself that you were here on behalf of Miss Carter. She also entered unannounced, dramatically sobbing threats."

"Who won the bet?"

Good heavens. The corner of his mouth quirked up in amusement for an instant. "Despite your charming demeanor, Miss Fenchurch, I'm afraid you'll have to take my word for the use of my carriages. None of them have ever been used to abduct anyone."

He was toying with me now. Bigger, meaner, uglier men had tried this same technique in the past. Of course, as a duke, he did it with more elegance. "I'm certain that's true, Your Grace, but I wish to clarify this matter so there can be no doubt in anyone's mind your coach is blameless."

He studied my face in silence. I fought down the urge to fidget as I watched him watch me. All businessmen and aristocrats wore unrelieved black and white, but no man had ever looked so exquisite in the absence of color. Perhaps because his skin was unusually tanned for an Englishman. Electricity seemed to crackle in the air between us.

Then he stalked forward, looming over me. Was he planning to physically throw me out of his study?

"Why do you want to find Drake?"

"Because he's missing, and no one deserves to vanish without someone trying to find him." I stared back in part because he cut a mesmerizing figure, and in part because I wanted him to know I was serious about my search.

"You're not looking for his stolen treasures?"

That surprised me. "What are you referring to, Your Grace?"

"That's not important."

"Did he steal something from you?"

"Not precisely, no." He was pacing around the room now. No, I paced around my bookshop. This room was large enough for the duke to stride about the room.

"Who did he steal from?"

"My sister and my late fiancée."

"I'd like to speak to your sister."

"I'm afraid that's impossible. She's staying at the castle, and there's no way for you to reach her."

Of course I would try. For now, I tried to sound deferential. "Perhaps you could speak for her. What is Mr. Drake accused of stealing?"

"A necklace and earrings from my sister, and a bracelet from my late fiancée. The thefts took place over two years ago, and nothing has been recovered."

"Was this reported to the police?"

"Of course." His tone said he was nearly out of patience.

"And did they determine Mr. Drake was the thief?"

"No."

I raised my eyebrows at that. "But you're certain he's responsible?"

"Yes."

"Why?"

He strode to where I stood before his fire and stared down at me. Intimidatingly close. He stimulated my nerves in a way I'd never experienced before while being threatened. I swallowed, expecting him to bodily throw me out of his study. Or ravish me with kisses. He was a man who made the air sizzle with the threat of a long-ago highwayman. Instead, he said, "Because the cur admitted it to me a year later."

"Did he return the jewelry?"

"He returned nothing."

I gazed into his rough-hewn face. What I suspected, given his ducal seat on the North Sea coast, was his pirate-raider ancestry. Behind the fragrance of clean linen and sandalwood was a hint of gunpowder and male sweat. "And you didn't pursue him in the courts?"

"It would have been his word against mine. My sister had no interest in reclaiming her property or having any more dealings with him, so I didn't . . . do anything." Behind the cold ducal expression, I saw passion flicker in his eyes.

But what passion? Hatred, anger, fear?

"How did you come to meet with him a year later?"

"He came up to me at a social event. He pulled me aside and he gloated." The last word poured from his mouth like poison.

I glanced down and saw his hands were in fists. His rage against Drake made him a good candidate for the man's abduction. But Drake lived in a very middle-class neighborhood. Under normal circumstances, these two men should never have met. "Why would Drake be at a social event with a duke?"

"He moves freely in society, befriending all the young people. He says his father was the younger son of a younger son, and his mother's family was related to French royalty."

"You didn't share your knowledge of his thievery with society? As a warning, of course."

"I should have." His tone turned bitter. "I had no idea he'd continued with his crimes until the Duke of Merville mentioned after his daughter's engagement party that certain items *and* Drake had left their lives."

The Duke of Merville suddenly sounded less like an alibi for the Duke of Blackford's coach and more like a fellow conspirator in a kidnapping. "When was this, Your Grace?"

"The party was over a week ago. Merville made the comment in our club a couple of days later." He dismissed my question and his answer with a wave of his hand.

"Did the two of you determine a course of action in regard to Mr. Drake?"

"We asked some questions around our club. We found three more members who'd had similar experiences with

Drake. He won't be invited to any events this coming season, I can assure you."

"You're going to ostracize him? That's all?" The man was accused of being a thief. Someone abducted him, and the Duke of Blackford's answer to all of this was not to invite the man to the round of society parties and balls that would soon begin again? My middle-class sense of justice couldn't begin to understand the duke's idea of punishment. Once again I was thankful I wasn't born to his class.

"It will make it more difficult for him to steal from us." Any sign of his interest in our conversation gone, Blackford took my arm and led me toward the door. Firmly and quickly, but without discourtesy.

I dug in my heels, more questions churning my mind. "Who were the others who'd had thefts? And why only you, the Duke of Merville, and those three?"

"Surely, Miss Fenchurch, you don't think I'm going to give you reason to burst into any more homes." His tone said he thought I was exasperating.

Despite my best efforts, we were nearly to the door of his study. "You don't think the matter of an abduction is going to disappear, do you?"

"It is, from my home. I've said all I'm going to on the matter." He pulled open the door and hustled me into the hall. The butler hurried toward us. "Good day. Stevens, see Miss Fenchurch out."

The duke let go of my arm, swung around, and entered his study. The door shut behind him with a firm thud.

I went to the front door ahead of Stevens, who seemed determined not to let me best him again. He needn't have worried. Blackford had given me enough to work on elsewhere. Had that been his plan?

As the butler helped me on with my cloak and handed me my furled umbrella, I said casually, "I understand the duke has quite a collection of carriages he keeps in London."

His eyes traveled toward the back of the house. "No, miss. Just the Wellington one and the ordinary coach."

I nodded to him and stepped outside, unfurling my umbrella as I walked. He'd told me what I needed to know.

Two minutes' walk in what was now a drizzle brought me to the mews in back of the duke's residence, where a two-story stone barn and carriage house stood.

The carriage door, much taller than most along the mews, stood open, and I took a step inside. The shining carriage nearest the door was magnificent. Tall and old-fashioned, it was black from its massive wheels to the driver's leather seat. The only spot of color was the crest painted in vivid colors on the door.

"'Ey, you can't be in here." A stocky man in rolled-up shirtsleeves, a rag in his hand, came around the side of the carriage.

"It's beautiful. Are you the one who keeps it in such magnificent style?"

"Aye."

"You are to be commended. It's quite old, isn't it?" I took another step inside, peering at the coach.

"Aye. The present duke's great-grandfather was given 'er for service to Wellington in the war with Napoleon."

"Do you get to ride on it?" I poured a helping of breathless wonder into my tone. At thirty, I was still young enough to bring out chivalrous instincts in most men. The dangerous duke was not most men. I hadn't made up my mind on whether that was a good or bad thing.

"Aye. I'm His Grace's driver. John Turner." He nodded.

"Oh, you are? Fortunate man." I nodded back. "I'm Georgia Peabody. I'm visiting down the road and they told me about this carriage. I had to come and take a look at something so beautiful." Georgia Peabody made appearances all over London when Georgia Fenchurch didn't want to call attention to herself or the Archivist Society.

"'Tis that, all right."

"I'm sorry, I must be keeping you from your work. But could you open the door for me so I can take a peek inside?"

"I guess it won't hurt. There, stand on the blocks so you can see in better. But don't touch nothin'."

Mounting blocks inside the coach house would have made it easy for me to climb inside if I'd wanted. "Thank you." I gave him my hand and he helped me up a step before opening the door. I didn't touch, because I could scour the inside with my eyes. Nothing seemed amiss.

"This must be difficult to drive in rain or fog."

"No more so than any other carriage. You got to know your team."

"And I imagine you're a man who knows his team well, Mr. Turner."

"Aye."

"I have a confession to make. I saw this coach out last Thursday night. I thought it the most magnificent sight I've ever seen. Where were you going?" I put a sigh into my voice that wasn't faked. I had a chance to learn something about the abduction carriage.

He frowned before saying, "Last Thursday? His Grace went to the theater and then to a late supper."

"He must have kept you up late, sitting around in the dark and the weather. How unfortunate."

"Not this time. The footman he took with us is the brother of a housemaid at Merville's. She worked it so we was invited in to a late supper while their lordships were upstairs dining."

"Leaving this beautiful coach and those magnificent animals in the rain? You must have had your work cut out for you cleaning them later."

He grinned. "Merville's coachman and I are friendly. We have a deal. When one of us is coming over, the other makes room for the horses in the stables. Then, working together, we unhitch, take care of the beasts, and then have tea and a natter until it's time to leave."

"How clever of you." I heard someone coming at the same time Turner jerked his head toward the house. He helped me down and shut the carriage door.

"Turner," a man's voice called, "His Grace wants you in front of the house in ten minutes."

"Aye. I'll be there."

When he glanced back at me, I mouthed, *Thank you,* and hurried out of the coach house.

The Duke of Blackford's coach appeared not to be involved. Why had Miss Carter lied? But while the coach was cleared of any involvement, the duke could still be Drake's kidnapper.

CHAPTER THREE

PHYLLIDA, formally Lady Phyllida Monthalf, had bowls of mutton stew and crispy bread on the table as soon as Emma and I reached our flat near the bookshop. The smells of roast and gravy and warm rolls reminded me how I'd not had time for even a cup of tea all day. I rushed through our prayers as my stomach growled in hope.

I'd told Emma all I'd learned that day and, while I dug in, she repeated everything to Phyllida. As Emma talked about the blood on the floor, I watched as terror flashed through Phyllida's eyes.

Ten years earlier, I'd seen that same terror when I first met her, at her brother's London town house. After a week of trying to interest Scotland Yard, a street lad named Jacob had learned from a policeman of the existence of the Archivist Society. He'd begged us to investigate the disappearance of an East End prostitute named Annie at an address in an upper-crust neighborhood belonging to Earl Monthalf. Our own inquiries convinced us that something was amiss and we decided to gain entrance to Earl Monthalf's home to search for the woman.

We'd discovered that our suspect and his sister lived there, but no one had seen his sister in a decade. Earl Monthalf came and went by the front door, but he allowed no one into his fortresslike house. The front door was locked and bolted. Ornate grilles covered all the windows, making entrance that way impossible. The easiest access was by the kitchen door, and by watching, we discovered Earl Monthalf opened it at ten in the morning for the daily deliveries.

Adam Fogarty, invalided out of the police force, took over for one of the regular deliverymen and I followed, planning to slip in while Fogarty kept Earl Monthalf busy. My job was to search for any sign of the missing woman and rescue her if possible. Jacob was outside to call the police if we were successful. We didn't think anything could go wrong.

When I slipped in the kitchen door, I encountered a cowering wretch, who stared at me, backing away until she bumped into the sink. Her frock was stained, sweat slid down her cheek, and I could see fading bruises on her face and arms. "Go away," she said. "It's not safe here."

Fogarty, Jacob, and I had wondered why we'd seen nothing of a domestic staff come and go from this house. "Who are you?"

"Lady Phyllida Monthalf."

She looked pitiful, and I immediately felt sorry for her. Seeing a lady, the daughter and sister of lords, in such a bedraggled state in this basement kitchen made me wonder what had caused her downfall. "You don't need to fear me. I can help." I moved forward and squeezed her hand.

She looked toward the next room, where we could hear Fogarty and Earl Monthalf's voices. She trembled as she pushed me toward the door. "You can't help. There's no escape. Hasn't been for years."

"Lady Phyllida, was there a woman here named Annie? Where has she gone?"

"She's still alive, poor soul. Chained to a bed on the first floor, but still alive when I took her breakfast this morning."

If this beaten, dirty drudge called Annie a poor soul, what would I find upstairs? "Has this happened before?"

"Dozens of times. Dozens of them. It's terrible." Her blue eyes flashed defiance for an instant, and I recognized an ally in this investigation.

I heard the men raise their voices in argument and knew I didn't have much time. "Thank you." Hurrying over to the back staircase, I climbed it as silently as I could.

Up two flights of stairs, I began to open doors. The first bedroom, opulently decorated for a man, was empty. The second, resembling a tidy jail cell, also was empty. The third contained an iron bedstead with soiled linens and a scrawny, filthy victim with big, staring eyes.

She was chained to the bed in such a way that her attempts to free herself had failed, leaving her with bloody fingers. By moving to the other side of the bed, I was able to unchain her quickly.

"Can you walk?" I asked.

She nodded and struggled to her feet. Leaning on me, we moved slowly and noisily down the two flights of stairs. She was surprisingly heavy and we banged into walls as I awkwardly hurried her along. I knew there was no way Earl Monthalf hadn't heard us. I kept looking behind and in front of us, but no one gave chase or blocked our way.

When we reached the basement floor, Monthalf stood between us and the door, a knife in his hand. There was no sign of Fogarty.

He walked toward us, smiling. "Two of you to have fun with. Where shall I start?"

Mesmerized by the blade, I didn't see Phyllida until her

brother tumbled unconscious to the floor. She stood staring at us, a cast-iron skillet clenched in both thin hands. Then I ran for the outside door, screaming for help and jostling Annie as I half dragged her along.

The police quickly arrived and medical aid was summoned for Annie and Fogarty, who'd been attacked by Monthalf. Fogarty was furious that his limp had given away his weakness. Monthalf had knocked his injured leg out from under him and then beat Fogarty senseless, leaving Monthalf free to attack us in the kitchen.

Monthalf awoke in chains and was taken to Newgate to await trial. I brought Phyllida home with me when the police began to tear apart the house to find the remains of other missing prostitutes. What started as a temporary refuge a decade before had quickly become her home.

"Will you two be safe?" was Phyllida's only comment once she'd smoothed her narrow-boned features into mild interest.

"Yes, Aunt," Emma said, using the honorary title we both employed.

"I doubt we'll be in any danger but I don't know what we have: an abduction, a runaway, or a simple misunderstanding," I told her.

Phyllida gave me a hard look, but she said, "You'll figure it out. In the meantime, I should plan meals that will fit in with your odd schedules. You are taking on the investigation?"

"I think so."

"Then your schedules will be disrupted." She took another bite of her stew. Despite being better fed living with me, she'd never lost her gaunt look.

I smiled. "You always manage to keep the household running no matter how much disorder Emma and I cause."

"I don't do that much," Phyllida said. As much as I was in her debt for the help she'd given me over the years, she still felt as if she wasn't earning her place. Her brother had left scars on her soul that Emma and I would never be able to erase.

"You save me dealing with the laundress and the grocer and the char. I can't run the bookshop and take care of our home, too."

Emma said around a mouthful of stew, "This is wonderful. You are the best cook in the world."

Phyllida dipped her head, but I saw the blush of pride on her cheeks.

After dinner, Emma and I hurried downstairs and out the door onto the street. In the shelter of the narrow porch, I put the hood of my gabardine cloak over my hat and turned in the opposite direction from the bookshop, wishing there was something equally rain repellent for the hem of my skirt.

Fortunately, the rain held off for most of our walk, and we were out at a time when we didn't have to wait as long to dash across the streets between carriages. What light there was, from street lamps, shop windows, and carriage lamps, made the wet, shiny pavement look smooth as silk.

When we finally reached Sir Broderick's looming six-story house, I hesitated, staring at the glistening raindrops starting to hit the pavement at my feet. "I don't want to listen to a roomful of critics tonight. I have no idea how to find Nicholas Drake. I don't even know if he's a victim or a villain."

Emma gave me a sharp look. "What's really bothering you?"

I looked up and down the road lined with elegant brick town houses. Lights shone behind draperies in many of the windows, looking welcoming on this dreary night. But how many of them hid secrets as dangerous as Nicholas Drake kept? And did one of them hide my parents' killer? "I saw a man today—oh, never mind." I couldn't tell her who I'd seen.

Emma took my arm and dragged me forward onto the steps. "You'll figure it out. And we'll help you." As she reached out and rang the buzzer, the hood of her cloak fell back. Her golden hair sparkled in the light of the lantern above the door.

Emma was born beautiful and lucky. She kept telling me beauty was a curse, but I thought it was better than being called "agreeable."

Jacob, the street lad who was now a young man and Sir Broderick's assistant, immediately cracked the door open, saw us, and swung it wide. Emma rushed in, rubbing her hands together. "It's bitter out. Be glad you don't have anywhere to go."

I walked in and gave a sigh. Everything I'd heard that day was a contradiction of something I'd learned from someone else, and I was certain to hear complaints about my investigation tonight. And at some point I'd have to tell Sir Broderick who I'd found.

Jacob gestured with a tilt of his head toward the brightly lit stairs for us to go up. Then he held out his arms for our cloaks.

I took off my damp cape, hat, and gloves, rejoicing in the warmth of Sir Broderick's home. The head of the Archivist Society insisted on keeping his house overly hot, but after my walk through the blustery night, I was grateful for the heat soaking my clothes and sinking into my bones. Following Emma up the staircase that wound around the iron lift, I found the double doors to the study open.

A cheery fire burned and Sir Broderick had parked his wheeled chair where he would gain most of the heat. I stepped toward him, feeling sweat begin to border my scalp and my spine as I moved closer to the blasting fire.

After his "retirement" into his wheeled chair a dozen years before, Sir Broderick had found his days to be never changing. With time on his hands, he'd gradually organized bored record clerks, antiquarian booksellers, policemen forced into retirement, and others with specialized knowledge into a formidable organization. He was the one who kept us marching in step.

While he said he acted to bring justice to this world, I

knew he needed to be active, to have a purpose for living. Crippled in the prime of life, he was too young and alive to spend his days collecting antiquarian books and solving word puzzles.

And as our leader, it would be Sir Broderick who would have the task of correcting me for my mistakes if the group found I'd mishandled the interviews.

Sir Broderick held out both of his chubby hands. "You've had an unsettling day. Dominique, a cup of tea for Miss Georgia and a couple of scones. She's looking thin and wan."

I reached for his hands and felt his callused palms and his firm grip. Hope flickered. Dominique's scones could never be considered punishment.

"Sit down, Miss Georgia. Dominique will take good care of you." The West Indian accent of the woman with skin the color of tea rolled over me, easing some of the tension from my shoulders.

"Thank you, Dominique." I settled onto a chair at a distance from the fireplace, shifting on the upholstered yellow and orange seat in a failed attempt to find a comfortable position. "Sir Broderick, the client I sent you the message about lied to me. I'm confused by what I've learned."

"We've been lied to during many of our successful cases. Don't let a client telling tales worry you. I've called a few of the members to hear your information so we can decide how to proceed from here."

I took a sip of tea to wet my dry throat and breathed in the fragrance of buttered scones. The buzzer sounded and a voice rang out in the front hall. "Terrible night out, Jacob. Am I late? Do we have a case? It's been weeks since I've done anything adventurous."

Then heavy footsteps on the stairs announced the arrival of Frances Atterby. She came in with a general greeting and enveloped Sir Broderick in a hug. "Ah, scones. Dominique, you are a lifesaver."

"Made especially for you, Madame Atterby." Dominique grinned and faded into a dim corner by the bookcases.

Frances savored a bite of scone while still standing by the tea table. "You look very fetching tonight, Miss Emma."

"I thought I should dress up, since Georgia spent part of the day with a duke."

Frances swung both chins from Emma to Georgia and back. "Any luck there?"

Emma briefly lifted her eyebrows. "He's single."

I stared at my employee. I'd spent the time since I'd returned to the shop resisting the urge to research the Duke of Blackford in Debrett's. Emma, who'd not been subjected to the duke's forceful personality, had eagerly searched for information on the man and his lineage.

So what if he was single? I didn't want to waste my time trying to comprehend the powerful, arrogant, mesmerizing, fascinating duke. Yet why, instead of Nicholas Drake, did my thoughts keep drifting back to the Duke of Blackford?

Frances walked over and sat on the sofa next to Emma. "Tell me all."

"You'll have to ask Georgia." Emma gave me an encouraging smile.

Enough of this nonsense. "Are you ready for me to begin?"

"No. We're still waiting for Fogarty. In the meantime, enjoy your tea." Sir Broderick adjusted his lap robe and smiled through hooded eyes at the group.

The buzzer sounded again, and as male voices were heard in the stairwell, Frances returned to the tea table for another scone. "Might as well tuck ourselves in for a long meeting."

I doubted they'd spend much time on Drake's possible disappearance.

"All right, the Archivist Society members I've summoned are now all here. Shall we begin?" Sir Broderick said, breaking into my thoughts as he wheeled his chair around to face me.

I looked around the study, the warmest, most brightly lit room I'd ever entered. Jacob had joined us, his legs stretched out from a settee, a plate of scones balanced on his lap. Adam Fogarty leaned against a bookcase, drumming his fingers on a shelf. Frances sat next to Emma, scone crumbs spread across her ample chest. Dominique had vanished.

I began by telling them everything Edith Carter had told me and my impressions of the woman. I passed around the photograph Miss Carter had given me of Nicholas Drake, and then Jacob set it on the desk to be taken to an Archivist Society member who was a photographer to have copies made.

"Why did Miss Carter have a photograph of her next-door neighbor? Not the usual thing to have, is it?" Fogarty said.

"No, but her concern made it clear she's in love with Nicholas Drake. Her possession of this photograph tells me he reciprocated her feelings."

The buzzer sounded. I fell silent and looked to Sir Broderick, who nodded to Jacob. The young man set down his plate and silently hurried down the stairs to the front door.

Moments later, I heard the door open and a commanding voice said, "The Duke of Blackford for Sir Broderick duVene and Miss Fenchurch."

"They're not available this evening, Your Grace."

"Oh, I think they'll see me."

Emma whispered, "That's him. That's Georgia's duke."

"He's not my—" I looked at Sir Broderick and gulped. This was worse than any nightmare. How did he know I was here? My friends would throw me out of their society after this debacle.

"Bring him up, Jacob," Sir Broderick called out.

My heart thudded with every step on the stairs. I glanced around the room. Every eye was trained on the doorway.

Maybe it was only a fluctuation in the gas pressure, but it seemed to me that the lights dimmed as the Duke of

Blackford entered the study. He was dressed in the finest of black evening wear, and it seemed to absorb the warmth and brightness of the room and replace it with chilled darkness. Every hair on his head was precisely combed despite the wind outside.

I didn't realize the room had grown silent and I was holding my breath until Sir Broderick said, "Come in, Your Grace, and state your business with us."

"You need to cease your search for Nicholas Drake."

"Has he been found?"

"No." The duke stood just inside the room, towering over the seated occupants. His eyes were like burning coals, a thin crust of black holding the flame within. I knew I'd be in awe of his passion if he'd direct it toward something beneficial. As it was, I was astonished at the tightly leashed power flowing from him like heat from the fire. How had he known we were meeting here tonight?

"Then why should we stop?" Sir Broderick asked.

"A slander has been made against my reputation. I am the one who should find Drake and prove my innocence in his disappearance."

"Our help could prove invaluable."

"I doubt it." The scorn in the duke's voice was unmistakable.

Sir Broderick didn't hide his anger. "You underestimate us, Your Grace."

"No. You underestimate us. Call off your search for Nicholas Drake." He faced me, his gaze piercing my brain. "Your help is neither wanted nor appreciated."

Then he turned back to our host. "This should conclude any business between us. Miss Fenchurch, if you'll see me out?"

I glanced at Sir Broderick, who nodded slightly. I rose and gave the duke my arm. He escorted me down the stairs in silence while I tried to plan a series of questions that might lead me to the reason a duke had descended on our meeting and ordered us away from the investigation.

Stunned, my mind spent those precious few moments absorbing the precision of his steps, the firmness of his arm, and the scents of soap and smoke. I couldn't think of a single articulate question.

"Please convey to Sir Broderick that I am serious about handling this investigation without your interference." He picked up his silk top hat and reached for the door handle.

I moved to stand with my back to the door, blocking his way. "We've not yet decided if we will undertake this search, but we might be more amenable to your request if you told us what was behind it."

"This slur on my reputation is my business, not yours."

"We've been asked to locate a missing man, not salvage your pristine reputation." My tone made clear what I thought was more important.

He stared down on me, standing close enough to let me study the grim set of his mouth and feel the heat coming off his body past the cold air trapped in his heavy wool overcoat. For the first time, I noticed tiny light gray flecks in his dark eyes. "You don't know what you're getting involved in."

"I'm going to find out."

"You said the Archivist Society hasn't yet decided to undertake a search for Drake." His hand reached past me to the door handle.

I decided on my first step. I would defy a duke to find Nicholas Drake. "You said 'us' upstairs. Who are the others? The men in your club who've also been victims of Mr. Drake's larceny?"

He opened the door by pushing me aside with it. "Why put yourself in danger?"

"Because a man is missing. He deserves to be found."

Blackford stepped outside. "No, he doesn't."

"Why not?"

"He brings misery into the lives of everyone he meets."

I stood on the doorstep, a cold mist blowing against my face, but I didn't want to shut the door on the duke and the challenge he presented. "I can't believe that."

His mouth twisted into a grimace. "You've never met him."

"Are you telling me this because he's a thief?"

"No."

"Then how can you say he brings misery everywhere? Who is he to you? You're much too concerned about a man who is unimportant in your circles."

He studied my face, his dark eyes losing the light gray flecks as I stared back. The mist stung with sleet but neither of us moved. I wanted to know his real reason for warning us off this case. I wanted to memorize his features. I wanted to consider the agitation raising my heart rate while I faced this powerful adversary. I had no idea why he didn't walk away.

Finally he said, "Don't exert yourself finding him. He doesn't deserve your sympathy or your pity." He set his top hat on his head, covering his thick black hair worn straight as a soldier's back.

"Yes, he does. Everyone deserves that much. Good night, Your Grace." I shut the door and leaned against it, listening to my pounding heart. When I didn't hear any knocking on the outside of the door from an irate duke or his retainers, I wearily climbed the stairs, shoving back the messy curls that had come loose from my hairdo while I'd argued with the duke in the windy doorway.

Frances broke the quiet in the study when I entered. "That was the duke who's involved in this investigation? Oh, my. Not what I expected."

I couldn't resist a dry retort. "They're not all old and fat." He'd just dismissed my assistance in a very public manner, and it annoyed me. Why would he think he could do a better job than me? Than the entire Archivist Society?

Fogarty, who rarely sat and never stayed motionless, limped across the room. "How did he know you'd be here?"

"I don't know."

"How did he know you were investigating Drake's disappearance?"

I told them of my investigation of the carriage in question, and my earlier visit to Drake's home.

I was aware of every pair of eyes on me, every click of a tongue, every murmur. I plodded on through each detail. They were fellow Archivist Society members and my friends. And they all held accuracy in high regard.

Fogarty, assuming the line of questioning he learned during his years on the Metropolitan Police force, took down my description of the jewelry stolen from the two women and the approximate dates. "I'll see if this was really reported stolen." He snapped his little notebook shut.

"You think the duke told me a fib?"

"I think it's better to check."

Sweat slid down my back by the time I finished, and my throat was dry. I took a sip of my now-cold, too-sweet tea and said, "Any questions?"

Sir Broderick led the questioning. "What did he want with you downstairs?"

"To warn me off this investigation. He said it would be dangerous."

"What do you think happened to Nicholas Drake?"

"I don't know. I believe that the duke's carriage was not used in the abduction, but I also think Miss Carter sincerely believes the duke is involved. There can't be too many carriages fitting that description. Finding them and learning if they were used that night would be one place to start." I came to a halt and looked at Sir Broderick. "That is, if we're going to investigate this case."

Frances looked from one colleague to another. "I think we should continue. Something happened to the man and it wasn't a trip to Brighton."

The door buzzer sounded again, stopping any response. Jacob went downstairs and in a moment they heard a man say, "Is the Archivist Society still meeting?"

"And you are—?"

"Lord Edward Hancock."

Sir Broderick shut his eyes and shook his massive head. "Bring him up, Jacob."

Lord Hancock was an ordinary-looking man with fair coloring and lines around his eyes from a permanent squint. When he saw Sir Broderick's wheeled chair, he took a half step back and looked around for another person to address. His gaze lighted on Adam Fogarty, who now leaned on the back of my chair, tapping his foot against the chair leg and annoying me so I could barely concentrate on the new arrival. "I'm Lord Hancock and I'd like to ask you not to search for Nicholas Drake."

"Why?" Sir Broderick barked, and for an instant I expected to see him leap from his chair. Then I blinked and realized I was seeing him as he'd been the day I ran to him for help rescuing my parents. Seeing the man who'd put Sir Broderick in his wheeled chair was affecting my thoughts. I needed to tell Sir Broderick I'd found the killer—and admit I'd lost him again.

Hancock jumped when Sir Broderick spoke, but he recovered quickly and said loudly, "The man has been pursuing my ward, and any time they spend apart is welcome."

Sir Broderick said, "No need to shout. My ears work well. Do you believe Mr. Drake left because he wanted to avoid a closer friendship with your ward?"

Lord Hancock flushed. "No. I believe he left because his crimes have come to light, making his life in London unbearable. Mr. Drake is a thief."

"Is this your opinion or is this common knowledge?" Fogarty, who paced through our meetings like a caged animal, his limp more pronounced in bad weather, was now standing to the side of the fireplace.

"In the last week, several of us who've lost items of value to a skilled thief realized the common denominator was Drake. We were gathering information to confront him when he disappeared. Needless to say, my ward knows nothing about this, and I'd prefer to preserve her delicate feelings by preventing her from discovering that someone she thought a friend was truly reprehensible."

"Did Mr. Drake know you suspected him?"

"I don't know. We tried to ask questions discreetly."

Uneasiness crept up the back of my neck. "Was the Duke of Blackford someone you discussed this with?"

Hancock swung around at my question. "Yes. He's been more upset than most. An item he lost belonged to someone he loved who has died."

"Why don't you want us to investigate, my lord? We could be of great assistance, and we are very discreet," Fogarty said.

"He's probably already fenced the jewelry he stole, and I don't want him back in society spending time with my ward. We'd all be better off if he stayed in Brighton or wherever he's gone."

"Who is your ward?" Mrs. Atterby asked.

"Daisy Hancock, my late brother's daughter. He and his wife died on her eleventh birthday. She's out in society now. I've grown quite fond of her over the years."

I decided to chance learning the names of the other victims. "Who was in this group besides you, the Duke of Blackford, and the Duke of Merville?"

"The Earl of Waxpool and Lord Dutton-Cox. If Drake's stolen from others, they don't belong to our club."

"And you propose that the five of you handle this matter rather than the police or the Archivist Society?" Sir Broderick stared at the man from under hooded eyes, his large hands gripping the wheels of his chair.

"The police believe he's in Brighton. They also understand five peers don't want them looking into the situation. I hope you show the same wisdom."

"I doubt Mr. Drake would find such a course of action wise. Good evening." Sir Broderick swung away to face the fireplace.

Hancock glanced around the room before his shoulders drooped. When none of us looked him in the eye, he said, "Good night." His footsteps were slow and heavy going down the stairs.

Once the door had been shut and Jacob had returned, Emma said, "Have we ever been thrown off a case twice in one night by two people who've not hired us?"

"No. You've brought us quite a little puzzle, Georgia," Sir Broderick said.

"The duke told me he thought Drake stole from him. Now we know some others to investigate in his disappearance." I looked at Sir Broderick. "If we take the case on, of course."

Sir Broderick glanced at Frances and Adam, and they both nodded. "It's time you headed an investigation."

I was glad I was sitting. Otherwise I'd probably have fallen over. "I've never led an investigation before. You've always told me what questions to follow, Sir Broderick. I won't know what to do."

"You'll figure it out. And we'll be there to help you," Adam Fogarty said as he paced his way to the door.

Doubts and objections filled my mind. "We don't have a reliable client."

"Yes, we do. Drake himself. Don't you think he'd like to be found?" Frances asked.

"Well, yes, of course, but—"

"No buts. We're going to find Nicholas Drake. Or rather, you will. Don't you find it intriguing that we've heard from so many people who don't want him found?" Sir Broderick smiled at me.

I took a deep breath and tried to look at the puzzle rationally. Ticking things off on my fingers, I said, "Lord Hancock wants Drake to stay away from his ward. I understand why he doesn't want Drake to reappear if he wants to make a good marriage for her. The Duke of Blackford wants to find Drake so he can restore his name, but he doesn't want our help. You'd think he'd welcome assistance. And Drake's housekeeper refuses to believe anything untoward happened to her employer despite the blood and disorder in the house."

"What else is odd about this, Georgia?" Sir Broderick's eyes were half-closed like a cat sleeping in the sun. He was slumped back in his wheeled chair, his arms at rest on his lap robe. From previous cases, I knew his appearance was at odds with his lightning-fast mind.

"Two peers came here tonight for the same purpose. One worried about his niece, the other worried about his name. And there are three more just like them lurking in the background. Maybe more."

"What do we know about any of these people?"

"Nothing yet. Including Drake, whose ancestry may or may not be what I was told."

"Study the records. There should be plenty on the peers. Miss Carter and Drake might prove more difficult. Adam, Jacob, Emma, they'll be your responsibility. After you go through the records, find their friends. Talk to the neighbors. It's a new neighborhood. Try talking to them whilst pretending to take a survey for the Water Board. That ruse has worked well in the past."

Sir Broderick turned his gaze toward me. "We need to know the identities of all of Drake's victims. Talk to Lady Westover. She's a terrible old bat, but very useful. Then start with the records on Blackford and Hancock until you can tell me what they had for breakfast."

"There's no financial gain in this," Frances said.

"We're going to take on Drake's disappearance out of love for our fellow man," Sir Broderick replied. And then he smiled the way the cat smiled at the canary. "Frances, help Georgia with the records, please."

"You don't think this was a simple abduction," Adam Fogarty said as he paced in front of the bookcases, his footsteps making a th-thump, th-thump on the wooden boards. Then he stopped and rubbed his stiff knee, muttering something in a growl.

"No. If it were, we wouldn't hear claims that a duke was involved or that the victim was a thief," the baronet said.

I held up a hand, palm out. "To question our suspects, we're going to need to move about society."

Sir Broderick smiled. "Be sure to see Lady Westover tomorrow. You'll need her help to give an authentic performance. You're about to enter aristocratic society."

CHAPTER FOUR

AS the meeting broke up, I went to sit next to Sir Broderick. I couldn't bear the heat from the fireplace baking my skin, but I couldn't let it drive me away.

He looked at my face and said, "What is it, Georgia?"

"I saw him today. My parents' murderer."

"Good grief. You can't be certain. It's been a dozen years."

"Yes, I can. I spent time with him. I memorized his face. I remember his stride and how he carried a newspaper under his arm. I'll be able to point him out until the day I die."

Sir Broderick kept shaking his head. "He could be dead or have left the country. His appearance could have changed with time."

"This man looked older, but it was him. I saw him walking along Hyde Park Place. Perhaps it's time to again check on the land records for the cottage where my parents died."

"We do that every year. It's never changed hands, and the killer is definitely not the owner or anyone who works around there. Did you speak to him?" Sir Broderick reached out and patted my hand.

My shoulders slumped and I couldn't hide the mournful frustration in my voice. "I couldn't catch up to him, and I lost him. I feel like I failed again."

"You didn't fail, Georgia. Not then; not today. You did the best you could. If it was him."

My best wasn't good enough. "Have you learned any more about the Gutenberg Bible?"

He looked away for a moment, and I thought he wouldn't answer me. "Every year or two, I hear a rumor about one for sale here in London. I heard the rumor again about two weeks ago."

I reached out and took his hands. "Maybe he left and has come back because he heard the same rumor you did. Maybe that's why we haven't seen him until now."

"'We'? Georgia, please. I rarely leave this house, and I never saw him. And I know you've been looking for him on every street you walk down and in every carriage that passes you since the day your parents died. Can you be absolutely certain this man you saw wasn't very similar to your parents' killer, and you want him to be the one?"

"I was certain when I saw him. And now that I have an area to search, I'll find out if I was right."

He gave my hands a squeeze. "Good luck. I want the bastard found, too. If he can be found. But for heaven's sake, be careful."

I WAS ALONE in the shop the next morning when the bell over the door jingled and a middle-aged man walked in. Portly, bearded, and balding, he was a caricature of a peer. Knowing a potentially large purchase when I see one, I hurried over to him with a welcoming smile. "May I help you? I'm the proprietor of Fenchurch's Books."

He glanced around the shop rather than at me. "I'm the Duke of Merville."

I kept my smile in place with effort as astonishment nearly made me miss the man's next words.

"I understand from my man of affairs that you deal in antiquarian Bibles."

"I have a small selection, Your Grace, and I can check the catalogs for more." I hoped my face reflected a helpful expression, since my mind was searching for a way to bring up Nicholas Drake's thieving and Merville's ride in the Duke of Blackford's coach the night Drake disappeared.

"I'm looking for something with gilt edges, no wormholes or brown spots or water stains. New Testament only, or just the Gospels. A good leather cover. Original, not rebound, in quarto or octavo size."

The Duke of Merville was obviously a collector of the best examples of antiquarian books. He sounded like a man who would appreciate the care I used in storing the rare books in my possession. "I keep the old books over here, away from outside walls, the floor, and the ceiling to keep the temperature constant, and behind brass wire rather than glass to ensure air can move freely around them."

He followed me behind the sales counter to the antiquarian shelves. Ordinarily, I'd have insisted he stay on the other side of the counter, but I didn't want to start off by telling a duke to behave like a mere mortal. I put on my pair of cotton gloves, handed him a pair from the counter, and unlocked the ornate grille.

"How much do you plan to spend?"

"How much is a volume meeting my expectations?"

"I have an octavo-sized Gospels meeting your requirements for"—he was a duke and I wanted this sale—"twenty pounds." I pulled the book out and held it away from him while I stared at his hands.

With pursed lips, he yanked off his leather gloves and put on the cotton ones. Then he held out his hand. I passed him the volume and held my breath. The duke was knowledgeable, but was he careful with fragile things?

He examined the cover, which was cracked in a few places from heat sometime in the past, and ruffled the pages enough to send up a puff of dust. "Eighteenth century?"

"Possibly late seventeenth. The printer worked in both."

"Do you have something a little more modern, with a cover in better shape?"

So he was one of those, who only cared how the cover looked on his shelves. I put back the book he'd examined and pulled out a quarto New Testament covered in pristine black leather. "This is late eighteenth century and kept in very careful circumstances. The price reflects its condition."

I believed it had been kept at the bedside of the first owner, a woman who'd possessed it for all of her long life, which explained the book's still-elegant condition. I gently stroked the beautiful volume before I handed it over.

He examined the book briefly. "I'll give you fifty pounds for it."

I'd never thought I'd hear those words. I'd expected to bargain him up to forty-five at most. "A most discerning purchase. I'll wrap it for you."

"I need something appropriate for my daughter to carry down the aisle at her wedding. Then I'll add it to my collection." He pulled off the cotton gloves and walked to the other side of the counter as he pulled on his finely crafted leather ones. He glanced around my empty shop again as if he were appraising it and its owner. "I see you don't have much trade."

Quick to defend my shop from his slur, I said, "Mornings are our slow hours. We also do more business when the gentry and overseas visitors come up to London to shop."

As soon as he handed over the Bank of England notes, I added, "The Duke of Blackford said you had something stolen by Nicholas Drake."

For the first time, he looked me in the eye. "You know Blackford?"

"Yes."

He looked at me skeptically. "And you know Drake?"

"I know he's now missing."

"Bad luck for him. He won't get another penny until he reappears."

"Oh? You pay your thief?"

He jerked back a half step and then snatched up his purchase. "Of course not." He turned and rushed toward the front door.

"Then why did you say—?"

The bell jangled as the duke yanked the door open and stepped outside between our two show bow windows. With a quick glance in each direction, he stepped onto the sidewalk and marched up the street.

LATER THAT DAY, I left my bookshop in Emma's care and traveled by foot and the Oxford Street omnibus to search Hyde Park Place. The day was brisk and the sun tried to break through the gray coal-tinged clouds, encouraging people to come outside. The sidewalks were full and there were plenty of top-hatted men, but not the one I searched for.

Turning my feet toward Grosvenor Square, I vowed I'd be back soon and I'd find my parents' killer. Now I had just enough time, if I hurried, to reach Lady Westover's neighborhood of grand town houses. I had the sidewalks to myself. No one but servants walked there except on the finest of days.

I made certain to arrive at Lady Westover's after lunch but before visiting hours. As was often the case, I found her ladyship in the south-facing greenhouse she'd built onto the back of her house.

She looked up when I entered, a mist sprayer held in one glove-swathed hand. "Ah, there you are, Georgia. Sir

Broderick sent a note saying you'd be round to see me today. How is the dear boy? Have you a new case? How exciting. Help me off with this apron, child."

I spent the next five minutes unwrapping Lady Westover from her apron, duster, gloves, hat, and boots. Underneath was a countess in pristine dress, unmarked, unwrinkled, and undeterred. "Come along," she said, taking my arm, "we'll find someone to get us some tea."

Once we were settled in front of the fire in Lady Westover's cheery yellow and white morning room with a pot of tea and delicate sandwiches, the countess said, "Now tell me all about this new case."

"Have you ever heard of Nicholas Drake?"

The lines in her face turned into deep furrows. "No. I haven't. Should I have?"

"Supposedly his mother is descended from French royalty and his father is the younger son of a younger son."

"Whose younger son?"

"So far we've not learned his name."

"Well, I really doubt that story. It's so easy to say these things if one can keep them general. Once the story is given specifics, it all blows away like dust. What has this Nicholas Drake done?"

"He's vanished. Either by abduction or by running away, depending on which story you prefer."

"And you want to find him."

"Yes."

"I'm afraid I can't help you with him."

"It's not him I came to ask you about. It's his victims. Nicholas Drake has been accused of being a thief by the Duke of Blackford, the Duke of Merville, the Earl of Waxpool, Lord Dutton-Cox, and Lord Hancock. We need to know what you know about these men, and whether you can deduce any other victims."

Lady Westover set down her cup and said, "Oh, my. Where

to begin. Dutton-Cox is a stingy soul, the kind who throws large parties and then is miserly with the food. The heir is in the country with his family. There were two daughters. One was supposed to marry Blackford two years ago, until she died just before the wedding. He had a lucky escape. She was a vain thing, just like her sister, who recently wed Viscount Dalrymple. Lady Dutton-Cox is still grieving the daughter who died and has become something of a recluse. Sad, really. I'm fond of Honoria." She glanced at me. "Lady Dutton-Cox. We've been close friends for years and I refuse to believe she or her husband could be involved in an abduction."

Lady Westover rose to pinch a dead leaf off one of the many ferns hung or set on stands around the room. While she examined three of the plants, I pulled my notebook out of my pocket and jotted a few notes in pencil.

She sat down and said, "Where was I? Waxpool is a sharp old man, an older version of the Duke of Blackford. At least five years my senior. His heir, a fat, puffed-up piece of buffoonery, will destroy all Waxpool has built up over the years. The old man prefers his grandchildren, a boy and a girl who take after him. The boy is at Cambridge and doing quite well, from all reports. The girl has been presented to the queen, but doesn't spend much time at social events. She's found the men swarm around her money rather than her, and she's been rather put off by it.

"I don't know the Merville family at all. By reputation, they are conservative, politically and financially."

"I met the Duke of Merville today in my shop. He offered more for an antiquarian Bible than I expected to receive after hard bargaining." I hoped to do more business with him. Much more.

"Odd. I'd heard he was given to underpaying." She was up again, closely examining a dead frond on a large and ugly fern.

"And while I was godmother to the last Lord Hancock's wife, I don't know his brother, the current Lord Hancock.

I wasn't asked to sponsor his ward, my goddaughter's child, when she came out last season." She made an expression of disgust, which could have been for the leaf or Hancock's failure to ask for Lady Westover's help.

"And Blackford. Oh, my. Sir Broderick said you'd met him."

I'd been enjoying the tea and sandwiches while I wrote. I swallowed and said, "Yes. He seems to have either a strange sense of humor or a kind nature behind his gruff exterior. I expected to get thrown out of his house on my rear, but he was polite enough to tell me his side of the story. He claimed Drake was a thief and they figured it out after the Duke of Merville's daughter's engagement party. He wouldn't tell me who 'they' were, but Lord Hancock supplied the names."

"I've never heard the Duke of Blackford described as kind, but I'd believe he has a perverse sense of humor. He hasn't been rumored attached to anyone since Victoria Dutton-Cox's death a week before their nuptials. He has a brilliant head for investments and has made an absolute fortune."

"What can you tell me about his sister?"

"His half sister. Margaret. He raised her after the deaths of both her parents. She was the old duke's child with his second wife. She was presented to the queen, but by the next season, after Victoria Dutton-Cox's death, she was up north at their castle and has never returned to London. Can you imagine a young society belle not coming to London for the season?"

"Was her season successful?" Maybe she'd been ignored by the men despite her brother's fortune. I considered the possibility and discarded it immediately. From the royal family to the poorest in East London, everyone gravitated to money.

"Oh, yes. She had her pick of men, but she was too busy having a good time to settle on one."

"Would her brother have made her miss the next season to be in mourning for his fiancée?"

"No. The two girls came to hate each other. He wouldn't have expected Margaret to do more than a token mourning.

He kept his mourning for the entire year, but it didn't keep him from conducting his financial affairs."

I looked out the window past the plants hanging there for a minute while I thought. "The only thing these men seem to have in common are young ladies in the family who were recently involved in the London season. Can you think of anyone else who fits into the same group and might have had something stolen from them by Mr. Drake?"

"Plenty of young ladies have been out in society the last few seasons. I don't know of anyone who had something stolen. Still, it's odd this Mr. Drake could get away with it for so long. Margaret hasn't been in society the past two seasons. Daisy Hancock just came out last season. Why didn't the word spread through society that the man was not to be invited?" Lady Westover raised her eyebrows before she took a sip of her tea.

"Blackford told me no one realized the connection until Merville made a comment after his daughter's engagement party."

"And you believe this?"

"On the face of it, yes."

Lady Westover laughed a wheezy rumble. "My dear child, this man Drake had no real standing in society, things were presumably stolen while he was around, and no one questioned the losses or his presence. Don't be naive."

I was no sheltered miss. I'd never considered myself naive. "What do these men have in common, then?"

"No. The question is why have they kept quiet so long, even to each other, but when they suddenly discover they have something in common, they immediately join forces. I believe if you look closely, you'll find they were all being blackmailed."

I nearly dropped my delicate china cup. "Blackmail? We hadn't considered that possibility." I thought over what I knew and what the Duke of Merville had said as he left my shop. "But it makes sense."

Lady Westover nodded and then took another sip of tea.

"Sir Broderick's note says we need to turn you into a society miss. Not an easy task when everyone knows everyone else's family tree back five generations. I'm afraid you'll have to have a questionable pedigree. Would you prefer slightly wanton or deliciously decadent?"

I RETURNED TO the bookstore and hung up my cloak and hat while Emma finished with a customer. Once the bell rang over the door marking the shopper's exit, I joined my assistant. "I've had an interesting meeting with Lady Westover."

Emma made a face. "Meetings with her are always interesting."

"She suggested Drake was blackmailing the men he supposedly stole from."

Emma looked startled. "I can't wait to hear how she came to that conclusion. When do we meet with Sir Broderick?"

"Tomorrow night. How do we find out who originally introduced Drake to society? Lady Westover didn't know him, so she's no help."

"You could try the Duke of Blackford. He was helpful before." After she finished speaking, Emma managed to keep a solemn expression for five seconds before she burst out laughing. When I frowned, she turned serious. "I have no idea who we could ask, since I've never been presented to the queen. Unless you count the queen's judges."

I wondered how Emma could joke about what must have been a terrible experience for a young girl. When I'd met her, she was in Newgate Prison awaiting trial for theft and as an accomplice in murder.

At the request of the victim's son, the Archivist Society had taken on the murder case. The victim was a wealthy manufacturer who'd been stabbed through the heart in his study. The son believed his father's business rival was the

murderer, but the rival claimed to have been home all evening.

At the same time the body was found, however, three
burglars were discovered hiding in the man's bedroom.
Among those three was an athletic child who'd climbed
through upper-story windows to let her accomplices in.

Emma was thirteen, dirty, undernourished, and bruised.
Pacing across the stone floor of the interview room, her blond
braid bouncing on her thin back, she had a Viking's defiance
and the wits of a pickpocket. I sat down at the table and
began to read the police report to her. After a moment, she
came to stand behind me.

"You can read that?" she said.

"That, and much more. Stories of pirates and princesses.
The news of the day and a recipe from a cookbook. Have you
never been to school?" I asked.

"Not much chance of that where I've been."

"If you help me prove who really killed that man, I'll
teach you."

"Big Ed won't let you."

I knew Emma was charged with breaking into houses for
the gang of thieves and extortionists he led, and he was the
nastiest brute in a slum full of rotten scoundrels. I made my
decision on the spot. "Big Ed won't have a choice if you're
living with Phyllida and me."

"Who's Phyllida?"

"My aunt." Honesty made me add, "Sort of."

"Sort of?"

"She needed a place to stay and I needed someone to help
me. I can't manage both the house and the bookshop alone."
I was ten years older than this girl but certain that my
responsibilities made me seem much older.

"You have a shop?" Her eyes gleamed with more avarice
than just love of books.

"It means enough money to feed ourselves and provides us with the wonders of a thousand stories."

She scowled, her dreams of a heist vanishing while her curiosity grew. "Where are your parents?"

"Dead."

Emma nodded solemnly and our partnership was born.

She was every bit as observant as I suspected and provided eyewitness testimony to the arrival and hasty departure of someone who turned out to be the victim's business rival. Sir Broderick hired an excellent barrister who convinced the judge Emma belonged with me and not in jail where she'd be corrupted by villains.

I smiled at the wonderful young woman Emma had become. "Perhaps Sir Broderick can help find someone who knows how long Nicholas Drake has been in society and who introduced him. In the meantime, let's take a look at the public information about our candidates for kidnapper. Maybe we'll get an idea about how any of them could be blackmailed."

Sitting across from each other at the map table, we began to search the thick volumes on noble families. Dust rose with the familiar smells of dry paper and old bindings.

"Lady Margaret Ranleigh, sister of the Duke of Blackford, has her birth date listed and the date she was presented to the queen, and nothing else." I looked up the page at the long listing for her brother. "Here's the list of companies Blackford advises or invests in. I recognize most of the names, and these are successful businesses."

"We know he wasn't blackmailed over his financial state."

I shook my head. "If I were going to blackmail him, it would have something to do with his fiancée dying a week before the wedding."

Emma looked over my shoulder at the book. "How sad."

"Was it sad for Blackford? His sister supposedly didn't care for her. And the fiancée's father is Lord Dutton-Cox, another one of the five names we have."

"Could they both be blackmailed over her death? What's her name?"

"Victoria Dutton-Cox."

Emma looked at the entry for the duke's dead almost-bride. "Date of birth, date presented, date engaged, date of death. We better start with the death certificate and then find the doctor."

THE NEXT DAY, I left Somerset House, home of the repository of all of Britain's birth, marriage, and death records, and the workplace of a fellow Archivist Society member, after we had a nice chat and I gained a good deal of information. My next stop that afternoon was at Lady Westover's, where I found her at the desk in her morning room reading from a thick book about plant diseases. She slipped her pince-nez glasses off and smiled at me. "Back so soon? You must have hit a wall."

"Your suggestion that Drake specialized in blackmail and not theft has made us look at the death of Victoria Dutton-Cox."

"Her death certainly started a lot of hushed talk at the time. It was all anyone could do to keep the gossip out of the papers."

"Was her obituary printed?"

"Of course. That and nothing else. Still, her funeral was very well attended, more out of curiosity than grief."

"What did she die of? I've just come from Somerset House, and her death certificate was uninformative."

"Have you spoken to the doctor? I believe one was called immediately."

"His death certificate was also on file at Somerset House. Typhoid."

"Never trust a doctor who dies young. If he can't keep himself alive, why should you believe anything he says? Take

my advice, Georgia. If you want to live to an old age, stay away
from careless doctors." Lady Westover shut the volume and
focused her pale eyes on me. "Why are you here, child?"

"I need you to call on Lady Dutton-Cox and take me along."

"So you can stir up the memory of her daughter's death
again? You are ghoulish."

"I wouldn't ask if it weren't important. A man's life is at
stake."

"Mr. Drake? I don't care what Sir Broderick says, he's just
not important enough for me to risk my friendship with
Honoria Dutton-Cox."

"And if her husband or a duke is going to hang for his
murder, is that important enough?"

"Heavens, yes! Think of the scandal."

Some things Lady Westover and the Archivist Society
would never agree on. Ignoring our differences, I said, "Good.
Then we need to get moving to the Dutton-Coxes'. I don't
want to call on her while others might be present."

"At least you'd save her that much embarrassment. Of
course, she may not be home to anyone, not even me. By the
way, Georgia, have you decided who you'll be for this investigation?"

I'd already given that quite a bit of thought. "Georgia Peabody, your poor relation, here to see London, but there's no
danger of my seeing the inside of a society event. My mother
made an unfortunate marriage, but you see no reason to cut
me off entirely for her mistake." I gave her a big smile.

"Don't be too certain of that, young lady." She tapped the
table. "Mother is too recent. Your grandmother was the one
who made the scandalous alliance. Your mother was properly
married to a nobody; both parents are deceased. Yes, I think
that should do, Miss Georgia Peabody, to keep you scandalous enough to stay out of society."

CHAPTER FIVE

LADY Westover summoned coat, hat, gloves, and carriage, and soon we were off in more style than I was accustomed to to visit one of the suspects in the Drake investigation.

Luck was with me. Honoria Dutton-Cox greeted us in her empty parlor. Or rather, greeted Lady Westover. I did my best self-effacing act until I was introduced, at which time Lady Dutton-Cox gave a nervous giggle and said, "What a shame you're here while the weather is so beastly and the season has barely begun."

I gave the appropriate curtsy and said, "There's no chance of my coming to London for the season, because I wouldn't be invited anywhere. On account of Grandmama, you see. But Lady Westover wanted so much to see you today, with the second anniversary of your great tragedy coming up, and decided since you were a kind and understanding woman that you wouldn't mind my being introduced to you in private."

The woman blinked at my tale, but Lady Westover gracefully stepped in before she could organize her thoughts to throw me out. "We all have tragedies in our lives. You more than most understand the truth of that. So I thought you wouldn't mind my bringing Georgia with me today, since I know how melancholy a season this is for you and I wanted to cheer you up."

"That's kind of you," the woman said to Lady Westover, her dark eyes narrowing as she made a move toward the door. *She's not going to talk to me.* I decided to weave the story into a thicker cloth. "My sister died at about the same time as your daughter. I still miss her terribly, and not a day goes by that I don't see something that I want to rush home and tell her about. But that can never be."

The story was true, except it wasn't my sister and it wasn't two years ago. But my real feelings came through in my voice.

Tears sprang to Lady Dutton-Cox's eyes and she wordlessly clutched my hands for a moment before motioning us to sit. In that moment, I smelled the liquor on her breath. I wondered if her family realized how badly she grieved for her daughter, and kicked myself for using her.

"How did your sister die?" she asked me.

I had read Victoria's death certificate. "A weak heart."

Instead of taking a seat herself, the woman paced the room. She spoke so quietly I had to sit forward to hear her words. "My daughter was murdered."

Lady Westover gasped. I mentally applauded her timing while I said, "What a tragedy. Called not by God's design, but by man's. Have they caught the monster who did this?"

"No. Between them, her fiancé and her father made certain there was no investigation." Remembering herself, Lady Dutton-Cox took a seat and rubbed her hands together. "I'm told this is only my fancy. She had a weak constitution and succumbed to a chill."

"Still, a very troubling death," I said.

Lady Westover shot me a warning look before saying, "And a tragedy for all of Victoria's friends. But I suppose you still see them because they'd be Elizabeth's friends, too."

"Not so much since Elizabeth married. We've been quite alone since last summer." The woman gave a wan smile.

"I suppose you haven't heard the gossip about one of her friends that Lady Westover told me. A young man has vanished. A Nicholas Drake." I hoped her loneliness or the liquor would cause her to speak freely and hated myself for increasing her misery.

"Drake. I didn't think I'd hear that name again. He and Victoria were great friends. Along with Lord Naylard," she quickly amended.

"Lord Naylard?" I turned a puzzled look from one lady to the other.

"Lord Naylard and his sister, Lucinda, introduced Drake to us. To Victoria, really. They thoroughly enjoyed each other's company. Always telling jokes and laughing. Victoria loved to laugh." Her mother sighed and looked away.

After a moment, Lady Westover glanced at me. It seemed Lady Dutton-Cox had forgotten us. "So the four of them made a little circle?" the older woman asked.

Another sigh. "Not Lucinda. She's very serious. Very religious. High Church, almost Papist, I think. But Lord Naylard and Mr. Drake were both keen on Victoria before the duke asked for her hand. Then he wanted an immediate wedding and Victoria wanted to wait until summer."

"Summer weddings are so beautiful," Lady Westover said. "Elizabeth had one, I believe."

"Yes. But the duke is very businesslike. I imagine that's why he's so rich. Why put off the wedding until summer when right now will do? But Victoria had her heart set on waiting. She didn't want to give up her friendship with Mr. Drake and Lord Naylard, who were both more fun than the brooding duke."

"The duke wouldn't cut her off from her friends, would he? That's so medieval." Lady Westover's tone didn't allow for disagreement.

"No, but Blackford's sister would. She also fancied Mr. Drake, always whispering to him, although the poor girl had no chance with him despite her wealth. No grace, no humor, just those flashing black eyes like the duke's and a tragic air like Shakespeare's Juliet. And so jealous."

As we heard footsteps outside the parlor's double doors, Lady Dutton-Cox leaned forward and whispered, "If anyone murdered my Victoria, it was that evil Blackford girl. And she was definitely murdered."

I RETURNED TO my shop wondering why two people had now insisted the sister of the Duke of Blackford had murdered Victoria Dutton-Cox. Less than an hour later a carriage pulled up in front of our door. An elegantly dressed couple alighted with the assistance of a liveried footman. While the footman remained outside, the gentleman held the door open for the lady. Once she was inside, he hurried around her and marched up to the counter to face me. "Georgia Fenchurch?"

"Yes. How may I help you?" From the tip of his shiny top hat to the toes of his polished, impractical shoes, I could see he wasn't a reader. Our customers seldom walked as far as the counter before being distracted by a shelf of books, and they never arrived without a smudge marring their hems or cuffs or shoes.

I glanced at Emma, who was helping our lone customer in the cookbook section. She gave a quick nod of her head and said something to the woman while pointing to a shelf.

"I want you to stay away from Lady Dutton-Cox," the man said. His voice as well as his clothes announced he was used to giving orders.

How had he found out my identity so quickly? I stood staring at him with a puzzled look on my face, while Emma and her customer watched with curiosity.

He lowered his voice. "I know who you really are. Lady

Covington, who called on my wife's mother immediately after you, told us of your true identity."

The Archivist Society had aided Lady Covington in a previous case. She had been exceedingly grateful for our work, and our discretion. Unfortunately, she must have recognized me when I hurried from Lady Dutton-Cox's parlor and probably sang our praises using my real name. With that thought, the man's identity came to me. "You're Viscount Dalrymple, and this must be your viscountess." Elizabeth, formerly Dutton-Cox. I dropped them both a quick curtsy. "Now, why do you want me to stay away from Lady Dutton-Cox?"

Elizabeth, who'd been standing back, stepped next to the viscount. She was a stunning brunette with pale skin and flashing eyes. Right then they were flashing with anger and aimed at me. "Mummy's been through enough by losing Victoria. I want you to leave her alone," came out in a hiss.

She tugged off one of her gloves. "She thought the sun rose and set on my sister." Her voice was so low I barely heard her words, but the bitterness of her tone was unmistakable.

"Your mother is being blackmailed by Nicholas Drake, who has since disappeared," This was only a guess, but I watched their expressions for telltale changes. I was rewarded by a look of surprise followed by discomfort that crossed the viscountess's face as she glanced at her husband.

"Good," the woman snapped, yanking off the other glove.

"Why is she being blackmailed?" I asked as the bell over the shop door jingled. The viscount and his bride blocked my view of the new arrival, and I hoped Emma could manage both customers.

"That is neither your business nor mine. The point is, she isn't any longer. I put a stop to it," the viscount said.

"Why did you put a stop to it? Why not Lord Dutton-Cox or their son?" I was whispering now, and both Dalrymples were leaning over the counter to hear me. In my peripheral vision, I could see that Emma and the middle-aged woman she'd been waiting on were standing frozen in place watching us keenly. A white-haired man in a clerical collar joined them and looked from them to the three of us in fascination. Maybe drama was good for business. It certainly had been for Shakespeare.

"Because Lord Dutton-Cox sent Drake to me to deal with. I imagine my poor father-in-law had had enough. His daughter had died and his wife was"—he paused—"distraught."

I would have bet anything the viscount had also smelled liquor on his mother-in-law's breath. "What could she possibly have done to be blackmailed by Nicholas Drake? They hardly moved in the same circles."

The viscount lifted his head to look down his patrician nose at me. "As a gentleman, I didn't think it right to discover their secret. I didn't ask if it was Lord or Lady Dutton-Cox who was being blackmailed or why Drake felt he could threaten them." He was slim, fair haired, and blue eyed. Handsome if you liked the classic English aristocratic type. Unfortunately, Blackford had ruined my taste for tame looks with the lightning he left in his wake.

"Could this have anything to do with Lady Dutton-Cox's claim that Victoria was murdered?" I looked from one to the other. Dalrymple looked puzzled.

Elizabeth stared at me for a minute and appeared to come to a decision. "Mummy's right. Or at least, I believe she is. Can you imagine the pressure the Duke of Blackford can bring to bear to keep a story like that quiet?"

Her words gave the duke's interference a whole new meaning. "You think he killed your sister?"

"I wouldn't be surprised to learn his half sister did. She was high-strung. Flighty. And Victoria called on her shortly before she died." She leaned forward slightly, her nose still in the air. "Speak to Lady Julia Waxpool about Lady Margaret Ranleigh. You'll find it more enlightening than speaking to my mother."

"How would Nicholas Drake have become mixed up in this business?"

"He was there that day. If you want to know why he was blackmailing my mother, you'll have to ask him. If you can find him." With a smile to her husband, Elizabeth walked to the door without a glance around her.

"Stay away from the Dutton-Cox family, and stay away from my wife and me." With his parting order, the viscount hurried over to open the door for his wife and they walked out, oblivious to the four pairs of eyes watching them avidly.

The man in the clerical collar spoke first. "Oh, my. Not readers, are they?"

AFTER THE DINNER of roasted chicken and vegetables Phyllida had prepared, Emma and I cleaned up the kitchen and then hurried to get ready for the Archivist Society meeting at Sir Broderick's.

"You're going to be very disappointed if we learn Nicholas Drake has returned home and is surprised by all the excitement his going to Brighton caused," Emma called out from her room.

I'd be mortified by the hurt I'd needlessly caused Lady Dutton-Cox if Drake was found safe and sound. I wasn't going to admit that transgression to anyone. "That would be the best possible outcome, but I don't think it's going to happen."

"Help me with my evening corset. I want to wear my blue dress tonight."

I went in to help her dress. "In case we have two peers drop in on our meeting again?"

"I noticed you put on your evening corset and a nice dress before you went to Somerset House." Emma caught my eye in the looking glass and raised an elegant eyebrow. If she ever played an aristocrat, she'd have to play a foreigner. She could never act the part of someone's poor relation.

"What's this?" Phyllida might be twenty-five years my senior, but there was nothing wrong with the spinster's hearing. "You have two peers involved in your newest investigation?"

I shrugged. "Actually, half a dozen."

"Anyone I know?" Phyllida stood in the doorway, staring at me.

It seemed kinder to rattle off the names and pretend these weren't the people Phyllida had daily rubbed shoulders with in her younger years than not to respond. I gave her the list.

"I was friends with Waxpool's daughter. She died, oh, it's been thirty years ago now. I remember Dutton-Cox as a stuffy little boy. The current Lord Hancock took off for Africa to study nature and make his fortune a quarter century ago. He didn't, of course. Nothing that would help you now, I'm sure." She smiled weakly.

Silence hung in the air. No one mentioned the years she'd suffered at her brother's hand before the Archivist investigation had sent her brother to the gallows and brought her into my home.

"This case revolves around young ladies just introduced to the queen and a man who's accused of using society balls to steal secrets. Everyone's more Emma's age than mine." I needed to change the topic as heat crept up my face. "Lady Westover introduced me to Lady Dutton-Cox during visiting hours. I didn't get a chance to tell you, Emma, with all the bustle in the shop when I returned." I slid the dress over her head so I didn't have to hear her rejoinder.

Once her dress was in place, Emma began reworking her hairdo. "Too bad there isn't some money to be made from this investigation so you could buy some nice clothes for your role."

"I'm playing a poor relation from some backwater, so nice clothes wouldn't be appropriate." I tried without success to tame my auburn curls.

"Good thing, because your hairdo belongs on a washer-woman. Here, let me do something with it."

In a minute, Emma did more with my coiffure than I could do in an hour. I now had a curly upswept hairdo that made me look like a Gibson girl and made me fear my heavy locks would tumble down at any moment. Then she finished her own with a high coil and waves from the newest Paris fashion plates, gave us both a critical look-over, and we left for Sir Broderick's.

It was a short walk, but we hadn't gone far when the crawling sensation on the back of my neck told me someone was watching us. "When we reach New Oxford Street, I'm going to stop. I want you to look behind me while you adjust my hat."

"Why?"

"I think we're being followed."

"This is a strange case if someone finds it necessary to follow two harmless women," Emma said, "especially if the person feeling so unsettled by our interest is someone with the power and money of an aristocrat."

When I stopped, she was ready to swing in front of me and look over my shoulder while she straightened my hat. "It's a good thing I did, too. Your hat wasn't at the right angle."

"Well?" I demanded.

"There are plenty of people around, but no one is looking or acting suspiciously. Are you sure we were being followed?"

My cheeks heated. "No."

Nevertheless, with few people around and thick shrubbery for an attacker to hide in along the paths inside Bloomsbury Square, we walked around the edge of the park instead of through it.

When we arrived at Sir Broderick's town house, unharmed but slightly out of breath from hurrying, Jacob opened the door as soon as we rang and took our cloaks, hats, and gloves. We waited for him and then walked upstairs as a group to enter the study.

Frances Atterby and Adam Fogarty were already seated with Sir Broderick, who waved a sheet of cream-colored note-paper at us. "Lady Westover has graciously set up a family dinner for her relation, Georgia Peabody, which will include a couple of the peers involved in this case. Lord Naylard and his sister have already accepted. Her grandson will also be in attendance."

Emma and I fixed tea from the pot kept warm under a tea cozy while Jacob helped himself to Dominique's digestive biscuits. Then we settled into chairs at a distance from Sir Broderick's roaring fire. "How does Inspector Grantham feel about being dragged into one of our investigations?" I needed to know how angry he was going to be at me for involving his grandmother.

"He's threatened to lock Lady Westover up in her home, but she writes that he knows how far that will get him."

"He'll be taking it out on me, then." I shrugged my shoulders. "That's not a problem unless he gives me away."

"He won't, Georgia, unless it's necessary to save his grand-mother's life."

I knew Sir Broderick was right. Inspector Grantham had worked with us before and not given us away. "When is this family dinner?"

"Tomorrow night."

"That doesn't give us much time. What has anyone learned?"

Fogarty answered my question first. "I played the chap from the Water Board. I was suspicious of a woman with a colicky baby across from Drake's and one house over. I sent Grace back, thinking it needed a woman's touch. The mother had been up with the baby at about the correct time and looked out the window. She saw a very ordinary coach with no markings whose driver sat in the box the entire time. They were there at least five minutes, but not ten."

"Did she see anything of the passengers?"

He flipped over a page in his notebook. "No. She heard men's voices when they left, but she was on the wrong side of the street to see them. They seemed to be in a hurry getting away, shouting at the driver to get a move on."

"Not a shiny, tall, ancient carriage?"

"No. Just a rental you'd expect to see hired to take a group somewhere. She remembered one of the two horses was a gray. She thought the coach would look better if the horses matched."

"Definitely not the duke's carriage. Edith Carter lied about that. Why? And what else has been a lie?"

Fogarty said, "I talked to her maid when I went to her house on my rounds for our fictitious Water Board survey. She said it was just the mistress and her."

"No parents. Why did she lie to me about that? What possible difference could that make?" I'd been badly used by Miss Carter.

"I'm sure she has a reason for every lie, Georgia. The story about the coach may have been to point our attention at the duke." Sir Broderick smiled, his eyes half-closed.

"He and his fellow club members are the only people we've found so far who might have a reason to abduct Mr. Drake," Frances said. "Of course, there's no reason why he would choose his victims from only one club. Once we saw the connection between Mr. Drake and debutantes, I started looking at the parties he was invited to last season. He attended at least fifty balls, although none of the smaller entertainments."

Frances took a sip of her tea. "I talked to a couple of my contacts, middle-aged gently born ladies who act as chaperones at these balls so the mamas can go elsewhere. They remember Drake. He could always be counted on to fill out the dance cards of the less-popular misses and make himself agreeable wherever. It sounded to me as if he had ample opportunity to snatch the odd small, valuable trinket."

"And seek out signs of scandal for blackmail," I added.

"No one is ever more alone than in a crush at a ball," Sir Broderick said. "What else has anyone found?"

Jacob said, "I tried all the pubs in the area, looking for Nicholas Drake's friends Harry and Tom. Said I'd heard they were looking for me for a spot of work. I finally met up with Tom Whitaker. He said they didn't have anything planned at this time, but they'd keep me in mind if they did. I told them I'd talked to Drake a few days ago and he said there was work to be had and soon. That's when Tom said he'd not seen Drake in a few days and didn't know about any plans. And I learned Harry's last name is Conover."

"Good work, everyone." I filled them in on what I'd learned from Lady Westover and what Lady Dutton-Cox and her daughter Elizabeth had revealed.

"I'll track down Harry Conover and see if he and Tom are known to my former mates." Fogarty smiled as he limped in front of the bookcases. The retired police sergeant's eyes sparkled whenever anyone gave him the slightest reason to chat with his former colleagues.

"We need to talk to the duke's sister, but she's in the country," I said. I hoped I didn't sound bitter at the prospect of traveling four days to meet someone who'd probably refuse to talk to me, but I didn't want to leave my shop for that long for a trip that would probably prove fruitless.

"Where's the family seat?" Sir Broderick asked, stirring in his wheeled chair by the fire.

"Northumberland."

"Frances, see if you can learn who the duke's half sister, Margaret, was friendly with before she left town, and whether they've exchanged letters with her since."

I looked around the room. "I'll talk to Julia Waxpool. As

she's a debutante, Drake might be blackmailing or stealing from her, and her grandfather is on the list Lord Hancock gave us. I've heard she was acquainted with Lady Margaret. With luck, I'll be able to find out what she knows about Victoria and Margaret and whether there were truly bad feelings between them."

Turning to Emma, I added, "Could you follow up on where Edith Carter was born and if she's ever been married?"

"Do you think chasing down the person who brought the problem to our attention is a wise use of our time?" Sir Broderick asked.

I nodded. "She knows more than she's told us, she's lied to me, and I want to get that problem out of the way before we take on all of polite society."

Sir Broderick smiled. "Tomorrow, Emma, please find out everything you can about Edith Carter. After that, you may be too busy watching the bookshop in Georgia's absence to do much sleuthing for us."

Frances Atterby said, "Perhaps I can help Emma. I may not know the book business, but I know how to wait on people. And my son's wife has been making noises again that I'm underfoot and should be sent away to her family's farm to mind the chickens. Me? On a farm? Can you imagine anything worse? I can't allow that. And I can't stay not busy."

Emma and I made murmuring sounds. Frances might look like she was getting older and should be slowing down, but she wasn't. More to the point, she didn't want to.

The widow of a London hotel manager, Frances had come to the Archivists to find her husband's killer. It had taken us two years to bring the monster to justice, and in the meantime, her son kept telling her to sit down and put her feet up while he and his wife ran the hotel. Accustomed to an active life, Frances transferred her considerable talents and energy to the Archivist Society. As she told us, her son never noticed and her daughter-in-law didn't care.

"After you check on those young ladies for Sir Broderick, Emma and I would be glad of your help."

Sir Broderick said, "If there's nothing else, we can call it a night. Georgia, I'd like you to wait a moment, please."

Oh, great. What had I done? Or not done? Emma nodded to me and walked downstairs talking to Frances. I pulled up a chair across from Sir Broderick, letting his body block the worst of the heat from the fire. Sweat still rose on my scalp and under my corset.

"Georgia, I need to tell you something. From that time."

I knew what time he meant. Both of our lives had been irretrievably altered.

"Do you remember Denis Lupton?"

"I remember he had a bookshop on Piccadilly. He was murdered not long after my parents—" I gulped down a sob. Those days had been too much with me lately.

"His killer was never caught," Sir Broderick said.

"I remember every bookseller in London was terrified for weeks afterward. In the end, life returned to normal."

"Your father had a message from Lupton a few days before he was taken prisoner. About a Gutenberg Bible."

I grabbed the arms of the chair I sat in to prevent me from leaping up. "What did Lupton want? What did my father answer? And why have you waited until now to tell me?"

"I don't know what the message said, but your father was frightened. He told me he sent a message back to Lupton saying no. Your father wanted nothing to do with whatever Lupton proposed."

He'd ignored the question I most wanted answered. "Why have you waited until now to tell me this?"

"Because if I had told you before, you'd have gone off chasing the wind in hopes of finding the murderer. Now you're doing it anyway, so you might as well know what little I learned."

I settled back in my chair, ready to hear the rest. "You're certain this concerned a copy of the Gutenberg Bible?"

"Yes. I do know that much. Later, I learned Lupton's shop was ransacked when he was killed. A tall, well-built man in a top hat was seen strolling away just before the body was found, but he wasn't carrying anything. Could the murderer be your abductor? I don't know."

"Had you considered talking to Lupton about the Bible?"

"When you came running in here that day, I decided to question your father and Lupton as soon as we freed your parents. Instead, I found myself in agony with mangled legs. I was bedridden for months. Everyone who came to see me hovered, waiting for me to die." He smiled. "Except you, Georgia. Your determination to right wrongs, and forcing me to help you, saved my life and gave me a purpose for living."

I couldn't bear to have him thank me. I'd failed him as badly as I had my parents. "When did you find out the details about Lupton's murder?"

He brushed my words away with one hand. "No, Georgia, I need to say this. You saved my life twice, once at the house where your parents perished, and once when you came to me to help you prove you didn't kill Lord Westover."

"Scotland Yard should have searched harder for his murderer." I couldn't keep the bitterness out of my tone. I'd been eighteen, newly orphaned, and frightened of the police detective who'd questioned me.

"If they had, I never would have met Adam Fogarty and Lady Westover and we never would have formed the Archivist Society."

I had to smile at the recollection. "I nagged you night and day, brought you every scrap of information I learned, until you finally gave up. You brought Lady Westover, police sergeant Fogarty, and me together in this room. That was the day you began to build the Archivist Society. Now," I said, giving him an obviously false stern look, "when did you learn the details of Lupton's murder?"

"Much after the fact, a witness to the discovery of Lupton's body came to see me about an antiquarian volume. Given such an opportunity, I learned all he could tell me about the murder. He knew nothing about any bookseller possessing a Gutenberg Bible."

This was a new lead, at least to me. "I think we need to investigate Lupton's murder using the assumption he was killed by the same man who killed my parents."

"Georgia, we have to consider the possibility that the murderer learned about Lupton from your father."

My father would have only revealed that type of information to his abductor if he or my mother were tortured. I must have sounded grim when I replied, "We'll find out when I catch him."

But where was he now?

CHAPTER SIX

As it turned out, Emma was gone most of the next day on our investigation while I managed the shop and wondered what I would discover at dinner that night. She returned in time to help Phyllida dress me for the party with the warning that I'd better not stay out late because she had more archival research to do the next morning. Phyllida hushed her while reminding me what each of the fourteen pieces of silverware I'd face at dinner was used for.

I took a cab to Lady Westover's and entered through the mews at the back so as not to be noticed arriving. Fortunately, it wasn't raining and by carefully stepping and holding my skirt embarrassingly high, I entered without trailing dirt and wet footsteps. I didn't have time to brush mud off my skirt, and it probably wouldn't have helped. The fabric would be ruined if the hem got wet or dirty.

Glancing out from the back hall, I saw no one by the front entrance or the stairs. Hurrying up the steps, I caught my breath outside the door to her formal parlor. Then I nodded

to the butler and he opened the door. He announced me and
I found I faced a silent room full of stares.

My evening gown had too little fabric in the tiny sleeves
and too much in the front of my skirt. It was five years out of
fashion, and the guests were probably considering how far from
London and society I lived. I was well disguised to play Lady
Westover's unfortunate relative. Lifting my head, I stepped
forward, looking as pleased to meet them as I felt.

Lady Westover introduced me to Lord Naylard and his
sister, Lucinda, before she was called away by the butler. After
my curtsy, Naylard said, "It must be jolly to have family
visit." He had the coloring and eagerness of a golden retriever
puppy.

"Even more so for me, since this is a special treat. Do you
have a large family here in London?" I said.

"No. Miss Lucinda and I are on our own. We're not a
hardy family. But we have each other." He gave his sister a
look of pure devotion.

She looked at him benignly, like a woman gazing at a not
overly bright lapdog, and said, "My task in life is taking good
care of my brother." Her dark blue gown was high necked
and her widely puffed sleeves covered the tops of her white
gloves at the elbows. Her jewels at ear and neck and wrist
were almost as understated as my pearl earrings.

I gave her a smile and said, "Your dress is both lovely and
practical in these drafty houses. I admire your taste."

Lucinda gave me a gracious nod but said nothing.

How did these aristocrats handle social situations if they
didn't talk? Shifting the conversation, I said, "Lady Westover
told me this was to be a family dinner, so you must be related
to her, and, more distantly, to me."

"Lady Westover is my mother's cousin, once or twice
removed. How are you related to her?" Lord Naylard asked.

A detail she and I hadn't worked out. Aiming for vague-
ness, I said, "Through my scandalous grandmother. I think

Lady Westover takes an interest in me to make certain I don't repeat family history best left forgotten."

Another guest came up to us. Lord Hancock paid attention to only Lord Naylard, saying, "I'm glad I've seen you tonight. I have an opportunity I'd like to let you in on. I'll stop by your club tomorrow."

Hancock had seen me at the Archivist Society meeting he'd crashed. He apparently hadn't considered me worthy of notice that night, but I turned to face Lucinda Naylard and hoped he didn't recognize me.

Miss Lucinda ignored me and moved between Hancock and her brother. "He has no interest in investing in machines of war, Lord Hancock."

"The British army is fighting all over the globe for our empire. They should have every advantage," Hancock said.

"Our army already has the advantage over those poor natives in every way. You can't save the world by inventing noxious things and blowing everyone up. And that's all we've seen your inventions do." Miss Lucinda put a lovely sneer in her tone. I was impressed with her polished reserve. Apparently so was Naylard. He took a half step behind his sister.

Hancock matched her sneer as he said, "You claim to be concerned about saving the souls of all mankind, but I'm the one who's lived in Africa and met those savages. I've seen what they're capable of, and I think our soldiers should be protected from those heathens."

Lady Naylard sniffed indelicately and said, "What were you doing that made the natives respond with violence?"

Hancock narrowed his eyes and jutted his chin aggressively. "I was studying the medical properties of plants and insects. Nothing that should have upset them. But I saw barbarism that can't be believed in this civilized country, much less spoken of in polite society." He focused on Naylard and said, "Keep your sister home where she's safe to believe the natives have souls worth saving."

Naylard was saying, "Oh, I can't let her leave—," as a very young woman dressed in the height of fashion and dripping jewels joined us, Lady Westover at her side. Lucinda Naylard gave Hancock a scowl and turned to the new arrivals.

"Georgia," Lady Westover said in a tone designed to remind everyone they were at a dinner party, "I'd like you to meet Miss Daisy Hancock. Her mother was my dear goddaughter. And have you been introduced to Lord Hancock, her uncle and guardian?"

I dropped into my curtsy again, keeping my head down in the hope that Lord Hancock wouldn't recognize me.

When I glanced up, Hancock looked fully at me for the first time and scowled. I decided to stay in character and hope he only thought I resembled someone as I said, "Lady Westover has mentioned you're a famous scientist."

"More like infamous," Lucinda Naylard murmured.

Miss Daisy looked her over with a pitying expression and said, "My uncle's a brilliant man. Too bad you don't recognize his greatness. He's done vital work for the army and he's a fellow of the Royal Society. I've been privileged to live in London with him since my parents' death."

"Associate fellow, actually," Lord Naylard added with happy eagerness, and then dipped his head like a scolded puppy when Hancock glared at him.

"Oh, good for you," Miss Lucinda said with such finality the young woman was shocked into silence.

Hancock pulled Lady Westover aside and said in a loud whisper, "Really, should you be inflicting your unsavory relations on Miss Daisy? She's an innocent who was presented to the queen less than a year ago."

"Oh, Georgia is innocent of any trespass. It's her grandmother I wouldn't introduce to Miss Daisy," Lady Westover said blithely. "I had the worst time getting in contact with you. You really should let your friends know when you move."

"We moved last fall from Chelling Meadows to a more convenient and modern town house. I thought you knew." Hancock fixed her with a haughty expression. "No, I didn't. Your brother was the one who bought Chelling Meadows. I suppose it's hard to make someone else's house yours." Lady Westover matched his disdainful look before turning to her butler, who hovered at her shoulder. After a moment, she announced, "I've been informed dinner is ready. We'll go down now and hope our last guest arrives soon. Eddy, if you'd escort Miss Daisy down, and Georgia, you'll have to bring up the rear on your own."

Eddy, Lady Westover's grandson and a Scotland Yard inspector who much preferred to be called Edward or Inspector Grantham, winced but did as he was bidden. He flashed me a look that clearly said, *What are you up to?* before he offered Miss Daisy his arm.

We entered the dining room and faced Lady Westover's large square table with two seats on each of the four sides and a stunning floral arrangement in the center. With the amount of time and effort Lady Westover spent on her heated glasshouse, I shouldn't have been surprised at the gaily colored spring flowers that decorated the table.

Once we were all seated, the vacant chair next to me drew all eyes. Lady Westover had told me earlier my missing partner was the son of an old friend and suspected in Drake's disappearance, but she refused to give me the man's identity.

Naylard shared a corner of the table with me, giving me an excellent opportunity to question him about Drake. As soon as the soup course was served and the footmen retired, I said, "I've heard a friend of yours has gone missing."

His unlined face scrunched up in a frown. "Who?" he asked around a mouthful of creamy asparagus soup.

"Nicholas Drake."

"Yes. Shocking, isn't it?"

"How did you meet?"

"It's dashed embarrassing. How we met, that is." Naylard turned pink. "I was standing on the riverbank watching some friends practice rowing at Henley. I slipped and fell in. Drake fished me out. Saved my life."

"Can you swim, my lord?" I asked, staring into his eyes. Around us, other conversations were going on. No one was paying us any attention.

"Not a lick. I'm terribly uncoordinated."

"I imagine you keep that secret."

In the pause as Naylard took a spoonful of soup and then a sip of wine, I heard Lord Hancock touting the benefits of his newest invention to Inspector Grantham. Grantham's responses were toneless noises.

"Oh, no. Everyone knows I sink like a stone. This is the second time I almost drowned. The first was at school. Friends still tease me about it."

"How did you come to slip and fall in?" I took a quick sip of my soup. It was hot and creamy, the perfect thing on a cool, drafty night when I was expected to display a good deal of my neck and shoulders.

"The riverbank was wet and slick. I lost my footing when a wind gust hit me."

"Those strong winds must have made practicing rowing on the river difficult."

"No, there was no wind on the river." A startled look crossed Naylard's face. "Oh. Someone must have bumped me. I felt a nudge but I thought it was a strong breeze. Drake was the only one nearby to rescue me."

Just as I suspected. Drake helped Naylard into the river so he could rescue him. In the silence as distrust slowly penetrated Naylard's mind, I heard Lady Westover question someone about their favorite charity. I watched as Naylard's expression changed from cheerful to questioning to surprised and then worried.

Was the man really so naive? "So you've been friends with Drake ever since he saved your life," I said. "Any idea where he is now?"

Worry disappeared from his face. "No. I haven't seen him since Lady Florence, the Duke of Merville's daughter, had her engagement party last week. He's not been in any of our usual haunts."

"It is worrying when a friend vanishes."

"Quite. It's dashed disconcerting having people pop in and out of your life. Lucinda says it's God's will, but I'm afraid I don't share her faith."

I took a mouthful of soup, trying to think of a reply that would keep Naylard talking when the dining room doors opened and the butler announced, "The Duke of Blackford."

It was all I could do to keep from choking. Blackford here? I'd spoken to him under my own name at his house and then at Sir Broderick's. I'd told Lady Westover I'd met him. What was the old woman thinking of? He'd give me away.

My face heated as I stared at my soup, afraid at any moment my deception would be exposed. Mercifully, the Duke of Blackford began to talk to Lady Westover and Miss Daisy Hancock. I had only a few minutes before he would turn to face me and give away my true identity. I had to learn what I could from Lord Naylard.

I took a gulp of wine to wash the panic out of my voice. Hoping I didn't sound like a fool, I asked, "What interests do you share with Mr. Drake?"

"We both love a good practical joke. Drake has such a keen sense of humor. We both play cards, although I play badly. And we both like horse racing and horse trading. He's supposed to be looking for a new filly for my stables."

"You breed horses?"

"Yes." He started on a long story about horse breeding at his stables. All I needed to do was make appropriate noises at the correct moments and Naylard provided the rest of the conversation. Now I had the perfect opportunity to eavesdrop on other conversations around the table.

My interest quickly waned in Lord Hancock trying to sell shares in his latest weaponry to Lady Westover, and Inspector Grantham's increasingly forceful refusals on her behalf. I turned my attention to studying Blackford. His voice was a deep hum in answer to Miss Daisy's chatter. He ate neatly and sparingly. I dared not look at him directly, but I could glance in his direction as I sipped from my soup spoon. His jacket sleeve was made of the finest black material and his cuff link was a bloodred ruby.

I swallowed the last of my now-lukewarm soup and turned my attention back to Naylard just in time. A moment later, he finished his tale about his barns with "Don't you think?"

Giving him my best smile, I said, "I'm afraid I'm not an expert on raising horses, milord."

"We'll continue later," he said in a soft voice as the footmen picked up the soup bowls.

When the fish was set before us, Blackford turned to me with a cold smile. The clatter of silver and the rumble of voices faded in my ears. Apprehension must have shown in my eyes because my heart was pounding and I'd lost my appetite.

In a very low voice he said, "I didn't realize you were Lady Westover's country cousin, Miss—Peabody. Or should I say Miss Fenchurch? Does the presence of a Scotland Yard inspector have anything to do with why we're enjoying this meal together?"

"No." The duke deserved a better answer. He'd not given me away yet. I kept my voice low to match his. "The inspector's here to even the numbers and make it appear more of a family dinner. And he's curious about Drake's disappearance, although it's not his case."

"Scotland Yard inspectors don't attend dinner parties to even the number of men and women, even for as persuasive a hostess as his grandmama, and they don't get curious."

"I think they must. Curiosity is the most important characteristic an investigator can possess."

He took a bite of his fish and considered. "You're probably right," he said when he'd swallowed. "So what is this dinner in aid of?"

"Drake was introduced to Victoria Dutton-Cox by Lord Naylard. Lord Hancock was a victim of Drake's. I want to question them without them realizing what I'm doing."

He'd jerked in his seat when I mentioned Victoria's name, but by the time I finished speaking, he had himself under control again. "That'll be easy with Naylard. The man lacks both suspicion and brains." He took a sip of his wine. "Do you want to question me again?"

"Yes."

"Then it will only be fair if I question you, too."

"All right." *What does he want?* "Did Drake try to blackmail you?"

"Yes. How long have you been looking for missing people?"

I glanced around, trying to hide my surprise. I hadn't expected the duke to admit that Drake had blackmailed him. Fortunately, no one at the dinner was paying any attention to us. "Over ten years. What did Drake possess that would make him think he could blackmail you? You're a formidable man. He's very ordinary."

A smile flickered over his lips. "Letters written by my sister. I control her money; therefore, he came to me to sell his silence. Have you ever been someone's mistress?"

I felt my eyes widen and my cheeks burn. That was hardly a question one could ask in polite society, but then, the same could be said of questions about blackmail. I thought I had the upper hand until he'd turned the tables on me. The man had the instincts of a hunter hidden inside impeccable tailoring. This was a man I could understand.

Glancing across the table, I saw Lady Westover staring at me. Fortunately, no one else seemed to notice my discomfort. I gave a half smile and turned my attention back to the duke.

He raised his dark brows. "Surely you didn't think you could ask my deepest secrets without revealing your own?"

I took a deep breath and tried to steady my voice. "No and no. I'm not. Did you pay his blackmail and for how long?"

"No. I offered to buy the letters, but so far, we've not agreed on a price. Has a man ever made love to you?"

The soft growl of his voice as he asked me his impertinent question left me sweltering in the chilly dining room. I swallowed hard. "Yes. Who are the other men you mentioned who belong to your club who are also being blackmailed by Mr. Drake?" I wondered if he'd confirm the list I'd already obtained.

"Hancock, Dutton-Cox, Waxpool, and Merville. What did your parents think of your scandalous behavior?"

"It's not a scandal if no one finds out, and my parents were long dead at that point. Why is Lord Hancock being blackmailed?"

His gaze flicked across the table at the man in question. "It can't be over his inventions. They're both dangerous and disastrous. And it's no secret that his finances are shaky at best. With all that being gossiped about as common knowledge against Lord Hancock, I can't imagine what his secret is. Are you and this unnamed gentleman still lovers?"

I was saved by the next course. I turned my attention back to Lord Naylard, giving my heart rate a chance to slow while I tried with delicacy to learn why Drake would blackmail such an uncomplicated man.

"I keep thinking of Mr. Drake," I told Naylard. "He's out there somewhere and here you are his good friend, and you don't know where he is. Has he disappeared like this before?"

Naylard finished his bite. "This is very good roast. Try some. Drake hasn't disappeared before. I never went more than two or three days without seeing him, and it's been a week."

"Do you always see him in the same locations? Perhaps you haven't been to these places lately and Mr. Drake isn't really missing." I was already sick of looking at so much food and wishing this was Phyllida's simple cooking.

He chewed slowly and studied the far wall. "No. I either see him at my club, and I'm there almost daily, or at the race-course, but there haven't been any races lately. Perhaps he's gone somewhere to look at a promising filly. He'll turn up and make a joke at the thought of anyone being concerned."

"And as your sister says, it's all in God's hands."

Naylard seemed to back up a little in his chair. "I say, are you one of them?"

"One of whom, milord?"

"Is that why you're not quite eligible to go out in polite society?"

Had this man who appeared so simple figured out I was an impostor? "What do you mean, milord?"

"Lady Westover said you weren't eligible for polite society. Nothing naughty, I hope." He grinned as if he'd told a child-ish joke.

I grinned back. "No, but my grandmother was scandal-ous. Your sister hasn't done anything scandalous, has she?"

"Oh, no. Lucinda believes in following all of the com-mandments. She's very wise."

"I'm certain of that." Talking to Lord Naylard was useful, but I was beginning to develop a headache from all the verbal leaps we were taking. "Am I one of whom?"

"Papists, of course. Is that why you're not quite eligible to go out in polite society?"

Was that the reason Miss Lucinda Naylard was black-mailed?

Naylard had begun another long tale about his animals

when my roast course disappeared, replaced by the fowl course. I felt cold seep into every fiber of my being. Time to question Blackford again. My pulse began to race before I could turn my head.

The duke was already looking at me, a smile trailing off his face. The sort of look a cat gives a sparrow. Well, this sparrow was a determined little bird. "Was Drake blackmailing Hancock and the others in your club with letters their relatives had sent?"

"You haven't answered my last question. Are you still his paramour?"

CHAPTER SEVEN

I glared at the Duke of Blackford, unwilling to let him probe my feelings of loss. The man had been my fiancé, my hope for a life with a husband and children, after I'd lost my family at seventeen. I took a breath to steady my voice. "He's dead."

"My condolences."

"Thank you, Your Grace. Now——?"

"I don't know what papers he was blackmailing the others with. I know in Merville's case it is something going back more than ten years. When did your protector die?"

How dare he assume I was a kept woman. We were in love and planned to marry. The pain of losing him came out in my sharp hiss. "He wasn't my protector. We were of the same class. He died four years ago. What did the duke say to tell you it was an old scandal?"

"He said, 'I can't believe Drake found out. It's been over ten years. I'll be a laughingstock if anyone learns about this.' Did he tell you he'd marry you someday?"

I didn't know which was more upsetting. His questions

or his purring voice as he asked. "We were engaged and had set a wedding date. Rather like you and Miss Victoria, Your Grace." My comment about Victoria Dutton-Cox made no visible impression on him. He didn't even blink. "What do you know about the Earl of Waxpool's secret?"

"Nothing. He doesn't have one. Have you been in love since the death of your lover?"

I reached out and touched his sleeve. "Hold on a moment. He's being blackmailed but he doesn't have a secret? That makes no sense."

"If you want clarification, you must answer my question first."

"No."

"The answer is no, or you won't answer?"

I smiled. "If you want clarification . . ."

"Touché. The Earl of Waxpool has led a disgustingly virtuous life. You don't have to take my word for it; check with anyone. He said he had recently noticed irregularities in his accounts and suspected one of his relatives stole from him to pay off their blackmailer. If he suspected someone in particular, he didn't tell me." He ate another bite. "I believe you owe me an explanation on your answer about whether you've been in love since your fiancé died."

"No, I haven't been. Could you please explain what you said earlier about Lord Hancock?"

"He's constantly inventing something lethal and looking for investors so he can mass-produce it and have it deployed to slaughter the residents of some corner of the empire. Since his inventions are so destructive, our military is loath to use them for fear our soldiers would be among the victims. No one with any sense will invest with him." He shook his head. "I don't have any idea why someone would blackmail a man with so little money and so many lethal weapons at his disposal. Why are you looking for Drake?"

I was surprised at first because his question wasn't personal.

Relieved that it wasn't, I began with a simple answer. "Because that's what the Archivist Society does. We search for missing people and find the killers of those who are murdered."

Warming to my topic, I said more than he might have wanted to hear. "We believe what we do is important. And we do this for everyone, whether or not they deserve our help, because we decided long ago we wouldn't stand in judgment."

Blackford nodded. "I can understand that for some unfortunate wreck, some light skirt, but not for Nicholas Drake. He destroys people."

"Who has he destroyed?"

He stared into my eyes. I could feel anger and hatred flowing toward me. I stared back, but he didn't blink or turn away.

We were served the next course. I faced Naylard with only half my attention as he plunged into a long explanation of how his steward figured out what was wrong with one of his mares. What I really wanted to do was ignore the rules of etiquette and question Blackford further about Drake.

I glanced across the table at Naylard's sister. Lucinda barely touched any of her food and paid little attention to what Inspector Grantham said to her. "Milord," I broke in, "is your sister quite well? She's barely touched her dinner and looks quite pale."

"She doesn't believe in eating much or wearing jewelry or anything but praying."

"Is she heartbroken over a man?"

"Can you keep a secret?"

"Of course. I don't know anyone in society to tell anything to, except for Lady Westover, and I won't tell her. I promise."

"My sister wants to live in a convent, except she can't, because she's got to take care of me. I'd destroy myself and end up in a gutter somewhere if she didn't take care of things for me."

I looked into his guileless eyes and unfurrowed brow and said, "You're lucky to have her."

"I know. She can't leave me. She's always watched over me."

No one could blackmail Naylard. But someone could blackmail his sister if it meant keeping her brother safe.

The ices arrived, and I turned back to the duke. He said, "Have you had any luck finding Drake?"

"Not at all. But we won't give up."

"Wonderful," he muttered.

"Why did you say Drake destroys people?"

"I have the misfortune to have met him, and I've seen him ruin lives. I won't give you details because it's ungentlemanly to divulge other people's secrets, so don't ask me."

While I tried to think of another line of questioning, I tasted the ice. In an instant, I was savoring sweet and cold mixed with the flavor of bits of strawberry. Where had Lady Westover's cook found strawberries at this time of year? I didn't care if the berries were grown in a glasshouse or shipped in from Africa, I fell under their spell. The chill on my tongue made the fruit even more honeyed and almost made me miss the duke's next words.

"I didn't know something as simple as an ice could make a determined young woman like you melt."

Jerking my head to the side, the spoon still on my lips, I caught the laughter in the duke's eyes. I had a task to accomplish. I regretfully set down my spoon and said, "Is there anyone else who might be blackmailed by Nicholas Drake?"

"Not that I know of." His expression turned serious. "Have you considered this might be dangerous?"

"Yes. This wouldn't be my first investigation that involved ruffians." The worst ruffian of all was the first. He looked like a gentleman, but he'd killed my parents and possibly Denis Lupton for possession of a Bible. And I still hadn't found him.

Unaware of where my thoughts had traveled, the duke said, "Drake can't pay you for your efforts on his behalf. Even if he could, he wouldn't."

There was a little left in my crystal cup and I was enjoying the last spoonful, only half listening to the duke's words.

Then I turned to face him and felt my eyes widen at the intense way he was staring at me. I was immediately on my guard. "Sometimes we're paid for our efforts. The rest can be considered charity if you wish."

He leaned forward slightly and stared into my eyes. "Be careful Drake doesn't destroy you in your efforts to help him."

"Ladies, if you come with me to the parlor, the men can rejoin us later." Lady Westover stood and led the way out of the dining room. I followed, wondering whether it was Victoria Dutton-Cox or Blackford's sister who had been destroyed by Drake. And I felt decidedly uneasy about the unfathomable look the duke had given me.

When we reached the plant-filled parlor, Lucinda Naylard and Daisy Hancock chose opposite sides of the room. I decided to follow Daisy, who had settled on a sofa close to the only warm spot in the room, in front of the fire. Pushing aside the leaf of a rubber plant, I asked, "How did you enjoy your first season?"

The girl brightened. "It was everything I had hoped for and more. I danced every dance at every ball. I wore beautiful gowns and flirted with handsome men. There's nothing in the world as exciting and glittery. I can't wait for spring when it starts over again."

"But surely you'll marry soon and have other important duties to fulfill."

Daisy looked at me as if I had just spouted blasphemy. "My uncle says I must choose a husband this year and get married, but I want to enjoy this two more times at least. I don't think three seasons will qualify me as a spinster, do you? There's nothing more fun than shopping for clothes and going to balls and seeing old friends."

"It sounds wonderful," I said. If my doubt showed in my tone, Daisy didn't notice.

"My uncle says I need to find a husband this year or I'll end up like her," she said in a hissing whisper as she nodded toward Lucinda.

When I glanced over, Lucinda sat alone. She appeared to be praying. Lord Hancock needn't worry. Daisy would never be like Lucinda.

Inspector Grantham came into the room. "Grandmama, I'm sorry, but I must leave now. I've been called back to Scotland Yard."

"You work too hard, Eddy," she said as she kissed his cheek.

"Cousin Georgia, I'll speak to you later. Ladies." The inspector gave the room a bow and hurried away.

The other gentlemen joined us a short while later. Lucinda immediately pulled her brother into a corner and whispered in his ear. Coffee was served and Daisy gave Blackford a flirtatious look. He walked as far from her as he could, ending up by the window draperies, and set his coffee cup on a lace-covered table. "I don't think he likes girls," Daisy whispered to me.

"Perhaps he prefers women," I whispered back.

Daisy looked around the room with a pout. Her uncle, who'd cornered the duke in close conversation, wore a similar expression.

Lady Westover came over to join us, and I took the opportunity to say, "So, you've known each other a long time."

"I was godmother to Daisy's mother. After her death, I've tried to look after Daisy," Lady Westover said. "Lord Hancock has never married, and I thought a woman's touch would be helpful. I'm afraid I've been remiss in my duty to you, young lady."

Daisy gave a weak smile in reply. Her gaze darted as if she were looking for an escape from her hostess.

"You lost both your parents at a young age?" I asked. I had been seventeen when both of my parents were murdered. I understood her loss.

"My eleventh birthday. I was allowed to eat with my parents in the big dining room, and by the next day, both of them were dead."

"What happened to them?"

"Typhoid. Bad seafood. Something they ate. I don't know. I didn't like the strange foods served at adult dinners and refused to touch most of the dishes. I still don't eat seafood or spinach or asparagus." Daisy looked past me and smiled brightly.

The duke's voice came over my shoulder. "Lady Westover, I enjoyed dinner immensely. It's always good to see my mother's close friends. Please invite me anytime you have your charming family members visit."

I turned and caught his eye. After he nodded to me, he gave me a searching look. He knew our story was a lie. At least he didn't give me away.

We struggled to keep up a conversation for the rest of the half hour society dictated we should enjoy our coffee after the meal. I found myself between Lord Hancock and Lord Naylard while trying to think of something that would lead the conversation toward Drake and his disappearance. All I came up with was, "I'd love to tour your laboratory sometime, Lord Hancock. Your work on behalf of our soldiers sounds interesting."

"I don't give tours of my laboratory. It's not a museum," he said, glaring at me. At least he showed no sign of recognizing me from the meeting in Sir Broderick's study.

"He won't show his lab to potential investors," Lord Naylard said.

"Of course not. Creating chemical compounds requires careful measurements and undivided attention. I consider that room to be mine alone. I never let anyone in my laboratory. Not Daisy. Not the servants. Not visitors."

Daisy joined us and said, "After my parents died, I spent a lot of time trying to get into the laboratory. A challenge, I suppose. He keeps the keys to the doors on a chain on his waistcoat pocket, and all the windows have bars over them. I never found a way in."

I heard her stress the word "I." "Never?"

She shook her head.

"Never. I never let anyone in." Hancock caught Daisy's eye and she looked down quickly. "We must be going. Thank you, Lady Westover," Lord Hancock said as he took his niece's arm. The Naylards and the duke also said good-bye.

Lady Westover and I went to the entry hall to see the visitors off. Once the door was shut behind them, Lady Westover said, "Was the evening successful?"

"Yes, even though I ended the night with more questions than answers. Do you remember anything unusual about the Duke of Merville or his family ten or so years ago?"

"Merville? Nothing comes to mind. They've always been a bit dry and ordinary. Especially for a duke's family."

"And I thought you weren't in touch with Hancock. That was clever of you to invite them."

"I'm not. I loved her mother, but I've never cared for Daisy or the current Lord Hancock. I suppose I should have tried harder." Lady Westover grimaced. "At least they accepted my invitation for tonight."

"Tonight was very helpful. And enjoyable." I squeezed her hand.

"Shall I see you soon?"

"I hope so. I always enjoy my time spent with you. Especially when the man sitting next to me at dinner didn't give away my true identity."

Lady Westover stopped, one foot on the step. "Good. I'm aware Blackford knows you from the Archivist Society, but your place at table couldn't be helped, my dear. You had to sit next to him because of the order of precedence. Silly square table."

"I'll check to make certain your guests have left and then I'll go."

"Good night, child."

There were no carriages in view from the dining room window. I took my cloak and hat from the ancient butler and slipped out the front door. The street was still and empty, but I could hear the clop of horse hooves not far away. I'd catch a hansom cab on the main road.

Before I reached the corner, I had to pass the alley leading to the mews behind Lady Westover's house. I heard a scrape before I saw two men move out of the shadows. They grabbed for me. Dressed in evening wear and outnumbered two to one, I could do little more than strike at them and scream.

They tried to pull me into the alley, but a hard stomp on a foot and a bite on a hand let me escape to dash toward the street, holding up the fabric of my ripped skirt. A carriage pulled up, the horses reined in before I collided with them. The Duke of Blackford jumped out. My savior, or reinforcements for my attackers?

I started to dash down the sidewalk, but strong arms grabbed me around the middle, wrapping my cloak tightly around me. I kicked out and hit my pursuer by driving the back of my head into his nose. He let go and I ran. Behind me, I heard grunts and thuds, wood against metal, wood against bone.

I glanced back to see the duke thrash one figure with his cane. As my other attacker rose from the ground, he was pummeled down again. I'd have to pass the fight to return to the safety of Lady Westover's. Too dangerous. I rushed away from the fracas.

Horses whinnied and coach wheels creaked, but no footsteps pursued me. I slowed my pace to a brisk walk, staying as far from the street as I could as I approached the corner. Looking over my shoulder, I saw two figures prone on the ground behind me and a large carriage with four horses nearly at my side.

"Miss Fenchurch."

I picked up speed. So did the horses, pulling past me.

The duke's familiar baritone came from the coach. "Wait, Miss Fenchurch. I'm trying to rescue you."

"I don't appear to need rescuing." I held up my skirt to

step over a gap in the sidewalk, planning to hurry away from both my attackers and the duke's coach. Despite the duke's dispatch of the two thugs, I feared he was involved in the attack. His appearance was too fortuitous.

"Very well, then." The Duke of Blackford tapped on the roof of his high, ancient carriage and it began to pull away from me.

I looked back at the figures who were on their feet and limping in my direction. "Wait," I called after the coach.

Immediately the horses were reined in again.

I rushed to the side of the carriage as the two men started in my direction. "Could you drive me to a safer location?"

"Of course." The door bearing the ducal crest opened and I was faced with a daunting set of narrow steps lowered to allow me to climb the great height to enter the coach.

"My goodness. How do you climb in and out of this vehicle?"

"By using the steps. Of course, I wear trousers and am taller than you. I have it, John," he called to his footman, who had made a move to climb down and assist me.

Shaking my head at his literalness, I bunched up my skirts so I could reach one foot up to the bottom step. With satin fabric in one hand and the other gripping the handrail, I hauled myself upward.

When I reached the third step, the duke grabbed me by the waist. Since I was looking over my shoulder to see where my attackers were, I was startled to feel his hands inside my cloak and the smooth wool of his coat sleeves on my bare arms. My evening shoe slipped and my hand slid on the grip. The duke pulled me upward, off balance, into his carriage.

He barked a command and the carriage sprang into motion. I tumbled onto one of the seats. The duke had to grab a strap hanging from the carriage roof to keep from landing in my lap. Once he regained his balance, he pulled up the steps with one motion and shut the door. I tugged my ripped skirt around me modestly and looked out the window. My attackers were no longer in sight.

The duke sat down across from me and crossed his legs. "Do you have a lot of enemies, Miss Fenchurch?"

I doubted those men could have been hired by my parents' killer. He wouldn't know I'd seen him lately. I rose slightly to adjust my cloak and settled onto the leather seat. It was as hard as a board. "No. This rarely happens unless I'm disguised as a harlot."

His eyes widened.

My comment wasn't true; I didn't dress like a harlot. But any man with the effrontery to ask if a lady is a virgin shouldn't be shocked by what she tells him. I gave him a hard look. "So which member of your club has kidnapped Nicholas Drake and wants to stop me from finding him?"

He threw his hands up in a gesture of surrender. "It wasn't me. I rescued you."

"Which could have been a clever way of throwing suspicion away from Your Grace."

"I'm not that clever. But I will save the idea for the next time I'm in a sticky business negotiation, if you don't mind. Rescuing a foreign competitor would make me appear less threatening." In the light of a passing street lamp, I saw him smile.

"So why did you come back here?"

"I saw those two men loitering when we left. I wanted to see what they were after."

"Me."

"As it turns out. Where can I take you?"

"Somewhere where I can engage a hansom cab."

He made a tsking noise. "What's your address? You can pretend this is a hansom."

"I'd rather you not know."

"Still believe I could have set you up for injury?" He shook his head. "Not my style, I'm afraid. I use pounds and pence to inflict my injuries. And my combatants don't get up again."

CHAPTER EIGHT

"YOU handled the two men who attacked me very well." I was more impressed with Blackford's aggressive brawling approach than I should have been. The man was a duke. He should have men about him to take care of the unpleasant aspects of life. "Where did you learn to fight like that?"

"My grandfather. This was his cane. He told me we carry canes to represent the swords gentlemen used to carry. In honor of its role, he had this specially fitted out." He balanced the black wooden stick in one hand before tapping it on his other palm. He didn't offer to let me touch. "He had it specially weighted to inflict maximum damage."

"Why don't you have your footmen deal with thugs? I thought that was one of the perks of being a duke."

"I find it easier to take care of myself, with my footmen looking on to step in if I get into trouble, than to worry about my footmen being injured."

"Because it's harder to find a good footman than a useful duke?" I asked. We were far enough away from my attackers that I wasn't worried if he threw me out of the carriage for my sass.

"Because I'm a better fighter than any of them, and I like to deal with my problems myself. But this still doesn't tell me where I should let you off."

"Leicester Square, if you don't mind going so far out of your way."

"Not at all. I should have associated you with the music halls and theaters, since you have this other persona of Lady Westover's relation, complete with a scandalous grandmama to explain why you can't go out among society."

As long as he didn't associate me with the bookstores between Leicester Square and Covent Garden, I'd be fine. This duke had a sharp mind. Sharp enough to be devious, no matter how much he protested.

He turned serious. "Why are you looking for Drake?"

"Because someone wants him found. I told you that the first time we met."

"Anyone I know?"

He'd obviously forgotten Edith Carter. "No one you'd notice, Your Grace. Why do you not want him found if you want to retrieve your sister's letters? Don't you want him within reach so you can negotiate with him?"

"I don't negotiate with blackmailers if I can help it. If someone has kidnapped him, he has other things to worry about than destroying the reputations of good people. The longer he's out of circulation, the more chance there is that something unfortunate will happen to him and the evidence he holds against my family and friends. Or the more chance he'll decide it's safer to agree to my demands." A devilish smile crossed his face for an instant, and I feared I'd be devoured.

A new possibility came to mind. "Is his disappearance the result of the efforts of several people working together to keep Mr. Drake out of society and prevent him from causing them harm?"

"I would applaud such efforts, but I am not a party to them, if that is what you're asking."

"It is, Your Grace."

"No. I had nothing to do with his disappearance or the attack on you tonight."

"Would you tell me if you had?"

He steepled his fingers, showing off long, narrow hands inside pristine white calf gloves. "No. I wouldn't tell you if I had. While I know I didn't have anything to do with those events, there's no way I can convince you. Do you always find yourself running in circles during an investigation?"

"Far too often. It's part of what we go through to find the truth."

He gave a chuckle. "You expect to find the truth? Now, that is funny."

He hit a nerve. I glared at him and he composed his face into a somber expression. "The truth is very important to everyone in the Archivist Society. Otherwise we wouldn't bother to cut through all the lies we hear." We were getting close to my destination. "You know these men. Who do you think the most likely to have kidnapped Nicholas Drake?"

"None of them. Are you certain you don't want me to have the carriage drive down Charing Cross Road? You'd be much closer to Fenchurch's Books that way."

I closed my eyes and let out a sigh. Would I be able to hide anything from the Duke of Blackford? "How did you know?"

"Come, come, Miss Fenchurch. Did you think I'd have some strange woman walk around my study and not have her investigated?"

Curiosity is my downfall. I might not like what I heard, but I had to ask. "What did you learn?"

"That you've owned Fenchurch's Books since your parents died. That you live near the shop. That you pay your rent on time. That you handle some excellent antiquarian volumes.

That you have a modest success with the shop and employ one young woman who both lives and works with you. The blonde at Sir Broderick's the night I burst in on your meeting—is she your shop assistant?"

"Yes. Miss Emma Keyes."

He tapped on the front wall and the carriage pulled to a halt. "Here's the lane Fenchurch's Books is on. Will this do?"

"Very nicely, Your Grace." The footman helped me down the last drop to the street. I made a graceless, two-footed landing, but at least I didn't fall on my face.

I heard a snickering from the carriage, but when I turned to look, the duke wore a somber expression.

THE BELL OVER the shop door rang the next afternoon while I was helping a matronly looking woman find the right cookbook. Looking up, I saw Inspector Grantham step into the bookstore and remove his bowler hat. He nodded to me and glanced over a book while I finished with my customer.

As soon as the woman left the shop, Grantham walked over and said, "What were you and Grandmama playing at last night?"

"There's a man named Nicholas Drake whose disappearance the police don't want to investigate."

"I looked into it. We don't have any reason to. There's no sign of foul play. No ransom demand. Nothing. Can't a man just take off for a few days without his neighbors worrying?" He set the book on the edge of the counter and stared at me.

I gave up the idea of selling the volume to the inspector when I saw the title was *Household Hints*. "You may not be able to look into it, but the Archivist Society can. We've found evidence that Nicholas Drake was a thief and a black-mailer."

Grantham perked up at my last words. "Hard evidence?"

"Nothing anybody would share with you."

"But you could share what you've learned." He gave me a cold stare.

I did, briefly and without question. We'd been in the same position before, and Grantham had threatened to stop his grandmother's involvement if Sir Broderick didn't tell him everything. I respected Grantham as one of London's best police inspectors, and we needed Lady Westover's aid in dealing with members of high society. Sooner or later, in this situation, I was sure we'd need Grantham to make the arrest.

"There's something you can do for me in exchange."

Grantham looked at me uneasily.

"Find out the details of an investigation from a dozen years ago. No, not my parents," I said when he opened his mouth, "the murder of a bookshop owner named Denis Lupton."

His expression showed he was frankly curious, but he agreed.

As Grantham left the shop, Jacob came in, breathing hard from hurrying, his hair standing up from the wind and his scarf over one ear. "Georgia, Emma, this just arrived at Sir Broderick's. He thought you should see it right away. It'll need to be followed up on."

He handed over a letter. Emma crowded close to read over my shoulder. The flowery script said,

Dear Sir Broderick,

There are several people who do not want Nicholas Drake found because he is a blackmailer. He's an unprincipled swine who preys on the weak and helpless. Therefore, he generally chooses women as his victims, threatening to expose their sorrows if he is not handsomely rewarded.

I am one of his victims. I want the brute stopped and his evidence returned to me. You have the best people to accomplish this, but I dare not approach you in an obvious manner. Nor do I care to commit my story to paper. Since I am aware that

you cannot come to meet me in person, I request you send a female member of the Archivist Society to Portman Square on the next nice spring day we have at two in the afternoon. Have her wear a daffodil in her hair. I shall be wearing a green walking dress and carrying a green parasol.

Sincerely yours, a victim of Nicholas Drake

I looked at Emma and then at the dry leaves and paper blowing down the street in front of the shop. "We won't need to pick a daffodil from our garden today."

Emma smiled. "As if we had one. Or had the time to take care of one."

"What shall I tell Sir B?" Jacob asked.

"Tell him I'll keep the appointment. I'm surprised she didn't give me a code word to say." I glanced at the letter again and shook my head. "I wonder how she found out about our investigation."

"Something you'll need to ask her tomorrow. It should be nice out," Emma told me. "And bring home the daffodil. I'd like to try wearing flowers in my hair."

She gave me a haughty smirk. Jacob looked at her with devotion in his eyes.

EMMA WAS WRONG. The next day was cold and drizzling. Leaving Emma in charge of the bookshop at the lunch hour, I traveled to Grosvenor Square and watched the Naylard town house from the park. I couldn't picture Lucinda Naylard worrying overmuch about the weather, so I didn't believe she'd written the letter to Sir Broderick. After a few minutes, Lord Naylard left, no doubt for his club, and I approached the house.

As I reached the short steps to the front door, Miss Lucinda came out, bundled in a coat, hat, scarf, and gloves.

She put up her umbrella as I said, "Miss Lucinda, I was going to call on you."

"I'm sorry. I don't follow that custom." She looked wistfully at a passing hansom and then shifted her umbrella and plunged determinedly onward.

"May I walk with you?"

"You may do whatever you wish."

I decided to remain in my Georgia Peabody persona. "I hope you don't dislike me because of my grandmother."

"No." For the first time, I saw a fleeting smile on the woman's face. She shared the same blond coloring and features as her brother, but there was an intelligence in her eyes that I didn't see in his. "We have to answer for our own sins, not anyone else's."

"Do you know what sins Nicholas Drake must answer for?"

"Do you?"

"I've been told he's a thief and a blackmailer."

Her steps hesitated for a moment before continuing down the street. "What does Mr. Drake say about this?"

"He's beyond our power to ask him."

"Is he dead?" She sounded hopeful.

"No. Not that we know of. Only missing. Tell me about Mr. Drake."

"He's a good-looking man, well dressed, but cruel. Evil."

I would have to have been deaf to have missed the venom in her voice. "Isn't that a harsh judgment, Miss Lucinda?"

"No less than he deserves."

"Why don't you like him?"

Now her steps sped up. "That is a private matter."

I decided to force the subject. "I've heard he's tried to blackmail several people, so I understand why they don't like him. Did he try to blackmail you, too?"

Lucinda's face paled, but she sped up her pace walking

east. "No. No, he couldn't blackmail me. Only people who have something to hide are blackmailed."

"Everyone has something to hide. Sometimes people want to hide good news from their friends and neighbors."

"How could someone be blackmailed over good news, even if they didn't want to share it with the world?"

"Tell me, Miss Lucinda. Tell me how Nicholas Drake could do such a thing."

"He didn't."

"Lying is a sin."

She gave me a sorrowful look. "Something else for me to confess."

"Confess?" Then I understood. "Miss Lucinda, you've converted to the Roman faith."

"Yes." She lifted her chin and said the word more defiantly. "Yes."

"Nicholas Drake held this against you."

"He threatened to tell my brother if I didn't pay him. The fool didn't realize there are no secrets between Laurence and me. He's an even greater fool for trying to separate us."

Her expression told me how very foolish Drake had been. "Why would he do that?"

"So he could take advantage of my brother's good nature. He quickly learned he couldn't drive a wedge between us." She gave me a satisfied smile.

"Your brother already knew about your conversion before Drake tried to blackmail you?"

"Yes. Laurence has no problem with it as long as I don't leave him."

We both kept quiet as we waited for a break in the never-ending line of carriages, wagons, omnibuses, and horses crowding the street. Finally, a second's pause in the traffic let us scramble across the busy intersection.

"Prospective spouses for either of you might find this need

for a combined household difficult." Aristocrats have to continue their bloodlines. A requirement drilled into them from the nursery. I wondered if any of Lord Naylard's lessons had made an impression.

"I want to become a nun, so marriage is out of the question. And Laurence is in no hurry to wed. Once he finds a suitable wife who will both love him and provide his backbone, I will join a convent both for my own joy and for his domestic peace."

We were nearing Charing Cross Road. We would soon leave the boundaries of Miss Lucinda's world. "Where are you headed?"

"The chapel of St. Etheldreda near the Holborn Viaduct. It's an ancient church, used by the faithful long before the Reformation." Her face took on an otherworldly glow. "I feel so close to Christ there."

I envied her faith. "One last question if I may, Miss Lucinda. What did Drake do and say when you told him your brother knew and had no problems with your conversion?"

A smile crossed her face. "That was the only time I saw Nicholas Drake speechless. I thought for a moment he was going to strike me, but then he took a deep breath, said he was sorry he misjudged me, and walked off. He's made no attempts to bother me again.

"And he's been more circumspect in his efforts to get money from my brother. My brother considers him a friend, so I don't object to the occasional pound or two for dinner or the theater, and Drake limits his claims on my brother's purse. A satisfactory compromise." With a nod, she walked off.

It was a short walk from where I left her on her journey to St. Etheldreda's to return to my bookshop. Emma was finishing with a customer when I walked through to hang my cloak in the back hall and take off my hat and outdoor gloves.

I stayed in the back hall for a minute, wishing my thoughts

would lead me further into the investigation. Except for the certainty that the Naylards had nothing to do with Drake's disappearance, I was truly lost.

I had nothing to show for my efforts but a ruined evening gown. It was out of date, but it was a memento from my courtship. I'd worn it the night my love had taken me to the theater. The night he'd proposed.

Walking into the office, I shuffled papers until the tears stopped falling.

When I returned to the shop, Emma was the only one present. I told her how Drake had missed the mark with the Naylards.

"Well, that's one who didn't abduct Drake. Who shall we look at next?"

"The Duke of Merville was being blackmailed over a scandal ten years in the past. One that would make him laughed at. One that Drake learned of."

"What did Lady Westover make of that?"

"She had no idea. And to find out the Duke of Blackford's sister's secret, we'll have to travel to Northumberland to question her."

"Is that necessary? The Duke of Blackford is cooperating with you."

He'd saved me from my attackers, but I felt he was using us rather than cooperating. "Is he? I get the distinct impression he's holding something back. He wants to buy his sister's letters. That much is straightforward and understandable. But there's more. I'm sure of it. And it's the something more that could be the clue to Drake's disappearance."

"I think you need to have another talk with him," Emma said, a smile trailing her lips. "How did he know we were meeting at Sir Broderick's about Drake's disappearance, and how many other people did he tell?"

I returned the smile as another thought struck me. "With

the weather as it is, I should catch Lady Julia Waxpool at home. I was told she was a friend of the duke's sister. Maybe her answers will save me from traveling to Northumberland."

Before I could put on my cloak, a customer walked into the shop. He looked down in surprise and asked, "Is he yours?"

"Is who——?" I took a few steps toward the man and saw a brownish striped cat march into the shop, his tail up despite water dripping from his fur.

"Aaah." Emma grabbed some dust rags and followed the cat to the window ledge where he jumped up and looked out at the rain. She began to rub his back and sides with the cloths. "What shall we call him?"

"Gone."

The cat stared at me with regal disdain. A notch in one ear and a small missing patch of fur on one hind leg gave a hint to his less-than-royal lifestyle.

"Nonsense. He's purring. He likes us." Emma continued to pet the cat and I waited on our customer.

As he left with a mathematics text, the man said, "Looks like he's staying. What'll you name him?"

"This is a bookshop. We'll name him something literary. Shakespeare, perhaps." If he wouldn't leave, willingly or unwillingly.

"Voltaire," Emma suggested.

"He's an English cat," I said. "How about Charles Dickens?"

Emma smiled. "Perfect. Hello, Charlie."

The cat hissed his displeasure.

"I think we'd better call him Dickens," I said, glaring at the cat. I would swear he lifted his chin to look down his nose at me.

The man, laughing, said, "I think that'll be appropriate," and hurried off, umbrella clutched in one hand and book snug in the other.

Putting on my still-damp outerwear, I reminded Emma we were running a bookshop, not a foundling home for felines, and ventured into the cold drizzle again. Fortunately, the Waxpool town house was just our side of Berkeley Square. I didn't have far to go. Even more fortunately, Lady Julia agreed to see me.

I was taken to a small, cheerful parlor with a warming fire and plenty of burning gas lamps. Books and periodicals were scattered over every surface, from the pale pink sofas to the delicate writing desk by the window. The heavy pink draperies were pulled back, showing delicate lace curtains over windows with dim light shining through.

Lady Julia was standing near the fire as I walked in, glasses perched on her nose, looking at my calling card. "Do I know you?"

"I doubt it, my lady." I decided the room told me enough about the young woman to take a chance. "I'm an avid reader, but that's not why I'm here. Is this your room?"

"Really, it's Grandpapa's, along with the rest of the house, but no one uses this room but me. You came to see the room?"

"No, but I like it very much." I smiled with pleasure as I picked up a volume. "This is a room well lived in. Austen is one of my favorites." I set the book down gently. "But I'm afraid I came to see you on two matters of great delicacy."

She slipped off her glasses and set them carefully on the desk. "Then I suppose you need to come stand by the fire and warm up."

I did so, gratefully, while she rang for a servant and ordered tea. Then she joined me in front of the fire. "Have we met before?"

"No."

She glanced toward the window where rain could be heard beating on the glass. I was glad I had arrived before the downpour struck. "Why did you come here in this terrible weather, Mrs. Peabody?"

"It's Miss. I am unmarried."

She nodded at whatever she was thinking and then shoved aside two books to settle on one of the pale pink sofas. "Whenever you feel sufficiently dried off, please sit down and tell me what these two delicate matters are."

"Thank you."

Warmth had reentered my bones by the time the tea arrived. I sat while Lady Julia poured. Once we both had our cups and the servant had departed, I began. "I understand you were close to Lady Margaret Ranleigh."

"I thought we were at one time."

"You've not heard from her since she left town?"

"No. I wrote, but I never received a reply. I suppose her brother is keeping her locked up in their castle in Northumberland."

Having met the duke, I could believe he lived in a castle and not a manor house. "Is it truly a fortress?"

"According to Margaret, it's a massive stone castle overlooking the North Sea. The outer wall is medieval with ramparts and arrow slits and turrets." Lady Julia smiled at a memory. "She used to joke about it, saying how much she hated growing up among savages and all the while imagining Vikings coming ashore to rescue her from the tower."

"It sounds like you were great friends."

"We were. Or I thought we were. We had the same dream of marrying for love, but it's so hard for a woman with money. Neither of us could tell who was interested in us, and who was after our money. And Margaret had the extra problem of her brother. I'm glad mine isn't like that."

I felt an instant urge to defend the duke, but stopped myself. Lady Julia had known him much longer than I had. Perhaps, God forbid, her analysis of his character was correct.

"What is Lady Margaret's problem with her brother?"

"He has her imprisoned in that castle in Northumberland, doesn't he?" she snapped out.

"Why would her brother keep her locked up in a place she hates?"

Lady Julia's expression turned distant and she drew slightly away from where I sat across from her as if distancing herself from me. "I'm sure I don't know."

I decided to take a risk. "I know it has to do with the sudden death of Miss Victoria Dutton-Cox. Lady Margaret hated her, didn't she?"

"Yes."

I waited, and when nothing else was forthcoming, I tried again. "Lady Margaret saw her the day she died. Were you there as well?"

"Yes. Well, not when she died. I'd already left."

"Could you give me a clearer picture of what happened?"

"Surely it doesn't matter now."

"I'm afraid a man's life may depend on it."

Her eyes widened. "Who?"

"Nicholas Drake."

"There's a name I've not heard in a while. I spent last season studying at Oxford—well, at the ladies' college Lady Margaret Hall—reading history and economics. I didn't attend society events. I only saw Mr. Drake at balls the season before that. I know Victoria and Margaret spent a great deal of time in his company, but I avoided him."

My own eyes widened in surprise. I'd thought Lady Julia might be one of his blackmail victims. "Why?"

"He was too smooth. Too friendly. Too quick off the mark. Does that make sense?"

"I believe it makes a great deal of sense. He wasn't blackmailing you, was he?"

Amused disbelief flashed across her face. "No. My interest in books and banking is well-known. There are no secret lovers or torrid affairs in my past. I'm far too dull to be blackmailed. And now you want me to tell you what happened the day Victoria died, to save Drake's life?"

"I think it will help a great deal."

She took a sip of tea and set the cup and saucer down on the side table. "When I arrived at Blackford House that day, Victoria was already there. They each had a small teapot in front of them with their cup and saucer, and Margaret rang for a third one for me."

"Did you find that odd? Two teapots?"

"Yes, and then a third one seemed stranger still. Margaret said since it was such a blustery day out, everyone would want tea, and she hated stale tea. The pot gets cold and the tea bitter before the last cup is poured, so she was trying something new. Actually, she stole the idea from the tea shops and admitted as much. Fresh-brewed tea for each guest."

"How was Victoria that day?"

"Complaining of a heaviness in her lungs. Winter air bothered her, poor thing."

"Why did she go out and brave the weather to visit Margaret? You just said they hated each other."

"I don't know. There was a tension in the air, but they made every effort to cover it up when I arrived."

"Did all three of you fix your tea the same way?"

"Margaret never put milk in hers, while Victoria and I both did. We all took sugar, Victoria most of all. Margaret said something rude and Victoria added even more. I don't know how she stood it so sweet, but she drank her tea."

Julia smiled. "Margaret mentioned once she wanted to add sugar to Victoria's tea in secret, to see if Victoria could stand it after all the sugar she put in." The smile vanished. "Now we'll never know."

"How long did Victoria stay?"

"About a half hour after I arrived, she said she felt very tired, that her heart was pounding, and could she lie down. Margaret insisted we take her home and have her doctor called. I agreed. I thought she looked very red, and her skin was clammy."

"Did she complain about how the tea tasted?"

"No."

"You're certain about that?" If Victoria's tea was poisoned, it should have tasted bitter or metallic. Wrong, somehow.

"Yes, I'm certain. I was asked that later by both Lord Dutton-Cox and the Duke of Blackford. I told them both what I'm telling you. She said nothing about her tea tasting strange in any way."

I nodded. Victoria mustn't have been poisoned with her tea. "Were you served anything else to eat or drink?"

"Nothing, which was strange, but may have been why there was such an atmosphere in the room. Margaret was always on Victoria about her weight. I guess it was to pay her back for being on Margaret about her clothes, her manners, her interests, and the men she favored."

Was there anything the two didn't fight over? "What happened next?"

"Victoria said she felt so weak, she'd have to be carried. Margaret called her a silly fool and went to help her up. In the process, the tea tray went over. I was standing next to it and grabbed one of the pots, but the rest went over with a crash and splashed us all."

"Was she really that weak?"

"I don't know. Margaret said not to worry about the tea but to help her with Victoria. I did, of course, so I was standing close by when Victoria again said she'd have to lie down. Margaret said, in the duke's house before the wedding? Did she want to start a scandal by throwing herself at the duke and forcing him to marry her? Her brother would surely balk at marriage then. Victoria grumbled and demanded we give her a hand."

"Could she walk?"

"She could. All three of us tromped through broken china, with crunching sounds at every step. It would have been embarrassing, but no one noticed because Victoria had enough energy to stomp around and carry on dramatically. I think she hoped Margaret would back down and invite her to stay. Margaret rolled her eyes and made obvious she thought Victoria was trying to have her own way. Victoria was the type to always insist on having things her way."

Julia didn't sound like she thought Victoria's illness was too serious at that moment. "And then?"

"We all climbed into the Blackford coach and rode around to the Dutton-Cox house. By the time we arrived, Victoria was feeling nauseous and the footmen had to help her upstairs to bed. Margaret, Victoria's sister Elizabeth, and I went with her. Her mother called the doctor and sent word to the club for her father."

"Elizabeth didn't call on Margaret with Victoria?"

"Victoria fought with Elizabeth even more than she did with Margaret. It sounds terrible to say now, but Victoria only got along with men."

"Why? Did Victoria like to read and discuss politics and economics?" Elizabeth certainly didn't. She hadn't so much as glanced at the books in my shop as she walked by. If Victoria was intellectually curious, she would have found Elizabeth dull.

Lady Julia gave a deep-throated laugh. "No. Only men appreciated Victoria's flirtations. She hadn't a thought in her head."

And the duke was going to marry her? He would have quickly grown tired of her. Since Victoria didn't die of strangulation, I was confident the duke wasn't her murderer. "How long did you stay at the Dutton-Cox house?"

"Perhaps another ten minutes after her father arrived with the Duke of Blackford and Nicholas Drake."

"They all came together?"

"Yes. Apparently, the duke had received an anonymous letter charging—let's just say that Drake was involved in irregularities. The three men had been arguing about it when the message arrived and they all came back to the Dutton-Cox house."

Lady Julia Waxpool shook her head. "When the doctor arrived and Victoria began vomiting, we left the room. Margaret stayed with her brother across the hallway from where Elizabeth stood next to her father. There was quite a lot of arguing going on, and her mother was wailing the house down. All I could think was poor Victoria, to be ill in that atmosphere."

"And later? When she died?"

"I had already left. Victoria was known to have a weak heart, but I didn't think I'd never see her again. I guess between the cold air on her lungs and the illness, her heart couldn't take any more. When we met a few days later, Margaret and I agreed, we never expected Victoria to die."

CHAPTER NINE

B Y the next day, Emma had convinced me to question
the Duke of Blackford again. I took the coward's way
out and sent him a message. On my best writing paper, I
asked him the questions Emma had raised the day before. I
didn't ask the questions I most wanted answered. What was
he hiding? And where did his sister and his late fiancée enter
into the troubles Drake was now facing?

By noontime, a message was returned in a dark, bold hand
saying, *Come for tea today and I will tell you.* The message was
unsigned, but it was on the letterhead of the Duke of Blackford.

"Too bad it's raining," Emma said when I showed her the
reply. "What do you wear to take tea with a duke?"

I looked at the smock I had worn over my clothes while
giving the office a good cleaning that morning. I was filthy. I
shouldn't have chosen that day to straighten out the back room,
but it was a task I'd avoided for too long. "Not this. And I'll
need to bathe."

"I'll take over the shop for the afternoon." Emma started

to turn away and then faced me again. "Don't wash your hair. There's no time to dry it. And pin it up carefully when you bathe, or you'll catch your death of cold outside."

"It's a good thing I washed it for the dinner party. I'll need you to help me do my hair about three."

Emma nodded and then we both burst out laughing and hugged. After she brushed off the dirt I'd transferred onto her, Emma said, "Tea with a duke. You'll have to tell me every last detail."

I promised I would.

It was nearly two when I gave up on the office, said good-bye to Emma, and went around to the entrance to our apart-ment block near the shops. Our building was fairly new, with modern conveniences, but there were no internal stairs from shop to living space that had been so handy when I was a child. Those stairs were something I missed until I went to our cozy rooms and enjoyed our instant hot water and indoor plumbing.

I started the gas-powered geyser on the tap to heat the water and then Phyllida helped me undress. When I told her I was having tea with a duke, she only nodded.

"Anyone I know?"

"The Duke of Blackford."

"It would be his father that I remember. The former duke was on the lookout for a replacement for the current duke's mother. He chose a lovely, sweet-tempered young lady. I wonder how she fared, being married to an older, rather cross man."

"They had a daughter." I was in investigative mode and I didn't stop to think before I asked personal questions. "Are you sorry you never married or had children?"

"And put more children within reach of my brother?" She shuddered. "Besides, I have you and Emma for my family, without all the bother of childhood illnesses or hiring nannies. Now, get a move on. You don't want to keep a duke waiting."

She gave me such a smile I was glad I pried. I stepped out of my stockings and went in my shift to the small room where the mahogany-edged tub sat. I turned on the tap and let the steaming water fill the tub as the geyser gurgled and hissed.

I soaked in the tub in peace until the water began to cool. When I emerged, ready to dress, Phyllida was waiting to help. "Does the duke know you run a bookshop?"

"Yes."

She gave a last tug on my corset strings. "Then I'd suggest something businesslike. Your best shirtwaist is freshly ironed. Perhaps with your gray outfit."

I nodded. "What do you think the duke wants? I sent him a note with some questions. He could have sent back a reply. I wasn't asking anything personal."

The room was silent as she pulled my petticoat and skirt over my head. "Perhaps he wants to hire you and the Archivists to find that missing man."

"Perhaps." I considered the possibility while she did up my buttons.

"How old is the duke?"

"Mid to late thirties, I'd guess."

"And he doesn't have a family? I'd say he's interviewing you for the position of duchess. Or something like." Her voice turned dry. "He hasn't had any reason to get the wrong impression, has he?"

"I should hope not." But his questions about my virginity still left me uneasy.

I looked prosperous in my newest white blouse with a gray skirt and jacket. Emma nodded her agreement when I entered the empty shop, though she frowned at my hair. With a few extra pins, she gave me a tidy coiffure. I could only hope it would stay that way as I strolled from Grosvenor Square toward Park Lane. The drizzle had let up and the wind died down, but with it, fog had settled onto the city once more.

By the time I reached the duke's residence, the air was

that peculiar yellowish gray and smelled vaguely of sulfur. People and carriages sprang out of the cloud and then disappeared again. All in all, an ominous, depressing day.

The butler took my wrap and escorted me to a small parlor in the back. If he remembered me from my first visit to Blackford House, his manner never showed any recollection of me scooting around him in the main hall.

The view from the window of the duke's garden might be lovely on a clear day; today it was hidden behind an impenetrable film. A silent maid carried in a tea tray and set it on the low table by the sofa.

The duke arrived a minute later and found me still standing near the fire, looking about the pretty room and wondering what I, a middle-class bookshop owner, was doing there. He gestured for me to sit. I chose the sofa; he chose a wing chair. "My stepmother decorated this room."

"It's lovely." It truly was, done in pinks and yellows with striped wallpaper and well-padded furniture. It was a light, cheerful room, not yet darkened over time by the grime of coal fires and gas lamps.

"Would you pour the tea?"

"Of course." I hoped I wouldn't make a mistake as he watched intently. "Cream or sugar, Your Grace?"

"Sugar. One lump."

I handed him his cup and survived the ordeal without shaking too badly. He had a terrible effect on my nerves. His unblinking stare and pirate-raider expression made me wonder if he was going to lay siege to my honor or slit my throat.

After fixing my own tea, I looked at him expectantly. "You were going to answer some more questions for me?"

"I knew the Archivist Society was meeting at the time I arrived because I had you followed."

"Really? Neither Emma nor I noticed anyone following us that night. He must be very good."

"He is."

"Why did you have me followed?" I studied him intently. There was something battle ready about his appearance, from his helmet of straight black hair to his uniform of black suit and waistcoat, white shirt and collar. The gold chain leading to his pocket watch was like a band of medals from previous skirmishes. This meeting felt like a test of wills. Why had the duke chosen to fight me on his home ground?

"Because I don't want Nicholas Drake rescued by anyone but me. Since I wanted to speak to the Archivist Society, I decided sooner or later you would lead me to them. And you did. Thank you." He took a sip of his tea and then set down the cup.

"You weren't the only peer to visit us that night."

"I'd mentioned your involvement and that of the Archivist Society to my fellow victims of Drake's greed. Then, after I left your meeting that night, I ran into Lord Hancock at my club. He must have rushed over from the club to appeal to you to stop interfering."

I nodded my head in reply, while my skin cried for another bath. I felt dirty from being spied on. "Am I still being followed?"

"After you were attacked, I decided my interference was to blame and I told one of my men to keep you safe when you go out in the evening."

"Why?"

"I just told you why. My interference is to blame." He snapped off the words as they left his mouth.

He might think he was being prudent, but I needed to know if someone following me had evil intentions. "It might be wise to introduce us. I'd hate to disable my protector."

He gave one explosive laugh and then turned serious again. "That wouldn't happen. You're a lady."

"No, I'm not, Your Grace. I'm a shopkeeper. I have calluses from hard work. I don't have a houseful of servants and an estate in the country and a private income. I lost my parents at a young age. I've had to learn to rely on myself. My work for the Archivist Society makes self-reliance even more imperative."

He stared into his tea, considering my words for a moment. "Fair enough. But you are a woman. And until God sees fit to change the universe, you will always be the weaker sex. This man has military training and fought nomads in the desert."

"He sounds more capable than the ruffians I usually encounter. I'd like to meet him." I caught the duke's eye and smiled. He held my gaze as the edges of his lips curved upward.

"I'll send him to your shop when he goes on duty tonight." He picked up his cup and took another sip of tea.

As long as I was pushing my luck, I decided to see how far I could stretch the duke's hospitality. "You mentioned the Duke of Merville's reaction to Nicholas Drake included the words 'it's been over ten years.' Could something have happened to one of his children so long ago that the event would still be worthy of blackmail? Do they all join him for the season every year?"

He set down his tea. "Merville had nothing to do with Drake's disappearance. Of that, I am certain."

"Why are you certain?"

He rose and strode around the small room without brushing against any of the bric-a-brac. I was amazed at how silently and gracefully he moved among the lace and tiny framed photographs and seashells and polished stones that covered every table and shelf.

He'd circled the room three times before I said, "Your Grace?"

"Perhaps because the duke has used the police to pursue Drake since his daughter's party when her jewelry was discovered missing. Why would he ask the police to arrest Drake on one hand and take him prisoner on the other?"

"The Duke of Merville wanted to make sure if Mr. Drake escaped his attempts to capture him, the police would take him into custody. And who would suspect a man to both press charges and kidnap at the same time?"

He glared at me. "You're far too devious. Merville wouldn't think like that."

"But you would, Your Grace."

Before I could say more, he held up his hand. "I never pressed charges against Drake because I was not certain what he stole and what was given to him."

"You believe your sister won't ask for her jewelry because she freely gave it to Mr. Drake for some reason?" It made sense. So why did I feel the presence of some unseen force in this business?

"Drake has a powerful effect on women. My sister might have given him jewelry for a variety of reasons, including helping him out of a difficulty. Or he might have been pawning it on her behalf." He paused and looked at me. "And her jewelry is her own to do with as she wants."

"Clearly that's not what Mr. Drake blackmailed you over."

"Have you enjoyed your tea, Miss Fenchurch?"

I knew a dismissal when I heard one. "Very much, thank you. It's too bad you won't aid us in our search for Nicholas Drake."

"Why do you say that?"

We both knew he wasn't helping us, despite his civility. And because of his civility, or an unwarranted attachment I was developing for the man who cared about my safety, I was more truthful with my answer than I'd ordinarily be. I felt my face heat as I admitted, "You're a capable man. There aren't too many of those in the world, and it would be nice to work with you rather than have you try to block our efforts."

A crooked smile spread slowly across his face. "If I were

truly a capable man, you wouldn't have noticed my attempts to redirect you."

"Why did you say you don't want anyone to rescue Nicholas Drake but yourself?"

"I thought I'd managed to slip that mistake by you. But it's a fair question."

"I'd like a fair answer." I held his gaze and my breath.

"I'd rather purchase Drake's stolen papers and his silence so I can be certain no prying eyes read them than have the Archivist Society sort through them with their love of musty documents."

"We are very discreet." A thought struck me. "Unless you plan to abduct him to force him into a sale."

"No. Whatever his price, I can meet it without resorting to coercion or breaking the law. Miss Fenchurch, aren't there things you'd rather nobody knew, even if those who knew were discretion itself?"

I couldn't help smiling ruefully at his answer. We all had secrets we hide from the world and those closest to us. He held my gaze as I rose and then he strode over and opened the door for me. "If you decide to help us, we'll be glad of your assistance," I said as I walked up to him.

"Never, Miss Fenchurch." But he smiled in return.

"May I ask another favor, Your Grace?"

The smile disappeared. "What is it?"

"I'd like to speak to any staff who were involved in serving tea to Victoria Dutton-Cox and your sister the day Victoria died."

I braced myself for a quick rejection. Instead, he quietly asked, "Why? That was a long time ago."

"Two years."

"What can you possibly hope to accomplish?"

"I'm trying to discover what secret could be so dangerous that someone might want Drake killed rather than paying his demands or stopping him through legal channels. I've learned Drake was present when Victoria died. Did something happen that day to threaten Drake's life much later?"

He kept his expression rigid, but a note of anguish wavered in his voice. "Don't you think I've asked every single person who was involved in any way that day for everything they saw and heard? Asked them more than once?"

"I believe you. I still want to ask."

"What purpose could it serve?"

I didn't want to admit Lady Julia's comments about the teapots had captured my attention. "I want to make certain the right questions were asked. I'm a woman, not their employer, and they have no reason to keep quiet about the details with me."

"What details?"

"Things a duke wouldn't pay attention to."

"I assure you I pay attention to details. Especially when it concerns the death of the young woman I was to marry."

I looked into his eyes. I didn't see sorrow in them while discussing his fiancée's death, but I had seen sorrow after I'd asked to speak to his staff. "Perhaps your servants were trying to protect you from anything that might hurt you."

"She was dead. What more could possibly hurt me?"

"The manner of her death."

He held my gaze for a long moment before he said, "I'll introduce you to my cook, Mrs. Potter. She knows everything that happens in her department and who else was working that day and is still employed here."

I followed him along the hall and down the back staircase to the kitchen. Several women, mostly young, were sitting or standing at a long table carrying on various household tasks, from slicing vegetables to mending. They all immediately set aside their work and stood facing us.

"Mrs. Potter, ladies, this is Georgia Fenchurch. She wants to know what occurred in this house the day Victoria

Dutton-Cox died. Please give her any information she may require." The duke swung around and marched past me to the stairs.

I could hear his footsteps on the wooden steps as I faced the half dozen women in aprons. None wore a welcoming expression. Mrs. Potter was perhaps in her forties and looked strong enough to enforce her wishes on the others. "Mrs. Potter, I'm primarily interested in who fixed the tea and what happened to the teapots after the young ladies left the house."

"Sally always fixes the tea. She did that day, using Lady Margaret's new teapots. Ever so nice and delicate they were. Too delicate. When the young ladies were helping Miss Victoria out to the carriage, their skirts caught and knocked the tray over. The tea was spilled and one of the pots broke."

Was it an accident that the tea was spilled? I was being silly. Victoria didn't complain about the taste, so it probably wasn't the tea that was poisoned. "What happened?"

"We cleaned up the tea, threw out the broken china, and washed whatever was left," one of the girls said.

"That's Sally," Mrs. Potter said.

"You're the one who made the tea. And then you carried it up to the parlor where the young ladies were?"

"Yes."

"Only tea?"

"Yes. Lady Margaret told us earlier that Miss Victoria was getting too heavy to fit into her wedding dress, so not to bring up any biscuits with the tea."

"Did Miss Victoria complain that her hostess was being"—I searched for a word—"unwelcoming?"

Sally looked away. "I wouldn't know."

"Yes, you would. Those two were well-known for their disagreements. I would have listened, if only to warn the other staff if their mistress was going to be angry."

Sally and Mrs. Potter exchanged glances. Mrs. Potter

shrugged. Sally nodded. "Miss Victoria said, 'Can't wait to get rid of me, can you?' Lady Margaret said, 'Oh, sit down and drink your tea. You'll soon be able to order anything in this house that you want.'"

"Did you hear anything else?"

"No. I went downstairs then." Sally twisted her apron, obviously agitated over being questioned about what she'd heard between Lady Margaret and Miss Victoria.

I tried asking about that day from a different angle. "What china was broken?"

Sally let go of her apron. "The teapot Lady Julia Waxpool drank from split in two. Each pot had a different floral design. Pretty they were, and I remember distinctly which young lady drank from which. She arrived just a minute after I brought the first two and I was sent for another teapot and cup. Two of the cups and saucers and tea balls were so badly crushed I couldn't tell where all the slivers came from."

Lady Julia was still alive. There was no reason to break her teapot on purpose. I was certain the tea wasn't poisoned. "Is Lady Margaret that fussy about her tea that she'd have individual teapots for her guests?"

"She's always been," Mrs. Potter said. "Even as a little girl, tea cozies weren't good enough for her. Tea had to be fresh that minute and piping hot."

"Tell me how you fixed tea for her." Was there something special in the ritual that could have led to Victoria's death?

"Same as always." Sally began to sound mutinous.

"Please."

"When Mrs. Potter brought the water to a boil, I put some in the pots and then waited a moment before pouring that water into the cups to warm them up. Once I tossed that water, I filled up the teapots and put everything on the tray. Milk, sugar, cups, saucers, spoons. Then I carried it up."

"Who put the tea leaves in the pots?"

"I did. Well, I put the tea into tea balls and put them into the pots. Little things they were to match the teapots. Then I carried the pots up with the tea already brewing, ready for Lady Margaret when I reached the parlor."

"And the tea all came from one source?"

"Yes. That tin right there." Sally pointed to a tea tin over the stove.

"How often are the remaining teapots used? It sounds like Lady Margaret had a good solution to cold tea in the pot when someone arrives late."

Mrs. Potter answered. "She only used them that one day. Said it reminded her of Miss Victoria's death and she couldn't stand to look at them. The duke had us give the pots that were left to a charity drive a year ago."

I decided to try a different line of questioning. "Had the visit been planned long?"

"Miss Victoria sent a note that morning saying she'd call at teatime. The lady's maid, Ethel, came into the kitchen while the visit was going on and told us Lady Margaret grumbled that Miss Victoria would soon be here night and day, and couldn't she wait a week before ruining every one of Lady Margaret's days."

"Did Lady Margaret do anything to get ready for Miss Victoria's arrival?" I'd suspect sharpening knives except Miss Victoria wasn't stabbed.

"Just ordered flowers and arranged them."

"What did she order?"

"Lilies of the valley. Lady Margaret said they looked bridal. She was just cutting up the leaves when I came in to light the fire in the parlor," Sally said.

"Cutting up the leaves?" That didn't sound right.

"Yes. Into little pieces. Isn't that how you arrange them?" Sally asked.

I had no idea. Girls who were raised like I was to work

in a shop never had time to learn about flower arranging. But working in a bookshop had its rewards. Anything I wanted to learn was a hand's reach away.

And I would look up lilies of the valley just as soon as I returned after a walk down Hyde Park Place. It was the only clue I had until Inspector Grantham gave me the details in Denis Lupton's death or I heard more rumors about a Gutenberg Bible for sale in London.

After twelve years, it was time I solved my parents' murder.

CHAPTER TEN

I T was sundown and the light was quickly fading from
our street when the man came into my shop, tilting his
bowler hat to keep the light out of his eyes. He wore a jacket
and loose-fitting trousers of some cheap material, but his
muddied boots looked new and well made.

I came out from behind the counter. "May I help you?"

"You wanted to meet me." His deep voice was scratchy, as
if from disuse, and he kept his head down so I couldn't see
more than his mouth and chin below the brim of his hat.

He had to be the Duke of Blackford's man. "I do. I'm
Georgia Fenchurch. And you are?"

"Sumner." He took off his hat and held it in front of him
by one hand so I couldn't see his face. Then he held out the
other hand, which I shook. My grip let me feel the well-made
leather gloves that fit him like a second skin. His gloves and
boots wouldn't have looked out of place on the duke, but his
clothes were the same as my neighbor the greengrocer wore.
No one would give him a second look in our neighborhood,
unless they were examining him closely the way I was.

"May I see your face?"

"Rather you didn't."

"And I'd rather I could recognize you from my foes if the need arises."

Emma came out from the office and walked toward the man. As she did, he began to back up toward the door.

I held out a hand to delay him. "This is Emma Keyes, my assistant and a fellow Archivist Society member. You have nothing to fear from her." The words slid from my mouth like they would if he were a skittish child.

"She might fear me."

He lowered his hat then, and I'm ashamed to say I took a step back. One side of his face was normal, perhaps handsome, but the other was grotesquely scarred from his dented cheekbone to his puckered jaw. He'd kept his eye by sheer luck or the grace of providence. I wondered if his voice had been made raspy in the same battle.

Emma stepped forward, holding out her hand to the disfigured man. "I have no reason to fear you. But why would Georgia need to recognize you from her foes?"

"The Duke of Blackford hired me to guard Miss Fenchurch when she goes out at night."

Emma turned to me then. "Why would the Duke of Blackford hire someone to guard you at night?"

Blast. I hadn't planned to worry her or Phyllida. "There was an incident after I left Lady Westover's the other night. The duke witnessed the event and came to my rescue."

Her hands went to her waist and she tapped her foot. "When were you planning to tell me?"

When I finished crying over the ruin of my evening gown and all it represented. Happiness with the man I loved and all our dreams of our life together. I refused to admit my reasons in front of a man employed by the Duke of Blackford. "When I figured out which of the lords sent a pair of thugs to attack me."

"Or abduct you, like Mr. Drake was abducted. Georgia, think. This case may be too dangerous to undertake."

"Not with Mr. Sumner's help." I smiled at him, but I was still wary. "Did His Grace send you with something so I would know he truly sent you?"

Sumner grimaced, or perhaps he smiled. His face was so damaged I couldn't tell one from the other. He reached into an inner coat pocket and produced a note on the duke's letterhead.

This man, John Sumner, is in my employ and going about my business.

It was signed *Gordon Ranleigh, Duke of Blackford.*

I handed the letter back to him and he slipped it back into his inside pocket. "I don't plan to go out tonight, so I'm afraid you won't have anything to do. With this investigation, I doubt I'll have to go out at night. Thank you for coming by, but there's nothing for you to do here."

He turned to my assistant. "Are you going out tonight, Miss Keyes?"

She favored him with one of her most charming smiles. "No. I'll be at home all night."

He stared at her with adoration for a moment before turning back to me. "His Grace told me to give you this. He expects both of you to attend."

In his hand were engraved invitations to a masked ball to be held in several days. Not just any masked ball, but the crush the Duke and Duchess of Arlington held every year. All of society would be there, but in costumes and wearing masks, it would be difficult to tell one from another. Under the circumstances, no one would know we were interlopers.

"It appears we'll have to go out one night with this investigation. I hope the duke will employ you that evening. Did he tell you why he wants both of us to attend?"

"No."

"Did he suggest what costumes we're to wear?"

"You're to tell him when you know."

"What will His Grace wear?"

"Don't know. But he doesn't want your costumes to match his."

Presumably so no one would associate him with us. "Have you worked for the duke for long?"

"No."

Sumner mustn't like to talk. So far his answers had been short and barely informative. "So you don't know if the duke attends this ball every year."

"He told me he doesn't. Too many silly people doing silly things." His gravelly voice finally had enough expression to tell me he agreed with his employer. But when would Sumner have attended a ball? His wounded face would make him as ineligible as someone of my class if I weren't going to the dance at the order of a duke to find a missing man.

"If I were a duke, I'd want everyone to know who I am, costume ball or not," Emma said with all the assurance her twenty years gave her.

At thirty, I had some sympathy for the duke's position. "It must be tiresome to have everyone know who you are every moment of your life, scrutinizing your every move. In our work, we prize anonymity."

"Yes, but I'm not a duchess. If I were, I'd want to be the center of attention," Emma insisted. "I'd be proud of my works."

I turned to ask Mr. Sumner his opinion, but he was gazing at Emma and his rapturous thoughts were written in his eyes. Emma had won herself another devoted slave.

The bell over the shop door rang and fellow Archivist Society member Frances Atterby walked in muffled in coat, hat, scarf, and gloves so that only her eyes were visible. She huffed and puffed as she began to remove layers. "What a ghastly

night. Such a cold breeze. At least it seems to be breaking up
the fog. Thank you, Georgia," she added as I took her scarf
and gloves from her.

"Oh, hello," she added as she spotted Sumner. "You'll find
tonight a good one to stay in and read." She approached him
with a friendly smile, decades of working in the family hotel
ingrained in her manner.

"I'm here for the Duke of Blackford," he said in his deep,
scratchy voice. He remained motionless, his hat held to the
side of his face as if in the act of putting it on, so that Frances couldn't see his terrible scar.

"The duke is a good man," Frances replied and then drew
me to the side, leaving Emma with Sumner. "I found the most
extraordinary thing in the records of Somerset House. Nicholas Drake married Anne Carter four years ago in Northumberland. The records show Anne has an older sister, Edith."

"Then why does Edith, his sister by marriage, live next
door to him? You'd think he'd invite her into his household.
Where is Anne? And why all these lies when Edith came to
ask for our help?" My mind was swimming with possibilities,
each more ludicrous than the last. I felt used by her. She'd
deceived me, and that was something I couldn't abide.

"You need to ask her that and if she knows where Drake
is before we continue this investigation." Frances concentrated
on unbuttoning her coat.

I wished she and Sumner would both leave so I could tame
my unruly thoughts. They both appeared to be staying for a
while, Sumner listening raptly to Emma while Frances continued to unwrap herself after fighting the elements outside.

And then a customer came in, blinking at the brightly lit
room after the darkness outside. Emma pulled Sumner aside
to the biography section. Frances whispered, "You need to
hear the rest of what I've learned about Miss Carter and Drake
before you go any further with this. I'll wait until you finish
with him," and settled in the recent novels.

I put on my professional smile and stepped forward to
wait on the rabbity-looking man, but my mind was still
speculating on what other revelations Frances Atterby
brought with her.

THE NEXT MORNING, I rode the omnibus into the
suburbs where Edith Carter lived. I enjoyed the glare of
sunshine reflecting off the streets and buildings. A number of
people asked about the yellow ball in the sky, but their jests
were met with smiles. A warm, sunny day after a period of
rain and fog brought out the best in Londoners.

Children were out playing and mothers pushing prams
when I walked from the bus stop to Miss Carter's house. The
plain brick fronts of the rows of houses looked almost pretty
in the sunshine, and the tiny front gardens showed the first
buds on the plants.

I knocked on the door of Miss Carter's house, expecting
the maid to appear. Instead, Miss Carter herself answered
my summons.

When she saw I was alone, she looked crestfallen, but she
quickly recovered and said, "What are you doing here?"

"I'm looking for Nicholas Drake."

"He's not here. You should be out searching for him. I
repeat, why are you here?"

"While checking the public records, we found you've not
been completely forthcoming with us."

"I've not?" All her bluster fled her and she shrank back
from the door.

I took this as an invitation to enter and shut the door behind
me. "No. You didn't tell me you are from Blackford, the village
closest to Castle Blackford in Northumberland. That you know
the Duke of Blackford on sight. That Nicholas Drake is from
that same village. That he married your sister, Anne Carter.

That your parents, rather than living with you as you said, still reside in Blackford. And that you live in Canada with your husband, Mr. Norris, so we can't possibly be having this conversation."

She spun on her heel and marched into the parlor, leaving the door open. I followed her. She remained standing and didn't offer me a seat. "I came here following Nicholas, but I didn't want you to know I was living on my own."

"I'll admit it's unusual, but . . ."

"It's more than unusual, it's scandalous, and I'm finished with scandals." She wrapped her arms around her waist as she turned away from me.

I waited for what came next.

"I love him, but I want the respect due a married woman."

I kept silent, knowing she had more to say.

She paced quickly around the room, finally coming to rest behind a chair where she glared at me. "Don't look at me with that judgmental scowl."

"You said you were finished with scandals."

"I am." Her shoulders slumped. "Or I was until I moved down here, and Nicholas refused to admit to anyone that he had a wife. It was his idea that I live next door."

"Because he couldn't play the descendant of French royalty, the single gentleman, if he had a wife from Northumberland who wanted to live an honest life."

"You learned about my time in prison for theft?"

I nodded.

"Thank you for not throwing it in my face."

"I suspect you confessed to save Drake."

"Yes. How foolish could I be? But he promised to be waiting for me to start life over again where we weren't known."

"This wasn't what you had in mind. Why use your sister's name, Anne?"

"Edith doesn't have a police record."

"Does Mr. Drake?"

"No. Not really. Not much of one. I saw to that."

"Where is Drake now?"

"I don't know."

I was tired of playing games. I raised my voice. If Nicholas Drake was in the house and had any feelings for his wife, he'd appear. "Don't give me that. He's your husband. You know where he is."

"No."

Louder. "You've always known where he was. Even when you were in prison."

She yelled back at me. "No. That's why I came to you. To the Archivist Society. I want him returned to me alive and well."

"I don't believe you. You know where he is." I was shouting now.

"No, I don't. If I did, I would go there myself and get him." With the tears running down her cheeks and a fiery gleam in her eyes, she showed every sign of being ready to cross hell to bring him home.

I lowered my voice. "I believe you would. So believe me when I say we will find him, just as we found out your secrets."

Her plain face became beautiful as she smiled. "Thank you."

"Tell me what really happened the night you said Nicholas Drake was abducted."

"Sit down. Please."

We sat across from each other in front of an unlit fire on matching balloon chairs with red brocade seats. Anne Drake, or Edith Carter as I kept thinking of her, studied her hands for a moment. "Nicholas said he'd stay at his house that night because he'd be returning late from dinner with a lord and didn't want to disturb me."

"What lord?"

"I don't know. I don't sleep well when he's not here, and when I heard the carriage outside, I thought he was returning. By the time I rose and looked out the window, I only saw one man leave the open carriage door. That man was definitely not Nicholas. The driver stayed up in his box."

She rose and began to pace again. "I wondered if I should go down and ask what was going on, but Nicholas was always very strict about my staying out of his business arrangements. So I waited. After five minutes or so, two men came out carrying a third. I'm certain the third man was Nicholas."

"How certain?"

"As certain as I am those men worked for the Duke of Blackford, even if the coach was an ordinary hired hack. I told you the story about his antique carriage showing up on our street so you'd question him. I know he's behind this."

Her description matched that of the woman with the fussy baby across the street, but I needed to know more about Drake if we were to find him. "Tell me how you met Mr. Drake."

"We both come from the village of Blackford in Northumberland, so we've known each other all our lives. Nicholas was orphaned young and went to work in the duke's stables at age eight. He had a quick mind and big dreams, and he employed them to get an education and advancement to footman. That's where he learned how society behaved and entertained and hid their secrets."

She twisted her fingers as she continued. "The family brought him to London one season to help in the town house. He came back with more knowledge of society and a desire to escape to London. I was working in the castle as a nursery maid then, although I was not much older than Lady Margaret. Nicholas and I married. He began to steal things, little things they'd never miss, to fund our start in London."

"And he continued stealing in London."

"Did he? I don't know. I went to prison and he moved

here." She couldn't hold my gaze. Guilt over spending time in prison or guilty knowledge of Drake's continued thefts?

I hated to ask, but I needed to know. "How did you end up in prison in place of Drake?"

"When I saw they had all the evidence they needed to put him in jail for many years, I confessed to the crime. I threw myself on their mercy. Since I was young and lived a blameless life and my parents were well thought of by the duke, they gave me a short sentence. When I got out, I followed Nicholas to London."

"Was it Drake's idea that you confess?"

"No." Her chin rose. "It was all my own."

I wondered if Drake knew, or cared, how loyal his wife was. "Do you have any idea where he might be hiding if he's escaped from his attackers?"

She shook her head as her shoulders slumped and a sigh escaped her lips. "He couldn't have."

"There's always the chance he did. He might have fought his way free. Where should we look?"

She stared silently at me for a long time. Then she shrugged and said, "He never could have taken them in a fair fight, but he could have outsmarted them and escaped. If he's not hiding with Harry or Tom, he might be at his house in Hounslow."

This was news. I forced myself not to sit forward, eager to hear what she had to say. "What house in Hounslow?"

"It's a farmhouse outside of town on the Hanworth Road. He rents the land to a nearby farmer. The house is vacant except when he goes there."

I was excited by the possibility, but I didn't want to raise Anne Drake's hopes. She gave me directions to the farmhouse and swore me to secrecy.

That wasn't a problem. I wouldn't tell anyone outside the Archivist Society, and while there might be a chance Drake had escaped his captors, it wasn't a good one.

I rode back into the center of London, looking out the bus windows at our first springlike day. Perhaps the weather would bring my parents' killer out of doors, and the only place I knew to look was Hyde Park Place. I should meet Sir Broderick's mysterious letter writer at two that afternoon, but I had time.

I climbed off the omnibus as we neared where I'd seen the man before and walked slowly as I glanced at the faces of every male I passed. No luck. After a half hour spent searching, I knew it was time to go to Lady Westover's to obtain the signal the letter writer would look for.

When I told her what I wanted, Lady Westover laughed. "You don't need my greenhouse for that. My back garden will provide you a handful of daffodils."

"I only need one."

"Can you stay for luncheon? It's only a cold plate, I'm afraid, but the tea will be hot."

I accepted, and we moved into her morning room, where a maid brought tea, sandwiches, and cakes.

When we were alone again, Lady Westover said, "Are you making progress with your investigation?"

I had no problem telling my elderly hostess all we'd uncovered. Part of her role with the Archivist Society was to pass information to her grandson. Inspector Grantham, never happy with his grandmother's enthusiasm for assisting us, would demand to know every detail the moment he learned I'd been to visit. "I've eliminated the Naylards from the list of people wanting to kidnap Nicholas Drake. We've also learned Drake's next-door neighbor is his wife."

"How bizarre. From what you told me, he sounded so happy to be a bachelor, but you can't always believe what men say in that regard. I've long suspected men want wives more than women want husbands."

I looked at Lady Westover, wondering if I dared ask about the late Lord Westover.

She took one glance at my expression and didn't give me a chance. "When you marry, you'll learn what I mean. Now, tell me about this wife of Drake's."

After I finished giving her a few details, she asked, "Why this interest in my daffodils?"

I told her about the letter to Sir Broderick and the instruction to wear a daffodil in my hair.

"Portman Square? That's where the Mervilles live. I wonder . . ."

The thoughtful expression on her face made me ask, "What about the Mervilles?"

CHAPTER ELEVEN

"YOU asked me about what could have happened to the Mervilles ten years ago, Georgia. I don't think this was more than four or five years ago, but Lady Merville was quite ill. She didn't come up to London for the season. The duke came up and brought all four children with him. Only the older two children were out in society. But as I said, this was much more recent." Lady Westover took a sip of her tea.

"You're certain?"

"It seems like only last season. Time speeds by so fast when you're my age, and then you discover events happened further in the past than seems possible. No, I'm not certain." Her thoughts appeared to wander into the past.

I hoped I'd find out what happened to Lady Merville shortly. "One other thing has occurred. Emma and I have received invitations to the Duke of Arlington's masked ball."

Lady Westover gave me her full attention again. "Really? How did you arrange that?"

"The Duke of Blackford gave them to us with instructions to let him know what our costumes would be."

Her teacup stopped halfway to her mouth. "How very odd. What is he up to?"

"I think he hopes to set something up so we can learn more about Drake's blackmailing and who is most likely to have abducted him."

"Blackford? Being helpful? I should hope not. Next you'll see the queen frolicking in Hyde Park." She took a sip of tea, her eyes sparkling at the image.

Lady Westover's irreverent humor was one of the things I liked best about her. However, she raised a question I hadn't wanted to delve into too deeply. What was Blackford up to, and why was he helping us?

I finished the delicate fish paste sandwich I was eating and admitted, "I can't see any reason for him to go to the trouble of obtaining invitations for us if he weren't planning on helping us."

"Oh, my child, can't you see? He's not going to help you, he's going to use you. Emma's quite handy with a knife, but we must think about how you will protect yourself."

I WAS MAKING my sixth slow passage around the edge of the winter-blighted park in Portman Square, cursing the tardiness of the anonymous letter writer, when the lady in green with a green parasol decorated with bows approached me at a steady pace. She was matronly, a hat topped with flowers and birds sat on hair liberally streaked with gray, and she was accompanied by a hatchet-faced young woman I took to be her companion or lady's maid.

There were a few women strolling and plenty of children playing under the watchful eye of their nurses, but I was the only one in the park with a daffodil stuck over my left brow. The scent was already starting to fade from the flower and I knew it would soon droop. I'd set my hat back at a jaunty angle so the bloom could be seen, and as a result, I feared my straw boater would soon slide off my hair or pull a large chunk of my coiffure out of my scalp.

The woman slowed as she approached me. "I like your flower. One of the first harbingers of spring."

"It cheered me no end."

She came to a stop, the other woman hovering behind her. The fine fabric of her clothes and her well-fed, buxomly figure alone weren't enough to tell me she was the wife of a duke. But when I added in her upper-class accent and the patience of her warmly dressed, well-shod companion, the signs said this was a member of the aristocracy. "Do you think spring is finally here?"

"I've been noticing buds on all the trees and there are hyacinths in the center of the park." I wondered how long we'd be discussing the weather before she decided to trust me.

"Please show me. Helen, you may wait for me on that bench."

We took a few steps into the park, the maid settling onto the bench, before I released the breath I'd been holding. "I'm Miss Georgia Peabody."

"Mrs. Watkins."

"Pleased to meet you, Mrs. Watkins." I'd used a false identity. I was surprised she used something I could check as easily as the Merville family name.

"I expect a high level of discretion from associates of Sir Broderick duVene."

"The Archivist Society prides itself on its silence. Which makes me wonder how you found out about us and our investigation."

"The Archivist Society has performed a number of services for members of our class. If someone needs something . . . corrected, a few discreet inquiries will get them the name and address of Sir Broderick and the Archivist Society. Blackford told me about your inquiry. I need your silence because this blackmail has to stop without starting gossip."

"Nicholas Drake is blackmailing you rather than your husband?"

She nodded. "I assume you don't have children." She lowered her voice more as we walked through the park. The children running past showed no interest in us as anything but an obstacle.

"No, ma'am."

"The world believes I have four, but in truth, I have five."

My surprise slowed my speech and my steps.

She gave me a sharp look. "Come now. You must have met women before who had to hide, ah, an unusual child."

"Yes. Yes, I have. And I think it must be difficult for the mother to have to hide one child and show off the others."

She turned soft brown eyes toward me, eyes growing moist as she spoke. "But that child can't go out in society. He, and his entire family, would be ridiculed."

I'd seen enough children in London born weak of limb or eye or brain. Sometimes their families kept them in the circle of their lives, teaching them, feeding them, loving them. Others were dumped on orphanages or locked away in madhouses. "Where is this child?"

"In a cottage on our estate, cared for by a childless couple. They're very good to him. They can give him time we can't with our busy lives and our trips to London." She sniffed and looked around her. "We seem to have passed the hyacinths."

We had. After we turned back, I asked, "How did Drake learn of this child?"

"The boy was near death last year. The woman wrote to me, thinking I should know. I foolishly kept the letter. It disappeared after an event last season."

"How was the blackmail threat delivered?"

"In person. Here in the park. I let him think I had to raise the money from my housekeeping allowance, but in truth I told the duke. He gave me the money for Drake's silence, but he blames me for the blackmail, the child, everything." For a second, I thought she'd dissolve into tears. Blinking furiously, she pulled herself together as she glanced around to see if anyone was paying attention to us.

Everyone was too busy enjoying the day. Noise droned in the background as children shouted, nannies gossiped, and carriages were pulled by neighing, clopping horses. We could have been completely alone.

The duke was a coldhearted fathead for making his wife suffer the separation from her child, even if he was willing to overpay me for a volume for his antiquarian collection. And I was to blame today for her grief, because I had to dive into her pain. "Drake still has the letter?"

She nodded.

"And is still demanding money?"

"Money and invitations."

That surprised me for a moment, but it made sense. The more places Drake was invited, the more places he could rob. "Has anyone seen him at an event in the past week?"

"Few social events have occurred lately. I haven't received any demands for money, either."

"Was the child born ten years ago, when you didn't come to London for the season?"

"Yes. The duke said I was ill, but I was awaiting the birth of the child. Our other children were grown or nearly so, and the pregnancy was difficult. The doctor told us not to hold out much hope for a successful conclusion. I prayed he was wrong, and we'd be able to show off our little surprise. One look at the baby when he was born, and I knew he could never be part of a duke's family. How I prayed for him to die." She looked at me with sad eyes. "That sounds hard, doesn't it?"

"I can't judge what it's like to be married to a duke." I could, however, judge the duke, and I did.

"The couple who take care of him have been with us for a long time. I regret to say they take better care of him than I would, since they're simple people and can love him." She drew a shaky breath. "I visit them when we're at the estate. He thinks of me as the pretty lady in the big house. The duke has never seen the boy—"

"His son," I corrected.

She nodded. "His son, David, preferring to call the husband to his estate office if he needs to talk to him."

I'd spent enough time with her sorrow. "What do you want the Archivist Society to do, Mrs. Watkins, or should I say, Lady Merville?"

She sighed. "You knew Watkins is our family name?"

"Yes."

"Retrieve my letter from Drake and give it to me. Sir Broderick knows the duke will pay well for its return." She looked down at where we'd stopped. "You're right. The hyacinths are lovely."

Perhaps it was the word "duke," or perhaps the unbowing glamour of the hyacinths, but my mind immediately went to Blackford. "How many people in London know your secret?"

She flinched. "No one."

"Not even the Duke of Blackford? He and your husband appear to be political allies and friends."

"He's the duke's friend, not mine."

"You don't like him."

"No. He's a fine man. If one of my daughters had wanted to marry him, I'd have had no objections. It's his half sister I don't care for."

"Do you know Lady Margaret well?"

"No one knows Lady Margaret well. My older daughter was good friends with Victoria Dutton-Cox—and the stories she told me! Terrible. Lady Margaret was ungracious when it would have been just as easy to be courteous to the other girls." Lady Merville shook her head. "Do you know, she once threw a figurine when she didn't get her way."

I jerked my head back as my eyes widened. I thought the

aristocracy tried to hide that sort of behavior. "I hope she reimbursed you."

"It was her figurine, in her home."

"Does Blackford know?"

"I'm sure he does. It was Victoria Dutton-Cox, his fiancée, who was nearly hit by the object. My daughter witnessed the whole incident."

"Why would Lady Margaret do that?"

"They were in the morning room, and Victoria was criticizing the decor and saying as soon as she became mistress she'd change the wallpaper and drapes and rugs so it didn't look so tawdry. Turns out Margaret's late mother decorated the room."

I winced. If someone had spoken that way about my mother after she died, I'd probably have thrown something, too.

"Victoria had strong opinions and wasn't afraid to express them, even if they weren't always the most tactful. Still, Margaret never should have become so overwrought. She became upset and angry easily. More than once, she ran out of a room in tears over some little comment of Victoria's. No wonder the duke keeps her in the country." The duchess drew herself up and said, "Is there anything else you want to know? Any other tedious gossip?"

"I have to ask this. How do we know the Duke of Merville didn't abduct Drake?"

She looked me in the eye and said, "He wouldn't. He could deal with Drake blackmailing him because Drake never asks for too much. Horrid man is careful that way."

"Your husband is so embarrassed by his son, by David, he's never looked at the child. If his name was about to be tarnished, I'm sure he could do a lot more than abduct a man." I'd lowered my voice to a whisper, certain no one could hear, but Lady Merville looked around in terror.

Then she raised her chin and looked down her nose at me,

despite the fact I was a few inches taller. "Just retrieve the letter. Do not be so bold as to contact me until you do." Turning on her heel, she walked away.

I stared at her back. Both the Mervilles made good possibilities in Drake's disappearance. And then I realized we needed to consider the wives and daughters of the men we suspected as the possible brains behind Drake's abduction. A woman could hire thugs, and the women I was meeting in this investigation were strong willed and wanted Drake's threats removed from their lives.

But first I needed to confront the Duke of Merville and the other men who were suspects in this investigation. The best place to do that would be at their club. And to do that, I needed to return to Lady Westover's.

I arrived shortly before visiting hours, and she was surprised to see me when her butler showed me into the parlor. "Georgia, what are you doing back here so soon?"

"The House of Lords isn't in session today, is it?"

"No, so the members are probably in their clubs."

Good. "I need a couple of favors. A bunch of daffodils from your garden, some scrap paper and a pencil, and two items from your rag bin."

Leaving behind my straw boater to pick up later, I left Lady Westover's house with a battered and limp hat on my head, a ragged shawl over my neat blouse, a bunch of flowers in my hand, and printed notes for the Duke of Merville and Lord Dutton-Cox, complete with minor misspellings.

I walked directly to the massive Georgian club near Whitehall, ignoring the odd looks I collected from passersby. With fingers crossed, I rang the bell at the front door and waited for the club's butler to answer.

A man in full livery opened the door, looked at me, sniffed, and said, "The tradesmen's entrance is around the side."

Before he could shut the door, I shoved my calf kid

buttoned boot in the doorway and held out the note. "For Lord Dutton-Cox. I think he'll see me out here."

He took the note, I removed my foot, and he shut the door. At least he hadn't denied Dutton-Cox was there. Something I'd hoped but not been certain of.

And he hadn't noticed I wore fashionable, practically new boots with my disguise.

I lingered outside for five minutes, keeping an eye out for the local bobby in case the doorman summoned the police instead of Lord Dutton-Cox.

Finally, the front door opened and a balding, stoop-shouldered man appeared. He walked toward me with a frown and a glance over his thin shoulder before he asked quietly, holding up my note, "What is this about? I had no hand in my daughter's death, and I will call the police if you say I did."

"Nicholas Drake was there, and he says differently."

"I don't know what you're talking about. Go away." The paper I'd sent in to him shook in his hand.

"Drake told me what he saw that day. Now that he's missing, I'm willing to keep silent. For a price."

His eyes welled up with tears. "Then he saw more than I did. I lost my daughter at what should have been the happiest time of her life. Now I'm losing my wife to her grief, and we don't know why Victoria died. She was sickly as a child and we were always careful to coddle her. I've always believed her weak heart gave out, but my wife——. Please, if you know anything, tell me."

The mournful tone in his voice shocked me into silence. I hadn't expected his grief, and now I was mortified by my thoughtless prying. I stood there gaping at him, wishing I could take back my words. Since I couldn't do that, I hoped the sidewalk would swallow me up.

"You don't know anything, do you? You just wanted to

profit from our great misfortune. Go away and leave me in peace with my sorrow." He turned and rushed back into his club, crushing my message in his hand.

I stood on the sidewalk with my mouth open until I realized how ridiculous I must have looked. If the words I'd surprised out of him were genuine, and I thought they were, Lord Dutton-Cox knew what state his wife was in and was as heartbroken as she.

Drake was blackmailing them over something other than their daughter's death. Whatever it was, Dutton-Cox didn't act like he had any concerns about Drake, so why would he go to the trouble of abducting the missing man? I was certain I could eliminate him from suspicion.

At the sound of a carriage pulling up, I glanced at the street and recognized the Duke of Merville's crest on the door. I was in luck, but I'd have to improvise.

I stepped into his path between the carriage and the door to the club and said, "How is your son David?"

His face paled and his mouth opened and shut twice before he gasped out, "I don't know what you're talking about. Go away."

"There are those who know about David and are willing to keep silent. For a price."

"Name your price. Just go away." He didn't seem angry. He kept glancing around and the red creeping up his face appeared to be embarrassment at the danger of being seen with me.

"A pound."

"And you'll never come back."

"It's a deal. What was your deal with Drake?"

"Damnation. You learned about this from him, didn't you?"

"Maybe." I wasn't about to tell him his wife had told me.

"I don't know what he told you or why he put you up to this, but I wish he and you would just stay away. This is embarrassing for a man in my position."

"So you'll pay me the pound?"

"Gladly." He reached into his waistcoat pocket and pulled out a gold sovereign as a coach stopped behind me. "I'll take three of the flowers."

We made the exchange. Then a man stopped next to Merville and said, "Going inside?"

The Duke of Blackford. I peeked up from beneath my hat brim and saw his eyebrows rise. My disguise was a failure. He'd recognized me.

Over my heartbeat banging like a drum, I heard Merville say, "Yes," as he marched back into the building carrying the flowers.

Blackford gave me a shilling and a smile as he took one of the flowers out of my limp grasp and then walked inside.

All I could think was to disappear before he told Merville he'd been tricked by the Archivist Society. Clutching the coins in one hand, I hurried away, yanking off the shawl and balling it up in my other hand. I was certain Merville wasn't Drake's abductor. He was too happy to take any easy path to keep scandal from his door. And Dutton-Cox seemed to have no worry over what Drake might have known or seen concerning his daughter Victoria's death.

Therefore, Drake must not have been blackmailing Blackford about her death, either. So why was Drake blackmailing the duke and Dutton-Cox? I was becoming increasingly certain I'd have to travel to the wilds of Northumberland to learn the answer from the duke's sister, Margaret. I did not want to make that trip.

But first, I'd have to travel to Hounslow.

CHAPTER TWELVE

I T wasn't until the next morning that I had time to follow up on the information Edith, or Anne as I'd learned she was, had told me. Truthfully, I didn't expect to learn anything, and Hounslow felt nearly as far away as Northumberland.

I walked to the Embankment station on the Metropolitan District Railway, preparing for a long, smoky trip out to Hounslow. I entered by the wide, concrete stairs to the platform and was immediately reminded why I seldom rode on the railways beneath London. The platform was dimly lit due to the thick air and I expected the train cars to be crowded and dingy with coal exhaust from the engines.

At least I didn't have long to wait before the train arrived. I was fortunate to find a seat, wedged between a woman with a holdall on her lap and a man trying to read a newspaper. The windows were closed. With luck, no one would open them until we were aboveground and in the countryside. The white smoke from the engine hid the tunnels in a fog that broke apart as we sped along the tracks, but we couldn't escape the stench of sulfur seeping in from the train's boiler.

Once aboveground, passengers opened the windows and fresh air replaced the stale. The Heston and Hounslow station wasn't far from London, but it still retained its soot-free village skies along with its village appearance. I walked along Hounslow's main street searching for a hansom cab. When I didn't have any luck by the time I reached the Hanworth Road, I turned in at a stable.

"Hello?" I called out, walking forward. The stable seemed to be empty except for two horses.

"Looking fer someone?"

I turned around and found my retreat blocked by a short man holding a pitchfork. His clothes were battered and dirty from his cap to his boots, except for a clean, light blue woolen scarf wrapped around his neck.

I backed up a step, keeping my gaze on the scarf rather than the menacing pitchfork. I hoped someone else was nearby. "I'm looking for a conveyance to take me to Nicholas Drake's house about a mile and a half to the south."

"You want a conveyance?" He cackled with mirth. "What's wrong with your feet?"

"Nothing, but I don't wish to show up muddy at my brother's house." Until that moment, I hadn't decided who I was going to be and how far from the truth I planned to travel.

"Drake's your brother?"

"Yes."

"If it's Drake you want, you'd best go down the street to the police station."

What was this odd little man up to? "Has Nicholas been locked up? What's the charge?"

"You might say that. And it's a charge we all have to face." Chuckling to himself, the man shoved the pitchfork into the hay in an empty stall.

I hurried outside, afraid I'd feel the tines in my back at any moment. The police station was two blocks back up the road I had followed from the railway platform. I walked at a quick pace to the redbrick building and entered the lobby. The sergeant's counter was across a well-scrubbed pine floor from the door. A gray-haired uniformed constable leaned on the other side of the barrier.

"I've been told you're holding Nicholas Drake here," I began.

"You've come to collect the body?" the man asked, straightening.

"What? Nicholas Drake is dead?" Was it an accident, or had his abductor succeeded?

I must have looked as shocked as I felt, because the constable called for one of his mates and came around the counter to me. "Are you all right, miss?"

"What happened to Nicholas Drake?" I demanded.

"Are you Mrs. Drake?" he asked.

"No. I'm his sister."

"We didn't have any leads on his family, so it's a good thing you came by here today."

I had failed. The Archivist Society had failed. But how did Drake die? I wanted to beat the information out of the constable, who was asking more questions than giving answers. "What happened to Nicholas?"

"If you'll come back here with me, we'll find you a cup of tea and talk about this," he said in a soothing voice, but he watched me warily as if he expected me to become hysterical.

I nodded and followed him to an office down a long corridor. He had me sit on a hard wooden chair while another uniformed constable brought me a hot cup of tea. I took a sip and found there was too much sugar in the tea for it to be an unfortunate accident. They must have feared I'd wail and cry copious tears, but I'd already decided I'd learn more by being calm.

"Are you all right, miss?" the first officer asked.

"Quite. What happened to my brother?" They needed to tell me this instant what had happened or I'd scream, and not from grief.

"There was a fire in his house last night. Since his house

sits on its own, well, no one could reach the building until it was burned through and ready to collapse."

"You found his body inside?"

"When we could get into the rubble this morning, we found the body of a man. We believe it's your brother."

"You believe?"

"The body was burned beyond recognition. The doctor says it's a man in his thirties and about Mr. Drake's height. Nicholas was in the Red Lion last night until closing time, when he headed home. The fire occurred not a half hour later."

"He burned to death?" The timing was suspicious. Especially when blood was found in Drake's front hall the day he disappeared and he stood accused of blackmail.

The policeman patted my hand. "We talked to the regulars at the Red Lion and they said Nicholas had been staying here, well, at his house, for the past week. He'd lived there from time to time before. He was well-known around here and well liked. He was seen heading toward the Hanworth Road just after closing time. I'm sorry, miss."

"His house was on the Hanworth Road. How did no one see the fire until it had consumed the house?"

"Hanworth Road is well traveled, even at that hour. There were a few people at a distance who saw the fire begin and heard the explosion. It only took a moment to turn into a raging fire, much quicker than they could reach the house. It was so fast, he wouldn't have suffered."

An explosion? It sounded more and more like his abductors found him before I did. "His house wasn't old and decrepit?"

"No. It was a solid house, if old and small." The constable kept his voice calm and his manner reassuring. How many times had he talked to a bereaved family? I wasn't bereaved, and I wanted answers.

"And no one was seen running from the house?"

Shaking his head, the constable patted my hand. Again. I'd have gladly ripped off his arm if it would get me the answers I was looking for in a more timely fashion. "No. There's no sign it was anything but an accident."

"Who did he buy the house from?"

The constable drew his hand away and gave me a piercing look.

Oh, bother. I'd raised the policeman's suspicions. Trying to sound aware of his doubts and innocent of prying for information I should already have as Drake's sister, I said, "Nicholas and I hadn't kept in contact often in recent years. He was never a letter writer and I don't travel much. He told me something about it, but I don't remember now and I'd like to remember happier times."

The policeman nodded, apparently believing my story. "Old Lady Caphart owned several of the farms in the area. Your brother's was the smallest, not big enough to farm properly. Shortly before she died, she sold it to your brother. None of us had ever seen him before he came down here with the deed, and then it was only days later that we heard she'd died."

I nodded, belatedly remembering to pull out my handkerchief and take another sip of the rapidly cooling tea.

"How did your brother meet Lady Caphart?" the constable asked.

I wove together some details we'd learned about Drake and told him, "He'd done some work for her. He was a broker of artworks, and he'd found her some pieces she wanted. I had the impression the farm was in payment for something." Had he been blackmailing Lady Caphart? That would have to be looked into.

"Are you from a big family, and will you want to take the body home for burial?"

"We're not a big family, and we've all moved away from the village we grew up in. I'm sure he'll be buried locally."

"That's the shame of these modern times. People are starting to move out of their hometowns into the cities looking for work. No one knows their neighbors anymore." The constable shook his head.

"Are you local? I imagine you can remember all the changes coming to this area." Like Nicholas Drake. I hoped he'd start talking and I'd hear something that would help with my investigation.

"Aye. The railway into London just came out here five years ago. Or maybe ten. And with it came chain grocers buying up farms for a steady supply of produce in the city and we got new, bigger stores on the high street. Why, your brother had a friend come out from London yesterday on the railway."

My pulse jumped. Was it Drake's abductor? "Who was it?"

"A friend from London. Met him in the Red Lion." The constable flipped over the pages in his notebook. "Harry Conover. Left him just before the last train back to London. Just a few minutes before closing time."

One of the two friends Drake's housekeeper and his wife had mentioned. Now the Archivist Society would have to find him and learn what they'd talked about so close to Drake's death. Then I realized with a sinking feeling that this would be someone else we'd have to find to give them the bad news.

"What is your name, miss?" The constable had his pencil ready.

"Georgia Drake."

"And your address?"

Blast. I hadn't planned on that. "I'm nurse-companion to Mrs. Ellis of Winchcombe in Warwickshire. It's a village. No other address is needed." I remembered passing through the village during one investigation and Mrs. Ellis, of London, from another.

He wrote all that down. I felt guilty lying to a police officer, but not bad enough to tell the truth.

"Where will you be staying while you make arrangements for your brother?"

"London. I have family there." I stood up. "And they don't

know. I need to tell them. You will excuse me until one of us gets back to you about—about Nicholas."

He nodded.

"Thank you for your kindness." I nodded to him and left the police station, heading directly to the railway station to make the miserable underground journey back to London.

I WALKED INTO my bookshop to find Emma facing an insistent footman in Blackford livery. I paused, amazed because I'd never seen a male not immediately surrender to Emma's whims. She looked up at the man, her delicate chin jutting out, and said, "If you don't believe me, ask her yourself. She's standing right behind you."

The footman spun around and said, "Miss Fenchurch."

"Yes." Wanting to show Emma held authority in my absence, whatever the subject, I faced her. "Any customers or anything else of note?"

"A few customers. Nothing of note until His Grace sent him with a message." She growled the word "him."

"About?" I asked her.

"What you are wearing to the masquerade ball," the footman replied.

I'd just learned the abducted man we were searching for appeared to have been in hiding but recently had been killed, and the duke's footman was worrying me about something frivolous like costumes. I wanted to scream. Instead, I asked, "What is His Grace wearing?"

"I'm not at liberty to say."

"Which means you don't know. Until you tell us, I won't tell you, either."

"His Grace will not be happy with your response."

"He'll survive." Unlike Drake. "Now, unless there's something else?"

"No, miss." The footman nodded to us and strode from the shop, stiff-backed and head held high.

"I think you hurt his pride," Emma said.

"I don't have time for pride or nonsense now. Drake is dead, probably murdered in the fire that destroyed the house he owned outside Hounslow. A house and land he may have gained by blackmailing a Lady Caphart." I had to spill out my findings before anyone else came into the shop to overhear, and I didn't want to hold off any longer from telling Emma.

Emma took a step back, eyes wide. "Oh, dear. Your trip to Hounslow netted more than we expected."

"The Archivists will have to meet tonight."

"And we'll have to plan our costumes for the Arlingtons' ball." When I gave her a frown, she said, "We're now on the trail of a murderer. And he's bound to be one of those aristocrats at the masquerade."

AFTER ARRANGING FOR an Archivist Society meeting that night, I went to visit Lady Westover in hopes she could help with our costumes. When I followed the butler up a flight, I found a tall man with an angular face waiting outside the parlor. The butler paid the man no attention and announced me. Then I discovered she already had company in her green, flower-filled front parlor.

Her guest appeared even older than Lady Westover, formally dressed, wearing old-fashioned side whiskers and in possession of two canes. He started to rise feebly when I entered the room.

"No, please, don't get up. I never would have intruded if I'd known Lady Westover had a visitor already. Shall I return later?"

"Nonsense, Georgia. You sound as if Lord Waxpool and I are having an assignation in the middle of the day," Lady Westover said, smiling as if they had been.

The old man gave a wheezy chuckle. "Perhaps at the beginning of the queen's reign."

"Really, Harold, we're neither of us that old." Lady Westover was still smiling. "Georgia, have you ever met the Earl of Waxpool?"

"No, my lady." I swept them both a deep curtsy.

"Then I think now might be the time to ask the questions you have of him," Lady Westover said. "And do sit. We can't have you hovering over us."

As I sat, Lord Waxpool said in a quiet voice, "I get enough of that from Price. The man cares for me twenty-four hours a day. I couldn't do without him, but sometimes I get tired of him being there, carrying out my every wish."

"Would he do anything for you, milord?"

"Of course."

"Even murder?" If these aristocrats had servants who were incredibly devoted, the number of potential kidnappers rose dramatically.

His pale blue eyes bore into me. "Even murder. And before you ask, he's the only servant I've ever met I could say that about. He knows I would kill for him, too. We both have old-fashioned notions of loyalty." Then he smiled. "Now, Amelia has been telling me about your investigation into this blackmailer. I'm afraid to disappoint you. I wasn't one of his victims."

"Someone in your family, perhaps?"

"My son, George. The boy has been a terrible disappointment."

When he stopped, Lady Westover said, "Tell her the rest."

"It's private," he said.

"It's abduction and possibly murder," I said.

"What?" Lady Westover exclaimed as Lord Waxpool said, "Not George."

"Tell me the story. If we can verify it, we may be able to keep a police enquiry from your door."

Lady Westover nodded at my words.

"All right, young lady, but this goes no further than this room. George was responsible for part of the family investments. Not satisfied with his allowance, he embezzled from the family. From me. This Drake person found out, got hold of some records of George's that showed the embezzlement, and began to blackmail him. George's response was to embezzle more to pay the man. Idiot. I found out and put a stop to everything. The embezzlement and the blackmail." Waxpool stomped his cane into the rug twice for emphasis.

"You weren't afraid Drake would spread the story?"

"He saw it wouldn't do him any good. George has been sent to the south of France. I've done nothing wrong. If anything, it should win me sympathy." He laughed wheezily again.

"You met with Nicholas Drake? How long ago was this?"

"A month ago. I told him there would be no more money, and if he persisted in trying any more of his nonsense, I would press charges."

Curiosity wouldn't let me drop the subject. "But won't your son control all the investments one day?"

"He'll have the title, but that's all he'll have. I've organized my affairs so my grandchildren, a boy and a girl, will manage the investments and see to his allowance. My grandchildren take after me. Sensible, reliable, intelligent. I have no fears for the family fortune or name after I'm gone."

Into the silence that followed, Lady Westover said, "Georgia, why did you come by today?"

I couldn't hide my smile. "I mentioned Emma and I received invitations to the Duke of Arlington's masquerade ball. Time is getting short and I have no clue as to what to do about costumes."

"Something unusual," the Earl of Waxpool suggested.

"Yes, shepherdesses and Marie Antoinette have been done to death. You want to stand out, so whoever is looking for you can find you," Lady Westover said.

"What is this in aid of?" Lord Waxpool asked.

I answered him the way I would respond to Blackford. "In aid of justice for the blackmail victims and their families, and justice for a killer."

"A killer?" Lady Westover looked concerned. Whether for me or for her police inspector grandson and the dangers he faced, I wasn't sure.

I made a quick decision. The house fire that led to Drake's death would remain a secret for the time being. "Drake has been abducted and no one has seen him. There's always the chance he's been murdered."

"That's terrible," Lady Westover said.

"But what is the problem?" Waxpool asked.

"If this person would kill Drake to keep his secret safe, he'll kill again if he thinks his secret is in danger. And," I added, giving the old man a hard stare, "Drake's abductor doesn't have the right to kill the first time."

"Blackford obtained invitations to the Arlingtons' ball for Georgia and her friend Emma," Lady Westover broke in before the Earl of Waxpool and I could begin a heated row over Drake's right to live.

"Blackford? Did he? How extraordinary." Waxpool smiled. "Then you must find these young ladies singularly unique costumes. Amelia, I always enjoy seeing you." He rose shakily, using both canes. "Good luck, young lady."

I rose and walked across the parlor to open the door for him. His man Price immediately appeared and helped the old man from the room. I went back to my seat on the sofa with Lady Westover.

Before I could say anything, she smiled at a jest I didn't see. "Can you close the shop early tonight? I want both you and Emma here by six. I have an idea. We're going to work on unique."

CHAPTER THIRTEEN

EMMA and I arrived at Lady Westover's town house just as the bells of the nearby churches were tolling six. Our hostess was waiting for us in the parlor with two other women who were introduced as Madame Leclerc and her assistant. The assistant stood by with tape measures, a notebook and pencil, and a bored expression. Madame Leclerc greeted us with, "Take off your clothes."

"Madame Leclerc is my dressmaker. I have in mind very simple gowns of rich silk for you both. Seeing you together, I'm sure my idea will work. A pale blue for Emma and a deep red for you, Georgia."

Emma and I exchanged one quick look before I said, "What idea, my lady?"

"Emma will be the Ice Queen, and you will be the Fire Queen. Show them the fabric swatches, madame."

The red silk was beautiful, catching the light almost like flame. If fabric could shimmer and smolder, sending sparks along its length, this fluid material did. I touched only the corner, expecting to be shouted at by the dressmaker. She mustn't have noticed. I was surprised by smoothness so soft it barely registered as more than air on my fingertips and didn't burn my skin. I looked up to see Emma was just as entranced with her shade.

"The fabric is perfect, Lady Westover, but queens? How will we appear as more than well-dressed women?"

"Leave that to me. Just be here in time to dress the night of the ball." She put her hands together as a look of pure joy crossed her face. "Oh, I feel like a fairy godmother."

Emma and I looked at each other, grinning with pleasure. Fortunately, we had chosen to wear our best corsets, because once we were out of our skirts and blouses, Madame Leclerc and her assistant measured us so these gowns would be snug against our current undergarments.

"Lady Westover," I began.

"Don't move!" Madame Leclerc sounded like an angry schoolmistress.

I made certain only my mouth moved. "How am I paying for this?"

"You're not."

"That's a relief. But I can't expect you to—"

"I'm not."

"Then who?"

"The Duke of Blackford."

"What?" I spun around, knocking Madame Leclerc off balance and into a fern.

"Don't move!" came in a chorus from Madame Leclerc, Lady Westover, and Emma. Madame Leclerc straightened herself from the plant, stomped over, and swung me around again.

I obediently took up my pose and she went back to measuring me, a palm frond stuck in her hair.

"He's also lending you the tiaras for your crowns," Lady Westover said. "And your jewels for the night."

"Tell me they're paste." I couldn't guard a fortune in jewels and find a murderer at the same time. Certainly not in evening clothes. We wouldn't have any place to hide a hand-kerchief, much less a knife. The idea of going to a glittering ball in a beautiful dress was growing less appealing by the second.

"I doubt very much that the jewels will be paste."

I had a bad feeling about this. "Then I hope someone will be on hand to guard them."

"Oh, Georgia," Lady Westover laughed. "You'll be in a sea of diamonds. The jewels will be perfectly safe."

Madame Leclerc began to measure my face. When I jerked my head back, she said, "For your mask. It shall be of the same silk as the dress."

I held my head still, my eyes closed, and heard her mur-mur close to my ear, "A half mask. More dramatic."

"I don't know what the duke has planned." Lady Westo-ver sounded worried.

"When did he say he would pay for these gowns?" I asked.

"I sent him a note, suggesting my idea. He came to visit me at luncheon. As soon as I said you'd be dressed all in red, he murmured, 'It'll be easy to follow her,' and pulled out a stack of banknotes. He wasn't in the least interested in Emma's costume."

Emma gave me a raised-eyebrow look with a sly smile. Sometimes that girl can try my patience. The duke was a suspect, not a potential lover.

I was now beyond worried. I was confused, appalled, and frightened. These dresses would cost a fortune. What was Blackford up to? Why would he want to follow me? Or was he setting me up for somebody else?

NEITHER EMMA NOR I spoke on our trip from Lady Westover's until we were almost to Sir Broderick's doorstep. I was too busy listening to the duke's man, Sumner, following us as he'd been ordered to do, and wondering why this was the first time I'd heard his footsteps when Emma said, "You're really worried about this ball, aren't you?"

"Yes," came out in a hiss.

"In that crush, how will anyone find anyone? I suspect it will be a great deal of bother for a wonderful night and nothing more. Even a duke can't stage-manage unmasking a murderer, if indeed Drake was murdered." Emma reached out and rang the buzzer.

As Jacob, Sir Broderick's young manservant, opened the door, I had a sickening thought. Either the duke had already deduced who had tried to abduct Drake, or he was the one after Drake and that meant he was a murderer.

We hurried in, glad of the light and warmth after the cold and fog. Jacob took our cloaks and we walked upstairs to the study, where we met with the rest of the Archivists who'd been summoned for our meeting.

"There've been developments?" Sir Broderick asked from his wheelchair parked by the fire.

I ran down everything new, from confronting Edith Carter, or Anne Drake, about her real name and marriage to Nicholas Drake to the fire at Drake's house in Hounslow where he'd been hiding, and from meeting blackmail victims the Duke and Duchess of Merville and the Earl of Waxpool to the Duke of Blackford's involvement in our attending the Duke of Arlington's masked ball.

"Harry Conover. I'll look him up again. When Jacob talked to Tom Whitaker, Drake's other friend, he'd not seen Drake or Conover lately. Maybe Conover can tell us who Drake feared and what happened when someone tried to abduct him," Adam Fogarty said, limping across the room to the fireplace, head bent in thought.

Sir Broderick caught my eye and winked. I knew Fogarty's contacts inside the police force were valuable to the Archivist Society. Apparently, he was well liked by every constable and sergeant he'd ever worked with. Why the higher-ups let him go after he sustained his injury was a mystery he refused to discuss. If Sir Broderick knew, he wouldn't say, and he wouldn't allow the rest of us to ask.

"Find out what the police report says about the fire and the body," Sir Broderick said to him. "I'll have my man of affairs arrange a burial in the closest cemetery unless the widow has other plans."

I felt heat rise up my cheeks. "With everything else, I haven't told her yet."

"First thing in the morning, Georgia. You can't put a thing like that off," Sir Broderick said.

"Do you want me to come with you?" Frances Atterby's gray hair and ample bosom made her the perfect person for breaking bad news.

She'd spent decades working with her husband in their hotel before his murder. She'd developed a ready sympathy and an ability to talk to people that made everyone her friend. And I hated the bad-news part of the job. "Yes. Please. Thank you."

"So," Sir Broderick said, looking around at us, "who's going to figure out what the Duke of Blackford is really up to?"

"The answer to that is at Castle Blackford, and none of us are going to have time for that trip until after the ball." I looked around. "We need to attend Drake's funeral at the very least. We need to find out what Lady Dutton-Cox is hiding besides a belief that her daughter was murdered. My guess is Drake stole letters from her daughter Victoria before she died, but neither Lord nor Lady Dutton-Cox seems at all concerned about blackmail or Drake. We need to find out the particulars of Lady Caphart selling or giving the house and land in Hounslow to Drake. Was she also a blackmail victim? And can someone attend the ball as a footman and bring a weapon? We don't know what the duke plans, and I want to be ready for any eventuality."

"You don't trust him," Sir Broderick said. He didn't make it a question. He didn't need to. I think he shared my suspicions.

"No. The Duke of Blackford is paying for our very expensive dresses, providing us with jewels and tiaras, and arranging for us to attend the ball. When I know why, then I might trust him. A little."

Emma laughed. "Georgia, he might just fancy himself as your protector."

I remembered his questions at Lady Westover's dinner party about whether I was someone's mistress and shuddered at the word "protector." If he planned to make himself the protector of a trollop, he'd be sent away with firm words. If he wanted to extend his ducal protection to the work we were doing, that might be acceptable. As long as Blackford knew his bounds. I hadn't taken orders from any man since my father was murdered, not even my fiancé, and I wasn't about to start again now.

"We'll get someone in as a footman to the Arlingtons' masked ball. Who'll look into Lady Caphart?" Sir Broderick said.

Emma raised her hand.

"Emma, check out her connection to Drake. Georgia, you've met Lady Dutton-Cox. Go back there and see what you can learn. And I'll have my man of affairs sort out Drake's funeral after I hear from Frances. Is there anything else?"

"One thing," Jacob said, glancing around the room as if making certain none of us objected to him speaking up at a meeting. "Sir Broderick has me studying accountancy and I asked my tutor about the suspects Lord Hancock listed. He showed me how to look at public records about shares and companies."

Jacob looked at Sir Broderick, who nodded. "The Earl of Waxpool's son couldn't have been stealing from the family. Their wealth has grown nicely each year for the last several. The earl has a brilliant mind for business. My tutor introduced me to his man of affairs, who was willing to tell me the earl is very hands-on. He won't let his son, who has no interest in commerce, near any of the accounts. He never has let his heir have any role in their financial affairs."

"So the story the earl gave me was just that. A story," I said. Had he lied to hide the real reason, a compelling reason, why he was having Nicholas Drake hunted down?

"Sir Broderick's having you trained as an accountant?" Emma said.

"The lad can't be my valet and errand boy forever. He's far too bright. If he picks up some extra skills, he can help the Archivists long after I'm gone." Sir Broderick cleared his throat. "Is there anything else?"

I studied our leader's face. He looked healthy to me. He often planned ahead. This must just be another instance of Sir Broderick's foresightedness. I hoped.

"Just finding Drake's murderer," Fogarty said from where he'd momentarily stopped in front of a bookcase.

When Sir Broderick suggested we take a hansom cab home, I jumped at the idea. Even knowing it was Blackford's man who was following, I was still anxious from the footsteps constantly echoing behind us.

"Georgia, one moment if you please. It'll take Jacob a minute to find a cab."

I sat down by Sir Broderick, trying to ignore the sweat springing up under my clothes.

"You've been spending a lot of time in Hyde Park Place lately."

"That's where I saw my parents' killer."

"Where you thought you saw him. What's next? Knocking on the door of Surrey House and asking Lord Battersea if he knows any murderers?"

"Does he live along there?" I matched Sir Broderick's sarcasm. I wasn't going to stop hunting for the murderer. This was too important.

"Number seven."

I'd thought the first time I saw the killer that he was a powerful man. Considering the neighborhood where I'd seen him, I'd have to add rich to powerful. "Then I'll have to be more circumspect, because I'm going to continue to search for him."

"Be careful, Georgia. You don't know him, but he knows you."

"I doubt their killer remembers me." So far, everything had gone his way. But one day, he would slip up and then I'd find him.

Emma and I rode home to find Phyllida waiting for us. "Is the weather improving? Your skirts don't look as dirty."

"We've been more careful, Auntie," Emma said, grinning.

Phyllida pressed her lips together, but the corners edged up. "None of your cheek, young lady. I know better than that. I heard the carriage outside. Take off your skirt so I can dry it in the kitchen before you brush it."

Both of us obediently took off our skirts and handed them over. From the kitchen, Phyllida said, "You had a caller this evening."

I walked into the kitchen in my stocking feet and petticoat. "Who?"

"Lord Hancock. He wants to sell a rare book. He said he'd come by the shop first thing in the morning."

"Did you let him in?"

Phyllida heard the concern in my voice. "No. He didn't get past the landing. Why?"

"How many rare book collectors have you ever seen come to this flat rather than the shop?"

We stared at each other as the temperature in the room chilled. "None."

LORD HANCOCK ARRIVED the next morning as soon as I flipped over the Open sign. Walking to the counter, he laid a wrapped parcel on the smooth wooden surface and looked at me expectantly.

At least I had no reason to have worried about Phyllida's

safety. As I unwrapped the package, I said, "My aunt said you'd be here first thing this morning."

"Phyllida Monthalf is your aunt?"

"Yes." I looked at him suspiciously.

"We introduced ourselves last evening. Is she a member of the mad Monthalfs?"

They'd earned that reputation long before her brother had inflicted his depravity on the city. "A cadet branch. They're only slightly mad."

I looked down at the book I'd unwrapped. Definitely old and in good condition. Damp marks and a moldy cover, but no bookworm holes. "How much do you want?"

"One hundred pounds."

He was madder than the Monthalfs. "It's not worth more than ten." I'd go up to fifteen, thinking I could eventually sell it for twenty. One hundred? Never.

"It's the subject matter. It's an alchemist book of formulas."

"I don't sell rare books on subject, but on the worth of the book to a collector. I'm sorry, Lord Hancock, but we're too far apart to try to negotiate."

"You won't reconsider?"

"Ten pounds. That's the best I can do." I hoped he wouldn't take it. I didn't want a book on alchemy in my shop. I doubted people still believed such things were possible, but I didn't want to take any chances.

He rewrapped his book with rapid, jerky movements. "You'll be sorry," he mumbled.

I hoped I'd misunderstood him. "What did you say?"

"You'll be sorry. One day, you'll all be sorry." His package tucked under one arm, he stormed out of the shop, nearly knocking Frances Atterby over as she arrived to travel with me to visit Anne Drake.

I was already sorry. Nicholas Drake was dead, and I had to tell his widow.

*   *   *

I LEFT FRANCES later that morning dealing with Anne Drake's grief. Now that she'd been forced to admit she wasn't her sister, Edith Carter, she had no reason to hide either her identity or her love for her husband. Her carefully crafted world of lies, and the need for them, fell apart with Drake's death. She broke down into a gasping, soggy mess.

Frances ordered Anne's maid to bring heavily sugared tea and laudanum. Years of managing the family hotel with her husband had left Frances with the ability to handle any crisis, no matter how difficult the person or the situation. For now she sat with Anne, holding the new widow against her well-padded bosom as she rocked and crooned. Promising to do everything I could to find justice for Drake, I departed in haste.

My guilt followed me to Lady Westover's. When I marched into her greenhouse and stared at her, she looked up from her spraying and said, "You're in a temper."

"I've just come from Nicholas Drake's wife, informing her she's a widow."

She set the sprayer down and walked over to me, stripping off her large canvas gloves. Taking my hands, she said, "I am so sorry. That can't have been easy for you. Always seeing your parents' death and Sir Broderick's accident whenever you have to deliver bad news."

"No, I just—"

"Georgia, I am far too old to be put off by your denials."

I pulled my hands away and studied the terra-cotta tile floor, fighting the tears that threatened to rend my heart.

"It's been a dozen years since you lost your family and Sir Broderick ended up in a wheeled chair because of his injuries. You've grown up, but you haven't lost your pain."

I gritted my teeth. Swallowing my sobs, I forced my voice into something approaching normality. "I have to give

Nicholas Drake justice. Then maybe I won't grieve so much because I failed my family."

She took my hands again. "I know, Georgia. I know."

We stood in silence while the early spring sunshine shone through the glass panes, heating the air around us. The fragrance of moist soil and delicate blooms filled the air. This room always helped to ease my wounded heart. Once again I was reminded of how much time Lady Westover spent here on the anniversaries of events she wished had never happened.

I helped her off with her hat. "You must not tell anyone but your grandson that Drake is dead. We're keeping it a secret for now so that the killer is the only suspect who knows."

"All right," she said with a feeble smile but a businesslike tone. "What do you plan to do now?"

"I need to speak to Lady Dutton-Cox again."

"No, Georgia."

"She believes her daughter was murdered. I believe Drake was murdered. If they both died by the same hand, we have to stop the killer."

"If. Don't you hear yourself?" Lady Westover shook her poufy gray à la concierge hairdo. I knew if I tried such a move, my hair would be around my shoulders in an instant. A knot worn on top of the head might be fashionable, but I wasn't born to be fashionable.

Drawing my attention back to her words, I said, "You're afraid your friend is behind Drake's death, aren't you?"

She took a half step back from me and looked out the window at the blooms in the garden. "I know you were terribly rude to her last time I took you to see Lady Dutton-Cox. I don't want a repeat."

"I only want to know if she or her husband received blackmail threats because of letters their daughter Victoria had written. Or if they were blackmailed due to something else entirely," I added, not wanting to miss any possibility. I knew there wouldn't be a third chance to question her.

"What will that prove?" Lady Westover's blue eyes sharpened inside her scowl.

"Something Lady Dutton-Cox's husband said makes me suspect Victoria's death has nothing to do with Drake blackmailing them. Drake's thefts are part of a pattern, and the reason why he was killed in a fire."

"Someone wanted to burn the letters they couldn't get away from Mr. Drake." She nodded and walked away from me, sliding out of her enveloping apron. "I hope we can assure Honoria Dutton-Cox that her letters have been burned."

"If they were in that house, they were destroyed." I helped her out of her canvas duster.

"*If* they were? That's not much comfort, Georgia."

"That's all I can give at the moment." I went to follow Lady Westover into the main part of the town house, but she stopped me in the doorway.

"I've visited Lady Dutton-Cox since you saw her. She's grown more reclusive. More fragile. I also lost my favorite child, and I thought for a long time I would lose my mind. Perhaps I did. Honoria was there for me. I won't have you making her life more difficult. Do you understand?"

"I have to stop a murderer."

"Not at the expense of making Honoria Dutton-Cox suffer more for something she didn't do."

I nodded. I understood Lady Westover's determination to spare her friend, but I couldn't chance letting a murderer go free. "This is the only way she can see her daughter's murderer punished."

Lady Westover looked at me and shook her head. "That's not what she wants. Or needs." Nevertheless, she called to her maid to get her ready to go out.

CHAPTER FOURTEEN

LADY Westover decreed the day was suitable for walking, so we arrived by foot at the Dutton-Cox town house. We found Lady Dutton-Cox in her morning room with a piece of half-finished embroidery on her lap. She immediately sent the footman away to have someone bring us tea and bade us sit, all without rising from her chair.

"How are you enjoying your stay in London, Miss Peabody?" she asked as soon as we were settled. She took a sip from the nearly full teacup on the table at her side, but I saw no sign of teapot or sugar or even a spoon. I wanted to get close enough to smell the brew in her cup. Brandy, most likely.

The skin beneath her eyes looked faintly bruised, as if she hadn't had a restful night's sleep in some time. Her face looked puffy, and she gazed at me without appearing to really focus on my face. And it was early afternoon. I glanced at Lady Westover and she threw me a warning look.

I managed a few bland comments about London, the weather, and the traffic one saw at all hours of the day. "For a while I was afraid to send any letters home. I kept hearing stories of Mr. Drake, that friend of your daughter Victoria, stealing letters and blackmailing the sender."

Lady Dutton-Cox looked me over, scorn in her expression. "You have nothing to worry about. It's only rich, beautiful girls like Victoria and Elizabeth who need to worry about Drake stealing their letters."

Silence fell as the tea tray was carried in. Lady Westover fixed tea for herself and me. When she offered to pour some for Lady Dutton-Cox, the woman smiled slightly and shook her head, sipping from her own teacup.

The silence lengthened. I glanced at Lady Westover, who narrowed her eyes before taking a sip of tea. I needed to know if Drake had stolen letters from Lady Dutton-Cox or her daughter, and this brittle quiet was doing no good. "Did Drake steal any of Victoria's letters and then try to blackmail her?"

"You certainly are a nosy young woman."

"Did he?"

"No."

"Then he had obtained letters you wrote?"

"I rarely write letters. Hadn't you noticed? I'm a recluse. It would hardly do to be a recluse and then send letters all over the isle." She drank the rest of the liquid in her teacup in one gulp and then swayed slightly in her chair.

"So Mr. Drake didn't blackmail anyone in this house?" I must have sounded amazed, because the woman laughed at me.

"Not in this house." She rang for her servants. One appeared immediately. "My teapot."

"Do you think . . . ," the footman began and quickly made his voice fade.

"My. Teapot."

He disappeared and was replaced by a maid, who poured her mistress a cupful from a blue-flowered teapot and then left.

"Honoria, do you want us to leave?" Lady Westover asked.

Before I could glare at her, Lady Dutton-Cox said, "I don't care. I haven't cared since my beautiful Victoria died before she became a duchess. She should have been a duchess. It's not fair. Nothing matters anymore."

Lady Westover rose and crossed over to her friend. There was no place to sit near our hostess, since her chair was in a corner with tables standing sentinel on both sides of her. I pulled over a chair for Lady Westover to sit facing her friend. She was more likely to get the answers I needed. And I had failed twice today in being sympathetic. I was completely ashamed of my lack of tact. Not ashamed enough to stop this investigation, but embarrassed by my dearth of compassion.

"Honoria, look at me," Lady Westover said. "You have other children. You have grandchildren. Don't they matter to you?"

"My son has taken his family to the country and refuses to see me or let me see my grandchildren until I behave the way he wants. He says I have no shame." She gulped from her teacup.

Lady Westover patted her free hand. "I don't expect you to put away the pain of Victoria's death. That's impossible. I know. But Victoria wouldn't want you to quit living. She was happy and carefree and would want you to enjoy life."

Lady Dutton-Cox looked away, but she set down the teacup with a clatter.

I was only trying to be helpful when I said, "Your husband is beside himself with sorrow over Victoria's death, with the blackmail and your melancholy. Talk to him. Share your grief."

The lady took a quick drink, nearly spilling the liquid in her hurry to pick up the teacup again. Lady Westover looked daggers at me.

"Oh, he's beside himself all right. Elizabeth always was his favorite. He had to pay a pretty penny to Drake to keep him quiet about her letters until we married her off to the viscount. Not our problem anymore." She wagged a finger at me and then rang for the servants. "Bloody Drake. Bloody Elizabeth. Bloody servants." Her voice raised in pitch with every word.

A footman entered and she yelled, "My teapot!"

"Milady . . ."

"My teapot, you fool!"

A maid returned with it a moment later and poured. She hadn't left the room before Lady Dutton-Cox took a gulp.

"And you might get her lady's maid," Lady Westover said to the servant's retreating back.

I knew I only had moments to learn anything else. "Who did Lady Elizabeth write?"

"Bloody Drake. Bloody shisters fighting over the same man. Elizabeth, the little fool, wrote compromising letters to Drake. Victoria would have won. She was the prettier. But then Blackford ruined it all. Ruined it all. And Blackford's bloody sister, Margaret, killed my baby." Tears ran down the woman's pudgy face.

Lady Westover ran a gloved hand over Lady Dutton-Cox's brow and murmured comforting sounds.

I had to ask. "Does Elizabeth's husband know?"

"'Coursh he does. He's a swine. Refused to meet Drake privately. Jush what Elizabeth deserves. And Drake, too." She gulped down the rest of the contents of her teacup before it slipped from her hand. Then she started mumbling as her lady's maid dashed in.

I tried one last time. "Lady Dutton-Cox, talk to your husband. He's in mourning, too, for Victoria. Let him share your grief."

She looked in my general direction with unfocused eyes and said, "Go to hell."

Lady Westover marched past me on her way to the door. For an old lady, she moved fast. I didn't catch up with her until we were outside the house.

"Lady Westover . . ."

"Good day, Miss Fenchurch. I'd almost forgotten that you are not one of us." Her nose in the air, she stormed off. I'd lost an ally, and it was my own clumsy fault.

I stood on the sidewalk, looking from the house to Lady Westover's retreating back and feeling miserable. I didn't want to hurt anyone, but I'd spent the day ripping people's hearts from their chests and waltzing on them. Sadly, Nicholas Drake wasn't the only victim of this abduction and murder.

Unfortunately, my day of treading on the feelings of others wasn't finished. I still had to find out if there was any merit in what Jacob had said at our meeting the night before about the Earl of Waxpool. I couldn't ignore the earl's possible involvement. And the best way to learn the truth was to revisit Lady Julia, his granddaughter.

When I arrived at their home, I was shown into the same cheery morning room as before. Lady Julia set down a heavy history tome to greet me and took off her pince-nez spectacles, leaving her squinting and with a mark on the bridge of her nose. Standing to greet me, she said, "How can I help you, Miss Peabody?"

"It's about your father—"

She braced herself so she wouldn't back away from me. "He's—he's in the south of France."

"I know. Your grandfather told me he sent him there. After the blackmailing started."

"He shouldn't have committed anything to paper. It was too dangerous." She wrung her hands.

"It's hard to keep track of the money otherwise, I would think."

"Who cared how much he paid that odious Drake? That horrid man sold my father's words to the highest bidder. That hurt."

"Drake sold your father's papers?"

"No, he bought them." She froze in place. "What exactly did my grandfather tell you?"

"That your father stole from the family accounts."

She smiled for an instant as she looked away. "Oh. Yes. That's right."

"Except your grandfather lied to me. Look, I don't care if your father ran with the Prince of Wales's crowd. Heaven knows there's enough scandals there to keep several black-mailers busy. I need to know what your family was being blackmailed over so I can judge the likelihood that it would drive a respectable family to kidnapping and murder."

She leaned forward as she faced me. "Oh, it wouldn't. There'd be no reason for us to attack Mr. Drake."

"Really? Why?"

"Why should I answer you?"

"Because I'm a member of the Archivist Society and we try to be careful of reputations." And because I wanted to know who killed Mr. Drake.

Lady Julia paced in front of the fire. Finally, she stopped and said, "You're a well-read woman. I expect it has made you broad-minded."

"I hope I am. Unless the subject is murder. I will not condone killing another human being."

"Oh, no. But my father has a secret. One that is considered illegal in this country. That's why Grandpapa sent him to the south of France. They're more forward-thinking there."

"And this stopped Drake's blackmail?"

"Yes. The scandal doesn't affect the rest of us, you see. Once Drake was convinced Grandpapa wouldn't pay to keep it secret, and my father was out of danger of being arrested, the letters no longer had any impact."

I looked at her blankly. How could it not affect the rest of them? So far I'd not heard anything that removed her grandfather from suspicion of hiring thugs to eliminate Drake from threatening his family. "I don't understand."

"There's a new play on the London stage. *The Importance of Being Earnest*, by Oscar Wilde. Have you seen it?"

"No. Is it good?" What did that have to do with——? Then I remembered the rumors of an upcoming trial involving Oscar Wilde and the Marquis of Queensberry, whose son was Wilde's lover. The son had reportedly hurried off to France to avoid arrest and the brewing scandal.

But that affair was illegal. The church pronounced it a sin. And yet her father—oh, dear.

"I can see by your face you understand why Mr. Drake attempted blackmail on my father, and the contents of the letters my father wrote," Lady Julia said.

"Even if your father stays safely in France for the time being, someday your grandfather will die and your father will inherit the title. If he returns to England?" I let the question hang in the air.

"Either the law will have changed by then, or something can be worked out to let my father stay in France and my brother inherit the title and everything entailed to the earl-dom. It's not a problem." She shrugged, moving her hands in an open circle. "Well, it's one that will someday be ironed out by solicitors. It's certainly not one that would have any of us paying good money to hire thugs to go after a blackmailer. What good would that do?"

I nodded and turned to go.

"Miss Peabody."

I turned back.

"Please don't repeat this. I'm trusting on your discretion in keeping my father's secret."

A lot of members of the aristocracy appeared willing to accept my promises of silence concerning their confidences. The Archivist Society had an excellent reputation. I was discovering just how good this reputation was.

I only had time to walk the length of Hyde Park Place once before returning to the bookshop, and I had no more success than on any other day since the first one. When I entered the shop, I nearly ran into Inspector Grantham in the doorway.

"Inspector, what can I do for you?"

"It's what I can do for you. The details of Lupton's murder a week after your parents'. I reviewed the file. There was no sign of a break-in, but it was business hours and the front door was unlocked. Lupton was strangled. It didn't appear that he put up any kind of a struggle. While the antiquarian books were ransacked, no cash was taken and his records indicated none of the old books were missing."

Grantham lowered his voice. "A man was seen walking away from the shop just before others walked in and found the body."

"This man. What did he look like?"

"Well dressed. Prosperous looking. Tall, average build, blond hair. Carried a newspaper folded under his arm. Inquiries led nowhere. We had a dead body with no motive and no suspects."

"Anything else?" I was holding my breath, hoping someone noticed something I hadn't.

"No. I'm sorry there's so little I can tell you. Lupton lived an ordinary life and he didn't die due to a robbery."

I shook my head. He could say the same for my parents. "No, you've told me a lot. The man who killed my parents killed Denis Lupton."

THE NEXT DAY, I strolled away from the Heston and Hounslow railway station with Anne Drake. While Fogarty walked to the chapel in Hounslow Cemetery for Drake's funeral, I found a tea shop where Anne—I was starting to think of her that way, and not as Edith Carter—and I could wait. She was determined to visit the grave as soon as the service was over and the dirt thrown in. Feeling guilty that

I'd waited a day before telling her Nicholas Drake was dead, and had then slipped off, leaving Frances Atterby to deal with her grief, I went along as support.

We stepped out of the gusty breeze and sat at a table, where I ordered a pot of tea and scones. "Who was the man you were talking to on the ride out here?" Anne asked.

"A colleague of mine. He's acting as Nicholas's brother and paid for the funeral."

"Oh." I realized this was the first time Anne Drake had thought of the cost. She remained silent until after the tea had been served and then said, "It's good of you to do this. Nicholas had no family, and I can't afford a funeral. I have no idea what I'll do. . . ."

Her voice trailed off and she took a sip of tea. "Mrs. Atterby was very kind to me yesterday, but she told me she wouldn't be able to come with me today. Thank her for me, please, and thank you for being here today."

I waited while she gave one sniff, took another sip of tea, and raised her chin. Purple bruises formed half circles under her red-rimmed eyes. She must have cried all night, making me feel even guiltier for not bringing Drake back safely. "I wonder if Harry and Tom will attend."

"We learned Harry Conover saw Nicholas Drake shortly before he died. We've not been able to find Conover, and Tom Whitaker hasn't seen him, but we'll continue looking."

"Harry came out here?" Anne asked me. "Why?"

"We won't know until we find him. Do you have any idea?" When she shook her head, I added, "It might help find whoever did this to your husband."

"I don't know," she burst out and then looked around the half-filled room at the eyes staring back at us. Lowering her voice, she repeated, "I don't know." She nudged her mourning veil forward so that it shielded her face from prying eyes on either side.

"Did you ever hear their conversations?"

She shook her head again. "Anytime either Tom or Harry came by, Nicholas took them out to a pub or he sent me back to my house. He didn't want me to hear. I suspect because they were up to something illegal, and Nicholas knew how I wanted to change our lives. To stay on the right side of the law."

When I didn't reply, she said, "You think that, too."

I didn't want to admit I thought her much-mourned husband was a thief and a blackmailer until the day he died. "What are you going to do now?"

"My house is rented, but Nicholas owned his. I'll move in there for a while until I decide what to do. For years, my life has revolved around Nicholas. I have no idea what to do now that he's gone."

With that, she grabbed up her handkerchief to stifle her sobs. After a few hiccups and a sip of tea, she said, "I wish I could have seen him."

"He was in a fire. It's better you didn't."

"I'll never be sure he's gone. I think I'd feel it inside if he were—oh, God." She sniffed. "And not being able to attend the funeral since I'm a woman makes it even harder to believe he's—. Instead, I keep expecting him to walk in and say it's all been a mistake."

I patted her hand. "It's no mistake."

In a whisper, Anne said, "I hope he didn't suffer."

Something she had said nudged at me. "When did your husband buy his London house?"

"I don't know. He owned it when I arrived. He was very proud of having obtained a house, since he came from nothing."

We finished our tea in silence, neither of us having any interest in the scones. When I guessed we had waited long enough for the service and burial to end, I paid the bill and we bundled up to face the chilly walk to the cemetery.

Fogarty was waiting outside the cemetery chapel for us, rubbing his gloved hands together. The wind howled around the building as if in mourning. "Would you like me to lead the way?" he asked.

Anne Drake nodded, and I fell into step with her behind Fogarty.

"It'd be a pretty day if the wind would just stop," he muttered after a vicious push by a hard gust of air.

Fortunately, we had only a short walk to the raw grave piled over with dirt. Fogarty stepped aside and let us go forward. Anne stared down at the soil, her soggy handkerchief pressed to her mouth.

I let my mind and gaze wander around the graveyard, giving her some privacy for her grief. I noticed movement behind a huge marble tombstone with an angel perched on top about thirty yards away. Keeping my head still, I watched the spot out of the corner of my eye. Finally, a man stepped out from behind the monument. Scruffy, needing a haircut and shave, and wearing clothes that hung limp on his body, but still recognizable from his photograph.

Nicholas Drake.

CHAPTER FIFTEEN

I glanced back at Fogarty and made a small gesture toward the monument. He looked in the direction I indicated, and I saw his eyes narrow. Then, as Drake moved to his right, Fogarty took a step backward and to his left. His quarry didn't appear aware of his movements, giving Fogarty the opportunity to cut the thief off before he escaped the cemetery.

Fogarty had only taken a half dozen steps when Drake glanced our way and then dodged behind tombstones, disappearing from sight. The ex–police sergeant took off after him, moving quickly around the large ornamental monuments despite his limp. Unfortunately, Drake had a head start.

I watched Anne, who appeared unaware of all the movement around her. How would she react when she discovered Drake was still alive? And who was the poor fellow who had been destined to lie under Drake's name for eternity?

Anne reached down and picked up a clod of dirt and threw it on the hump of loose soil covering Drake's coffin.

Brushing her gloves together, she said, "We might as well walk back to the station. I feel like everything is finished."

Then she sniffed and leaned her body against the wind to march away from the gravesite, her widow's veil streaming out behind her. I dodged the black fabric as we walked toward the chapel and, beyond the small brick and columned structure, the main road. I kept my head bent down, fighting for every breath as I moved forward into the blustery gusts, but I tried to search the cemetery with my eyes for Fogarty or Drake. Neither man appeared.

When we neared the chapel, I heard Anne gasp. Then she said, "Go ahead to the station. I want to stop in the chapel for a moment to say a last prayer." Rather than sorrow, she seemed to be hiding some great joy. Her eyes sparkled and the corners of her mouth twitched upward.

I caught a glimpse of a shadow near one of the pillars and guessed immediately who was waiting there. "Won't you introduce me to your husband?"

Anne Drake's gaze darted from the chapel to me before she demanded, "You know my husband's alive?"

"Yes. I saw him at the gravesite. Who's in the grave?"

Her eyes widened. "I don't know."

"Let's ask your husband." I took her arm and strode toward the chapel porch. I expected Nicholas Drake, after hiding so long and so well, to disappear before we arrived, but he waited in the shadows until we stood on the porch.

Anne flew to him, her arms outstretched. He took her into an embrace when she reached him and shushed her cries of delight. Then he stepped forward, an arm around Anne, and demanded, "Who are you?"

He looked good for a corpse. Actually, he looked good, period. Even better than his photograph. He had a nice height and a pleasant face, which currently looked delighted to see his wife.

She gazed back at him with devotion. "I hired the Archi-
vist Society to find you. To save you from your abductors.
You must tell her everything so they can stop these attacks.
Oh, Nicholas, I want you safe."

He gave her a squeeze and turned to me.

"I'm Georgia Fenchurch, a member of the Archivist Society. How many people are you blackmailing?"

Anne Drake looked at me with fury, but he grinned rogu-
ishly and said, "Please, Miss Fenchurch. You make it sound
like I'm some sort of evil creature. I'm not, I assure you. I'm
the one who should be the victim in that grave."

I couldn't decide if it was the smile, knowing and willing
to please, the voice, deep and smooth as a caress, or his eyes,
twinkling with sexual promise, that was the most devastating. I could see why others found him so charming. I glanced
around the cemetery. "Who died in your house?"

"Ah, that would be Harry. He found me in the Red Lion and
said he needed to lie low for a few days. Something about some
confidence trick that went bad. I sent him on to the house and
finished up at the pub. While I was walking home, I suddenly
heard a boom and then the sky lit up over my house. Someone
must have blown up my house. Harry didn't stand a chance."

"Couldn't it have been an accident?"

"You don't get an explosion like that from a fireplace or
an oil lamp. The house was out in the countryside where we
lack modern conveniences like gas lighting."

I shivered, both from the chilly air and from the knowledge that now we were dealing with a murder much like my
parents'. "And the blood on your entry hall floor?"

"It's from one of the three goons sent to drag me off.
When they forced their way in and grabbed me, I stabbed
one man in the gut. I know my way around the house in the
dark, so I was able to run to the basement and hide. They
searched the house but didn't find me. In too big a hurry to
get their friend to a doctor, I'd guess."

"Who's doing this?"

"I don't know." He looked genuinely baffled in a seductive way.

"I've been so worried," Anne broke in. Her widow's veil whipped to the side of her head in a gust of wind.

He focused his charm on her. "I know, love. I would have told you, but I was afraid I'd lead them to your door. I can't let anything happen to you."

I didn't believe him. About his not knowing who was after him, about his being worried for Anne's well-being, about his innocence. "You have a pretty long list of people who would be coming after you, Mr. Drake. Blackmail victims all, I'd guess. Who are they? And where are their letters?"

"Aristocrats all. Their letters are perfectly safe, and most of them have finished paying me." He smirked. He'd stolen from these people and then threatened them with what he had taken, and he had the nerve to laugh about what he'd done.

I stepped close to him, glaring into his face as I thought of his victims' fear of exposure. "I don't believe you'd let the wealthy loose from your grip so easily."

"It's not a matter of letting them out from under my control; it's a matter of circumstances changing so their letters no longer have value. Aristocrats have a talent for making new alliances to keep themselves above common gossip. That's the reason they've stayed in power for a thousand years."

I watched his face, searching for clues. He was bitter about something, but did it have anything to do with his attacker? "If the letters have no value, why don't you return them?"

"Because I don't know what will again become valuable." He smiled, as if we spoke of shares of a company and not the private correspondence of ladies and gentlemen.

I was so disgusted I could taste ashes. "But you still have them? They weren't destroyed in the fire?"

He laughed easily, a warm, seductive sound. Anne, in her

now-inappropriate black crepe, leaned on him, their arms around each other. "No. I wouldn't keep anything so valuable anywhere but in the safest of places."

Blast. I had hoped. "Where do you plan to hide now?"

"At home. Whoever my attacker is, he's made it clear I can't hide from him." His slight scowl said he wondered how he'd been followed.

I wanted to know the same thing. "How many people knew about your house out here?"

"Just Tom and Harry. I told the locals I worked somewhere up north and came down occasionally to look after things here."

"So Harry was followed when he came down here that night."

He winced at my words.

It didn't make them any less true. "Did you see any strangers in the Red Lion that night? Anyone you recognized from London? Anyone who didn't fit in?"

"No." He looked out into the distance. "It was just me and Harry and some locals I recognize by sight. It wasn't a busy night."

"What time did Harry Conover arrive?"

"Late. Ten, more or less."

Someone had to have followed Harry Conover from the station. Fogarty or Jacob would be good at finding out if another stranger was seen getting off the same District Railway train. Could it be as easy as that to find the murderer? "I suggest we head back into London before anyone else catches up with you."

We walked back to the train station, where Fogarty was waiting for us. The Drakes walked out onto the platform while Fogarty pulled me aside. "So he's turned into Lazarus. What next? Will the whole cemetery rise up?"

"There were no gas lines in the house. Harry Conover was murdered. And Drake is planning to go home where he'll be an easy target. There are a couple of things we need to see to." I gave him a big smile before rattling off some possibilities for the Archivist Society to consider.

WHEN I RETURNED to the bookshop, Emma waved a note at me before turning her attention back to a middle-aged woman searching through the novels. I hung up my cloak and hat and went out to face a man who looked like a bulldog browsing through our astronomy books.

A half hour passed before we were both free to talk. Emma held out the note and said, "Lady Westover has invited me to attend a lecture with her tomorrow afternoon."

She was bouncing on her toes. "I'm to be a barrister's daughter and will be introduced to Daisy Hancock. Lady Westover says she's the only possible blackmail victim left besides the Duke of Blackford's sister. No one else need fear a revelation by Drake."

So it wasn't the entire Archivist Society, but only me, who was in trouble with Lady Westover. Working up a smile for Emma, I said, "That's great. We need to know as much about Miss Daisy as you can discover."

I must have failed, because Emma said, "What's wrong?"

"Nothing. I'm just tired." I gave her a weak smile. "Nicholas Drake is alive. I met him today at the cemetery."

Her eyes widened as she reached out and grabbed my arm. "Good heavens. He's alive? Then who died in the fire?"

"Harry Conover, a friend of his who came to visit him that night. I think he was followed by whoever burned down the house and Conover was killed by mistake."

"You think whoever killed Conover didn't know what Drake looks like?"

"Hounslow isn't London. It's dark at night on their lanes. Possibly the killer thought whoever walked into the house had to be Drake and attacked."

The bell over the shop door rang. Emma gave me a sympathetic look, patted my arm, and walked over to our customer.

I stood between two bookshelves, suddenly drawn to Lady Westover's words that Emma had repeated. The Mervilles seemed to be willing to pay off Drake and anyone else aware of their secret, but they may have fooled me. The husband of the younger Dutton-Cox girl, Elizabeth, might be angry at Drake for blackmailing his wife or jealous if he knew Drake was the recipient of her daring letters. I couldn't see how Waxpool or the Naylards would be involved in the attacks on Drake, since Drake couldn't cause them any harm, but it might only be a failure on my part to dig deep enough.

Any of the threatened peers might be Drake's attacker. Even the Duke of Blackford. As much as I didn't want to discover that the fascinating duke, with his air of regal menace, was capable of murder, I needed to keep investigating.

I SPENT THE next afternoon alone in the shop except for a few customers who seemed particularly grumpy. It might have been the drizzling weather. It might have been my frustration with the case. And it might have been the prospect of traveling two days to reach the far end of Britain where the Duke of Blackford's sister was hiding from society. If Emma didn't find a good reason why Daisy, or Lord Hancock, was after Drake, and nothing else turned up, I would have to make that trip.

I jumped, my melancholy forgotten, as the bell jangled over the door and the Duke of Blackford strode in. After Nicholas Drake, with his suave good looks and seductive voice, the duke was like a drink of good brandy. Blood heating, sharp tasting, and molded by the very best. I bobbed a quick curtsy behind the counter. "What can I do for Your Grace?"

"First, I came to see your shop. Merville says you're well equipped to handle rare books. You use electric lights, I see."

"Yes. They became available on this street two years ago. It takes a little effort getting used to the brightness, but it's much easier on the books than burning those smoky gaslights."

"I'm thinking of adding them at Blackford House, at least on the ground floor." He studied our light fixtures for a moment. "And where are your antiquarian volumes?"

"Behind the counter, Your Grace." I led the way. To my surprise, he stayed on the customer side of the counter.

"Do you have any Shakespeare?"

I'd seen the antique globe in his library the day I stormed into his home. I didn't expect to get any of his business. I had nothing so grand. "I have a quarto-sized *Othello* from the early eighteenth century in pristine condition." I slipped on my cotton gloves and opened the brass wire cover. When I turned back to Blackford, he had already put on cotton gloves.

When I handed him the volume, he held it with reverence, carefully opening the book and examining the pages and cover. "There's no gilt to protect the pages from dust."

"No, but it's still an excellent volume."

"I'll give you twenty pounds for it."

I glared at him. "It's worth fifty."

"It's worth whatever the market will pay for it."

I held out my hand to take the book back. "If you don't want it, may I put it away, please."

He continued to examine the book, ignoring my hand. "You think this book is worth fifty pounds to a collector?"

"To a collector, yes. But not to a duke who's a sharp businessman." When he glanced over and glared at me, I said, "Financier?"

"Investor." He wasn't smiling. Aristocrats were so touchy about being associated with trade.

A blur of brown fur suddenly dashed from the back of

the shop, heading straight for the duke. I leaned over the counter to see Dickens with a mouse hanging from his mouth, standing next to Blackford.

"What is this?" the duke asked.

"Dickens. Paying his bill." I took a breath to cover my annoyance. "Your Grace. I know my business and the value of my stock. Please don't make the mistake of thinking I don't know my job, whether it's here in the bookshop or with the Archivist Society."

He gave me a smile and reached into his waistcoat pocket. "You're very sure of yourself."

"I have to be. I have only myself to rely on."

"Will you take forty-five?"

I stared at the Bank of England notes he held out and then smiled at him. I'd have taken forty. "Let me wrap that for you."

He changed back into his leather gloves and bent down to pet Dickens. "Is he yours?"

"He just showed up one day, and comes and goes as he pleases. Emma feeds him, so I'm sure he'll never abandon us." I watched Dickens's eyes shut as the duke scratched him behind the ears. "I suspect he thinks we belong to him."

Blackford straightened, still watching the cat. "You impressed me just then. You've done so well in your role with the Archivist Society, I expected your business would suffer. I was wrong to doubt the abilities of the Archivist Society. I want your help in contacting Drake."

Trying not to show the ridiculous amount of pride I felt at his words, I tied a bow in the string around the paper wrapping. "I'm glad to know I can surprise you."

"Is the mouse a bonus?"

"What?" I leaned over the counter again. Dickens had disappeared, leaving the mouse behind at the duke's feet. "Dickens!" I ran to the back, grabbed the broom and dustpan, and removed the body.

"I apologize about the cat, Your Grace."

The corners of Blackford's mouth edged up and his eyes gleamed with mirth. "I was honored. It's a tribute from one hunter to another. But please don't have too many more surprises for me. I'm hoping to count on you at the Arlingtons' ball."

Finally, we appeared to be getting to the point of his visit. "In what way, Your Grace?"

"I won't be able to tell you until that night. You'll have to trust me."

I'd rather trust Jack the Ripper. "Was there anything else you wanted?"

"You can tell me how the case progresses."

I didn't bother to pretend not to know which case. "It moves forward. Slowly. We keep eliminating suspects."

"And your costumes for the Arlingtons' masked ball?"

"I am to be the Fire Queen and Emma the Ice Queen."

"I know. I wondered how they're coming along."

"You'd have to ask Madame Leclerc that." Curiosity made me add, "The crowns. They will be paste, right?"

"No."

"Your Grace. We'll be weaponless, in evening clothes, surrounded and hemmed in by innocent revelers. We can't protect your jewels adequately and catch the person threatening Drake." The very idea scared me and left my stomach aching.

"I don't expect you to guard the jewels. I expect you to wear them."

I came out from behind the counter in a rush and marched up to him. A couple of locks of his rigidly straight hair brushing his high collar had curled up since he'd come into my shop, giving him a slightly rakish appearance. Looking up into that craggy, self-assured face, I said, "Then get an aristocrat to do it. They know about wearing jewels."

He stared into my eyes as he snapped, "I'm hiring you for your brains, not your bloodline."

"Technically, you've not hired me for anything."

He pulled a sixpence out of his pocket, tossed it in the air, caught it, and handed it to me with a bow.

I held his gaze, refusing to be intimidated. "If you're hiring me for my brains, then take my advice. Don't put your jewels at risk."

"A thief will recognize paste immediately."

"Not until he examines them, and we won't allow that close a perusal." Which was nothing compared to the scrutiny the duke was giving me. Our faces were mere inches apart, and I was growing nervous. He was the most magnificent man I'd ever met, stoic and fiery in one brilliant package, and he was out-of-bounds for a nonaristocrat.

He was out of my league in every way but one. I had the quicker mind.

He smiled slightly. "You will wear jewels."

"You're playing a dangerous game, Your Grace."

"Whoever is after Drake will recognize fakes by the lack of pride you show in them. Bring Emma to Lady Westover's tonight when you close your shop. You need to become accustomed to wearing jewels, so we'll practice."

Lady Westover's words *You are not one of us* rang in my head as the duke swooped around and strode to the door. "Aren't you afraid someone will steal them?" I asked.

"We're not dealing with a jewel thief. We're dealing with a madman."

His certainty alerted all my senses. "You know who it is?"

"No. But I suspect who it is."

"Who?"

"It's a suspicion based on only one thing. I need more evidence."

"And we're the bait." I was becoming very sorry I'd agreed to attend this ball. "Who will you be dressed as?"

"A highwayman."

How appropriate.

"And before you ask: my weapons will be real."

I never doubted that for a moment.

Not two minutes after the duke left, the bell jingled over my door again. I looked up, hoping for a paying customer, but I was sadly disappointed. It was Viscountess Dalrymple, Lady Dutton-Cox's living daughter, alone this time but for her footman. The carriage again waited outside my door. Remembering my regrettable confrontation with Lady Dutton-Cox, I expected another lecture from her daughter.

Instead, her tone was begging. "Leave my mother alone. Please."

"I will if you'll tell me what I want to know about your sister and Nicholas Drake."

She went from pleading to angry in an instant. "There was nothing between them. You shouldn't listen to malicious gossip."

"I don't. I have questions about both of them, but it was you he was blackmailing, wasn't it?"

She looked around the shop in panic. Fortunately from her point of view, it was empty. "No."

I'd rather be making a sale in my bookshop than listening to a silly young lady lie. "I know Drake was blackmailing you. I've had it confirmed." I wasn't about to tell her by her mother.

"You've found Drake?"

I suspected the key to keeping Drake safe was in not answering that question. "Drake isn't the only one who knows about his blackmailing you."

She pouted. *Really?* She was much too old for that sort of behavior. "Why should I tell you anything? I neither like you nor trust you."

"You may not like me or trust me, but believe me, I will find out all the details. It will make life for you and your parents much easier if you tell me." We were glaring at each other as we leaned over the counter, our noses nearly touching.

I took a deep breath and stepped back before I continued. "I have no desire to tell your husband anything or to blackmail you. I have other issues to investigate, but until I get this out of the way, I will haunt you."

"You're right. Drake was blackmailing me." The viscountess sounded so miserable I was certain I'd hear the truth. The electric lights overhead showed her frown lines and bitten lower lip in stark relief.

"Why?"

Elizabeth Dalrymple walked in a small circle, waving her hands. "I wrote Drake stupid, childish, idiotic letters. It was silly, impulsive, but he held them over my head. If the viscount had known, he would never have married me. As it is, if he knew, he'd never trust me again."

"Your father met Drake's blackmail demands until after you were married?"

"Yes. We went to the continent for our honeymoon and no one heard from Drake until after we returned. Then Drake approached my father, who'd had enough. He told my blackmailer he couldn't do any further damage and to go away."

"Instead, he went to your husband."

"Yes, but there Drake made his mistake. He asked the viscount for money to keep silent. Drake thought my father would have already told my husband about the blackmail. My husband, not knowing anything about the letters, demanded Drake give a full explanation of why he was asking for money.

"Drake was astounded. His business requires secrecy, and here the viscount was demanding he state his business in front of anyone walking through the lobby of his club. Drake kept asking for a private meeting, and the viscount refused. Perhaps my husband suspected I'd been indiscreet and didn't want to learn about my failings. In the end, he had the doorman throw Drake out of his club."

She faced me, both hands on the counter. "I nearly died when my husband told me the story that night. I wasn't certain if he was warning me he'd eventually learn of my stupid, silly mistake. For weeks afterward, I was afraid Drake would appear and demand money from me, but he never did."

I guessed it likely Drake thought the viscount had called his bluff, and, as he had with Waxpool and the Naylards, Drake simply gave up. "So your husband doesn't know about Drake's efforts to blackmail you or the existence of the letters?"

"No."

"You've had a lucky escape." And I could discount the viscount as a suspect in Drake's attempted kidnapping.

"So you won't bother my mother anymore?"

"One more thing. So much of this investigation has been about your sister Victoria and her death. What was she like? You must have known her better than most people."

For the first time since entering my shop, Elizabeth smiled. "After all this time, I've forgotten most of what we fought about and just remember her beauty."

"She seems to have been very popular but not well liked."

"Yes. I was her younger sister, always ordered around by her. And Mummy always took her side. She ordered our brother around until he escaped to school. She and Margaret Ranleigh fought constantly because Victoria tried to tell her what to do and what to wear, and Margaret would have none of it. Victoria even went so far as to tell her that after she married her brother, Margaret would have to do exactly as Victoria said, or she'd have the duke cut off her allowance and keep her home in Blackford Castle."

"I imagine Margaret didn't like hearing those words."

"Not at all. If Margaret had stopped and thought for a minute, she'd have realized the duke would never have stepped into the middle of that fight. But Margaret was not one to stop and think, and Victoria loved to trick people into doing what she wanted."

Elizabeth was now leaning on the counter, willing to tell

me all the gossip now the danger that her husband would learn of her indiscretion had passed. I decided to press a little more. "What was Victoria like as a person? What did she enjoy? What did she avoid?"

"Victoria loved a good time, to be the center of attention, to have the newest gown and the most admirers. She loved sweets and hated to walk and was already starting to get plump. Mummy was always after her about that, but she'd dump sugar and milk into her tea until there might as well not be any tea in the cup. The duke would have quickly found himself saddled with a fat wife."

The bell over the door jingled and Elizabeth jumped and looked around guiltily as Emma returned from her afternoon with Lady Westover. The viscountess looked back at me and whispered, "I trust you won't repeat anything I've told you in confidence."

"Your secrets are safe with me."

She nodded and strolled out the door without a glance at any of the books. For all her interest, the shop could have been empty.

CHAPTER SIXTEEN

EMMA, all blond elegance and aristocratic reserve, lifted one eyebrow and watched Viscountess Dalrymple leave. Her childhood in an East End criminal gang had made her an actress far beyond my talents.

"The lecture was interesting," she announced in an upper-crust accent. Then her eyes gleamed and she became Emma again. "Daisy Hancock is not our blackmail victim. No letters to Drake. She says he's fun, but she's worth more than 'fun.'"

"She actually said that?"

Emma giggled. "That girl is completely in love with herself. She gossips with abandon, probably shops with as much glee, and the only letters she writes are to accept or decline invitations and the thank-you notes she moans over having to compose afterward. She says she hates to write. Thinking makes her squint, and that will put lines on her face before her time."

"Really?" Daisy Hancock sounded incredibly vapid.

"Really. She loves balls, has never read a book, and proclaimed the lecture a crashing bore because there were so few young men attending. She doesn't commit anything to writing and her behavior in public is exactly what you'd expect from a debutante."

"I can't see Drake blackmailing someone like her. She'd be too careful to create a scandal." But we'd been told Lord Hancock was one of Drake's victims. "So it's the uncle, not the ward, who's Drake's victim."

"Perhaps one of his experiments went too far? Daisy said he spends all his time in his laboratory at Chelling Meadows, developing new weapons for our colonial troops."

"You got on well with her." I wasn't surprised. Emma made friends with everyone.

"I did. I pretended to be a bluestocking who's trying to convince her father to let her go to university. No competition, but keenly interested in everything she had to say."

"Did she say anything else about her uncle or the laboratory?"

"A few years ago, she tried to get into his laboratory. Out of boredom, I'd guess. She never was able to get the key away from him, and she never found another way in. She describes it as a fortress. She also complained he's in a hurry to marry her off, but she wants another couple of seasons."

"Money difficulties?" I guessed.

"Maybe. Or maybe he just wants the silly goose off his hands."

I nodded and began to turn away when I remembered my news. "The Duke of Blackford was by today while you were gone. We're to go tonight to Lady Westover's after we close up to practice wearing our jewels for the ball. Our real jewels."

Emma's eyes widened. "Is that wise?"

"The duke doesn't think anyone will go after the jewels. And he doesn't expect us to guard them."

She looked at me, comprehension dawning. "He has something planned, and we're the bait."

"Better us than a real aristocrat." I heard the grim tone in my voice.

"So, if someone will be after us for us and not for the jewels, who are we supposed to be? Surely not the staff of a bookshop or members of the Archivist Society."

I shrugged my shoulders. "We'll have to ask him tonight when we reach Lady Westover's. While we walk around unarmed and wearing jewels, he'll be armed to the teeth. He's appearing as a highwayman."

Emma nodded. "Appropriate."

The shop bell rang, and from that moment we were both kept busy with customers until closing. I locked up the proceeds for the day while Emma straightened the shop and then stood waiting by the front door. I'd nearly reached her when she said, "Forgetting something?"

I'd pulled out copies of the newest novels that came in that day for Phyllida and left them in the office. She'd never forgive me if I left them behind, considering she thought of them as her special perk for living with two booksellers. "Thank you. Go on without me. Tell Phyllida I'll be right behind you, but don't tell her what I forgot."

Emma nodded and left the shop. I went back into the office and hurriedly grabbed up the thin volumes of popular fiction featuring damsels in distress and brave heroes. Too hurriedly. I knocked a stack of papers on the floor. I piled them back on the desk, promising myself to organize them tomorrow.

Turning off the electric lights, I looked around the dim shop for a moment with a sigh of contentment. We'd made a little money, there'd been no disasters, and we may have made some progress on the Archivist Society investigation. Another successful day.

I stepped out of the shop, locked the door, and headed for the flat. The night was turning foggy, but it was still early enough to use our shortcut. I had just turned the corner and taken a few steps into the alley when a hand reached out and grabbed me.

I screamed and swung my umbrella. In a lucky stroke, I

stabbed my attacker in the leg. With a roar, he struck with his fist, knocking me over. My ears rang and my hands stung from hitting the rough, filthy paving stones. He kicked me in the corset. I couldn't catch my breath.

"Where's Drake?"

I doubled up, gasping.

He grabbed me by the hair. "Where's Drake?"

I tried to scream, but only whimpered.

"Hey! You!"

The grip on my hair loosened and I slumped to the ground as footsteps pounded down the alley.

"Miss. Are you all right?"

Hands lifted me up to a standing position and I found myself facing two young clerks. My hair was falling around my ears and my hat was trampled in the damp dirt of the alley, which also coated my clothes. The two men picked up my hat and the now-wrinkled books and handed them to me.

"Thank you." I burst into tears, ruining what little dignity was left to me.

When the clerks helped me to the flat, Emma and Phyllida thanked them profusely and Phyllida gave them the apple pastry that she had made for our dessert. Despite my protests, I was undressed and ordered into a tub of hot water.

It didn't take long for me to recover. My corset was tough enough to withstand any thug's boot and he'd only struck glancing blows. Getting dressed again was another issue. Phyllida didn't want us to go to Lady Westover's, since my attacker was still out there.

Emma slipped her knife out. "Either we'll be fine, or he won't be. Besides, I want to try on those jewels."

Phyllida threw her hands in the air and went to dish up dinner while Emma helped me dress. I was glad we weren't trying on our ball gowns that night, since I didn't want the stays on my corset pulled too tightly against my ribs and a bruise was forming under my left eye.

After a hasty dinner, complete with suggestions from Phyllida to keep our noses in the air if we wanted to look authentic in our jewels, we were ready to find out what awaited us at Lady Westover's.

The wind from the day before had died down and now fog muffled every street, alley, and path in London. While we heard occasional hoofbeats, no hansom cabs passed us, so we were forced to walk. We found our way to Lady Westover's in the dark by moving from one familiar landmark to another, one lamppost to the next. All the while, the footsteps I heard trailing us sent icy fingers skittering down my spine.

Emma slipped her knife out and showed it to me, but I still felt threatened. When we found an omnibus stop, we caught the next one and rode part of the way. As much as I wanted to, I hadn't caught a glimpse of Sumner, the man the Duke of Blackford had hired to guard me if I went out at night. After we left the omnibus near Lady Westover's home, I heard the footsteps again. Although I wanted to believe I heard Sumner following us, I was relieved to climb the steps to Westover House.

The butler opened the door and let us in along with a wisp of fog. As he took our wraps, he said, "Her ladyship is in the parlor. You're to go right up."

Lady Westover sat across from the Duke of Blackford, open jewel cases spread out on a table between them. Emma walked forward, staring at the sparkling riches for her to examine. My own stare was focused on a dim corner of the room where Sumner stood guard.

My heart thudded into my stomach. Sumner was here guarding the duke and the jewels. His couldn't have been the footsteps I'd heard behind us. I'd had no protection during or after my encounter with the ruffian. "If you're in here . . . ," I began and clenched my hands together as I shut my eyes.

The duke sprang from the sofa before I opened them. "You were followed. Good God, Georgia, what happened to you?"

I pointed to my bruised cheekbone. "This happened when

I left the shop tonight. I heard footsteps coming here, but I didn't see anyone. Too foggy."

The duke nodded to Sumner, who left the room. "Could it have been someone headed in the same direction?"

I remembered my last trip to Sir Broderick's. "How long has it been since Sumner stopped guarding us in the evening?"

The duke scowled. "I had him stop almost immediately. You never went out at night, so I decided there was no reason for concern."

I felt a cold breath on my neck at the thought of someone out there following us. And when I was alone, someone had struck. It made me wish I carried a weighted walking stick like the duke's or a knife like Emma's. "This is the second time it's happened. We were followed from here to Sir Broderick's three days ago."

The duke muttered a foul curse, looked around in embarrassment, and picked up a tiara. With a false note of heartiness in his voice, he said, "Now, ladies, time to start becoming accustomed to wearing jewels and tiaras."

I caught the duke's gaze and held it. Whoever had set those two ruffians on me after Lady Westover's dinner party had sent someone three more times. Two of those times, he'd not attacked. Was it because I wasn't alone? I couldn't spend my life with someone next to me every time I went out to keep me safe. I had to find this thug, and the person who'd hired him, and stop this horror.

The duke shook his head slightly as he returned my gaze and then handed Lady Westover a tiara. While Lady Westover adjusted Emma's tiara, the duke set mine on my head with the solemnity of an archbishop crowning a queen.

While he stood there admiring his jewelry, I said, "Why are you going to all this trouble to help us, Your Grace?"

"I want Drake to hand over the letters he's stolen. Surely the Archivist Society doesn't mind assistance."

"Not at all."

"Good. Start walking," he commanded.

Emma took to her diamond and sapphire tiara immediately, her bearing becoming more regal by the moment. I, on the other hand, held my head stiffly while keeping my eyes focused upward as if I could see the diamond and ruby confection resting atop my red-tinged locks.

Finally, the duke stepped in front of the path I was walking across the parlor while dodging ferns and flowers and said, "Georgia, look at me."

I did as he ordered and found myself staring into fathomless dark eyes. "I fear I can't guard your jewels properly, Your Grace."

"Don't worry about the jewels. They're insured. And I don't want you guarding them; I want you wearing them. Proudly. Like a duchess."

"More like a tethered goat, don't you mean?"

"There will be at least one hundred and fifty ladies there, all dressed in their finest jewels. Why would a jewel thief choose you? And why in a crowded room? No, you don't have to worry about jewel thieves. You need to keep a lookout for Nicholas Drake."

"You know he's still alive?"

His only indication of surprise was a slight rise in his eyebrows. "I didn't know he died."

Blast. I hadn't been going to tell him or anyone else outside the Archivist Society that I'd talked to Drake or that we'd thought he was dead. Until I knew why a duke was going to all this trouble for the Archivist Society, I didn't feel I could trust him. "We can't be sure until we see him."

"Hopefully, you will at the ball. I've set a plan in motion that Drake won't be able to resist. You'll be there as both sentinel and bait." He raised his head and his voice. "Lady Westover, will the dresses be such that no man will be able to resist them?"

"I certainly hope so, Duke. We have such good material to work with."

He looked me over from head to toe. "Yes, we do."

I held his gaze as heat crept up my face. No man had looked at me that way since I was barely older than Emma. I never thought I'd be flattered by a duke. Especially a duke who fevered my dreams.

After that, I was able to walk without thinking about the tiara. I was too busy trying to figure out what the Duke of Blackford had in mind. Sumner returned and whispered something in the duke's ear. Then he returned to the corner, where his gaze never left Emma.

"Georgia," Lady Westover said as she fell into step next to me, "I know what happened yesterday was not your fault. I should not have been angry with you. However, Honoria has been my friend for a very long time, and I hate to see her distressed."

"I feel badly for her, and badly for you to see her so"—I searched for a euphemism—"despondent."

"It would be terrible for her and the family if word were to spread of her . . . affliction."

"It's a shame her husband could drink himself under the table and no one in polite society would bat an eye, but his poor grieving wife can't."

Lady Westover's stern expression told me my opinion was not welcome.

"I spoke to Lord Dutton-Cox. He mourns his daughter as much as his wife does. She needs to try to rely on him. Encourage her to talk to him, Lady Westover."

"I'll see what I can do. In the meantime, she needs privacy to regain her composure."

"No one will hear of her lapse from me. I've already made the same promise to her daughter, Elizabeth. I can't speak for the Dutton-Cox servants."

"That's all I ask, Georgia. That you allow her to suffer in peace. And hopefully she'll regain her common sense." She gave me a sharp look. "You went so far as to question her daughter after that unpleasant visit with Honoria?"

"Elizabeth came to visit me at the bookshop. She told me about their problems with Nicholas Drake and what her sister was like. She doesn't seem worried that I'll bother her mother again."

"Good. I'm glad she's showing some interest in her mother. Honoria's going to need all the help she can get from her family."

I nodded, and the tiara stayed in place. I gave her a surprised smile, and she patted my arm. Apparently I could be trusted as much as one of aristocratic birth.

"What costumes will Drake's victims wear to the ball?" I asked.

"Waxpool and his grandchildren won't be attending. Neither will the Dutton-Coxes or the Naylards," Lady Westover said.

"The younger Dutton-Cox daughter, Elizabeth, will be attending with her husband, Viscount Dalrymple. They're going as Cleopatra and Mark Antony," the duke said, suddenly appearing at my side.

"This is her first masked ball as a married woman. Young women often run wild when they're first freed from their chaperones," Lady Westover said with a tsk.

"She couldn't get away with it if Dalrymple wasn't daring," the duke said. "They're well matched."

"I know what you're wearing," I told the duke. "What about the Mervilles and Lord Hancock?"

"The Mervilles go as Marie Antoinette and Louis XVI every year. I don't know about Hancock or his ward."

I glanced out of the corner of my eye at Lady Westover, who shook her head. "I don't know, either."

When the duke proclaimed us ready, all the jewels were put away and then loaded into a small chest. "Would you ladies like a ride home in my carriage?"

"That would be very kind, Your Grace," Emma said before I could open my mouth.

"I need to stop at Sir Broderick's house for a moment tonight, so—"

The duke gave me a gracious smile. "We will make a small detour."

Thanking Lady Westover, we went out and climbed into his tall carriage. Emma scrambled in with grace. With my muscles screaming from the earlier attack, I needed a hand to make my way up the folding steps and felt awkward.

Within a few minutes, we were at Sir Broderick's stoop. When the carriage door was opened, I looked at the pavement far below my feet and shuddered.

I was helped from the carriage by a footman while another of the duke's liveried servants rang the bell. Jacob opened the door in time to see me land heavily on both feet on the pavement. Fighting a grin, he said, "Georgia, do you need to see Sir Broderick?"

"No. Just a message for him." Sliding a quick glance toward the duke watching me from the carriage, I leaned toward Jacob and whispered in his ear. "Send word to Frances Atterby that she needs to come to the bookshop tomorrow to help Emma for the next four days. I'm going north to talk to the duke's sister. I need to know what's going on before this masked ball."

"What's wrong?" he whispered back.

"I don't know. None of this makes sense." Then, raising my voice, I wished him a good night and climbed into the carriage with as much dignity as I could muster, since I couldn't manage any agility.

I LEFT FROM King's Cross Station the next morning wearing my traveling clothes and carrying a few good novels in my holdall. I broke my journey in Durham at the end of the first day, staying in a small guesthouse and touring the cathedral. The next morning I started out again early by rail for the village of Blackford on the River Black.

For the last few miles I transferred from a slow-moving local train to an open cart, bouncing painfully on a wooden plank under the weak midafternoon sunshine. The water rushing in the river alongside the road raised my spirits and I hoped for a quick end to my journey.

I could smell the sea before we arrived. Then Castle Blackford's turrets appeared above the treetops, and soon I had my first view of the village.

The village, when we came to it, rose up the hillsides, probably looking much as it had when the Vikings arrived. The sea pounded against the river at the mouth of the rocky harbor. One bridge at the inland end of the village connected the stone and slate buildings on each side of the river above the docks.

Walking into the only inn, I found the grim-faced manageress in the reception room. She showed me to a tiny room on the first floor with an iron bedstead and a view of a single horse cart in the street. I reserved dinner and set out on the climb to the castle.

The lane constantly rose until I thought I'd reach the clouds, but I didn't mind. I was curious to see the home of the Duke of Blackford. The tang of salt filled my head and the call of seabirds rang in the breezy air. As the path curved back and forth, a stone fortress came in and out of view behind pine trees and the boulders that lined the road. It looked medieval and decidedly uncomfortable.

When I reached it, I was glad to see the drawbridge was down, because the tall, unbroken walls were unbreachable. I walked through the empty gateway and into the cobble-stoned courtyard. On either side were stables and other out-buildings against the protecting walls. In front of me, set in the center of the fortress, was a modern stone manor house with large windows. The edge of a flower garden peeked out from behind the house but in front of the surrounding wall. I headed toward a door facing me on the ground floor, hoping I'd find a bell to ring.

Before I reached the house, someone found me. A middle-aged woman in a faded dress and apron, her sleeves rolled up to her elbows and a kerchief around her hair, came out of a low door in a building to my left and crossed over to me. "Hello," she said, suspicion in her voice.

"Hello. I've come to speak to Lady Margaret."

She stared at me, her eyes widening.

"May I speak to her, please?"

"Oh, you can speak to her. I don't know whether she'll speak to you, though. Ask at the church in the village." At that, the woman turned on her heel and walked away.

Had Lady Margaret become a nun, or did she spend every day in prayer here in the middle of this wild landscape? I glanced back when I reached the gateway and saw the woman watching me through narrowed eyes.

As I walked downhill to the village, I caught the sparkle of the sea through the trees and boulders. All the buildings, from castle to shed, were built of stone. Wood seemed reserved for the boats I spotted in the small harbor.

The church was on the edge of the village, a small, green, tree-shaded graveyard spreading out on two sides. Seeing no one about, I opened one of the heavy doors and walked into the sanctuary. It was beautiful, with stained glass sending sparks of color over the pews, rich cloths covering the carved stone altar, and shadowy corners.

The vicar came out from the side and said, "May I help you?"

"I was told Lady Margaret is here."

"Yes, near the oak tree."

"I didn't see anyone outside."

He gave me an odd little smile. "Her grave is there."

CHAPTER SEVENTEEN

I felt, rather than heard, my gasp. None of the books on the peerage listed a date of death for Lady Margaret Ranleigh. "When did she die?"

"Nearly two years ago."

"Quite suddenly?"

"It was an accident. Drowning."

I lowered my head and said a silent prayer for this life cut short. Then I said, "Will you show me?"

He led me outside and walked slowly with me. Her grave was past the oak tree in the sunshine. Her gravestone was large, but it only said her name, her dates of birth and death, and *Beloved sister.*

"The duke must have been beside himself."

"Yes."

"Was he the one who found her?"

"He was in London. Took him until dawn the next day to return here after we sent the telegraph. He was on a borrowed horse, splattered with mud, and ready to fall out of the saddle he was so tired."

I couldn't picture the duke in that state. He must have been heartbroken. "Does he come back here often?"

"Once a quarter, to visit her and check on the estate."

Her death changed everything I knew about the Duke of Blackford. He'd kept his sister's death a secret in defiance of law and custom. Did he hold Nicholas Drake responsible? I could barely contain my excitement over this clue to our case and the duke's mind, but there was one more thing I hoped to discover in this village. "Did you know Nicholas Drake? He was from here."

"Before my time. I've only been here three years."

"And the Carters?"

He pointed. "That's their house over there. Second one from the end."

"Thank you." I started in that direction, but the vicar called after me.

When I turned, he said, "This is a close community. Don't bring trouble from the outside world to their doors. Especially trouble that doesn't concern them."

The priest must have known Lady Margaret's death was being kept secret from the outside world. I didn't know why he'd gone along with what had to be the duke's idea, but it didn't matter. "What trouble could I bring here? I'm sure no one here cares about the records of the peerage."

"Everyone is very loyal to the duke."

With a nod, I walked to the small, two-story stone cottage so like its neighbors. At my knock, an old lady opened the stout door a few inches. The doorway felt so low I ducked slightly. "I've recently spoken to the Carters' daughter Anne and would like to bring her greetings to her parents."

The door opened wider. "I'm Mrs. Carter. Anne's mother. Come in. You've seen Annie? How is she?"

There was a second door to enter, as low and thick as the first, and then I was in a dim parlor with lace curtains at the small windows, no fire in the fireplace, and stiff, uncomfortable-looking chairs.

When I opened my mouth to answer, she said, "No, wait. Sit down, please. I'll fix tea and call Anne's da." She bustled out of the room. "Papa, come here, please," she shouted to someone.

I sat, admiring the braided rug on the plank floor and wondering how long it would be until someone reappeared. And how long I could breathe the musty coal-fire smell in this chilly room without sneezing.

Finally, a man as ancient as the woman appeared and sat down across from me. "Ma says you've seen Annie."

"Yes, she's in good health and sends her greetings."

"She shamed us, she did. Did she tell you about going to prison? And all because of that lout she married." He stared fiercely through faded blue eyes set in leathery, wrinkled skin.

I stared back. "She's still married to him. They're in London."

"As long as they don't come back here." He waved a hand and looked away.

The old woman returned carrying the tea tray. "Annie's in London, you say?"

"Yes, ma'am. She's there with Nicholas Drake, in good health and spirits."

"I'm surprised she found him once she got out of prison. I would have thought he'd abandon her, him with his fancy ways," the old man said.

"They're together and quite happy," I reported, hoping my words were true. I could see their daughter loved Drake. I wasn't certain of his feelings.

"Good," the woman said, handing me a cup of tea. "It must have been a long journey to reach here."

"Two days." The tea was hot and weak.

"Why'd ye come? It wasn't to see us," the man said.

"I had business at the castle. Shame about Lady Margaret."

"Annie helped in the nursery in her first job when Lady Margaret was small. She thought Lady Margaret was the most beautiful creature. And she was. But no one ever said no to her until she went to London. The shock was too much and destroyed her," the woman said.

I took a sip of tea while I considered her words. Trying to sound only mildly interested, I said, "But drowning. How terrible."

"Not as terrible as it was for those who had the watch of her, letting her escape. They didn't find her body until daylight, caught on some rocks at the mouth of the river." The man sounded like he relished the story, giving a jerky nod when he finished.

"Letting her escape? She was a prisoner?"

"Aye, orders of His Grace. She'd already tried to run away once before."

"Why do you think she didn't take the road and the bridge if she was running away from the castle? What would she gain by trying to escape by sea?"

"Perhaps it was a different escape she had in mind," Mr. Carter said.

"Oh, don't say that. 'Tis a sin and you know it. Lady Margaret loved life. 'Twas an accident, was all," his wife told him in a sharp voice.

It took me a moment to take in the full measure of their words. Steering the conversation away from this new possibility as I digested it, I asked, "Do your daughter and Nicholas Drake know what happened to Lady Margaret?"

"Of course. At least Annie does. I told her when I visited her in prison. Terrible place," her mother said.

"What did Annie tell you about Lady Margaret as a child? I heard she liked to pretend the Vikings were coming to Blackford Castle."

"Aye, she did that. Imaginative little sprite she was. Spent a lot of time in the garden asking all sorts of questions about the flowers. Then when she got a little older, she became interested in the healers and apothecaries of the olden days. She knew good flowers and plants from poisonous ones before she could read well or do her sums. Her painting and sketching were marvels, but she hated to do needlework. Said it was too predictable." Mrs. Carter smiled.

"Too imaginative by half, I'd say. Left on her own with no one but servants and governesses, and if you told her no, you'd be out on your ear," Mr. Carter grumbled.

"You told her no a time or two, and you kept your post," Mrs. Carter said.

"Only because the duke, father and son, respect a man for the work he does, and I did good work until the arthritics took over my body," Mr. Carter said. "And she couldn't drown me like she did her pets."

"She only did that the once, and it was an accident."

"What about all those kittens and puppies we found drowned over the years?"

I shuddered at the picture forming in my mind.

"But we know that wasn't her, don't we?" Mrs. Carter said.

"We do know it were her. The whole village knew."

"That was only a daft rumor."

"There seemed to have been a lot of rumors about Lady Margaret. Whether she meant to end up in the water, whether she was the one who drowned kittens and puppies. Are there any other rumors?" Hateful things, rumors, but I needed to know what was being said in the village where people knew her better than anywhere else.

"'Twasn't rumor. 'Twas fact," Mr. Carter said.

"It was all nasty rumor. She was a spoiled, lonely little girl, and not well loved around here for it. That's the truth," Mrs. Carter said.

"Rubbish," Mr. Carter said.

I didn't want to get sidetracked by what sounded like an

old quarrel. "Drake worked for the family, too, didn't he? As a footman? So he must know the duke."

I must have spoken too eagerly, since the old man looked at me sharply. "Aye, he did and knows the duke. The duke knows him, too."

Then why didn't the duke point out Drake's lies when he was engaged to Victoria Dutton-Cox? What would make someone like the Duke of Blackford put up with Drake infiltrating polite society posing as an aristocrat?

Unfortunately, the Carters didn't know any more, or they weren't willing to tell me. Whatever secrets Lady Margaret brought here wouldn't be revealed to me.

I walked around the village and returned to the inn in time for my dinner. I needn't have hurried. I was served, alone, by the hatchet-faced proprietress in the parlor bar while men's raucous laughter could be heard from the main bar. I was certain no one in the other room was eating overboiled potatoes, mushy greens, and stringy mutton, or they wouldn't have been laughing.

I had nearly abandoned the effort of struggling through eating deliberately bad cooking when the manageress returned with an equally grim-looking woman. "You have a visitor."

Smiling, I said, "Won't you sit down?"

The two women stood looking down at me. "Why are you here?" scowling woman number two said.

"I didn't realize it was your business."

"I'm His Grace's housekeeper. You came to the castle. That makes it my business."

"I came to see Lady Margaret."

"She's dead."

"Yes. I saw her gravestone." This conversation was almost as unpalatable as the dinner.

"And then you spoke to the Carters."

"Yes."

"Why?"

"I was bringing their daughter's regards."

"You know Anne?"

"I also know His Grace." I expected her to threaten me with telling Blackford I'd been there. I thought I'd better nip that nonsense in the bud, and then maybe I'd find out what she really wanted.

"I find that hard to believe."

"Then don't."

"If you've finished with your business with Lady Margaret, I suggest you leave in the morning."

I saw a chance and decided to take it. "Not quite finished. Perhaps you can help me. What's the truth behind the drowning of puppies and kittens in this village?"

The two women looked at each other and the room grew quiet. Even the noise from the bar lessened, as if the men were waiting for a reply. "You know about that?"

"Yes."

"'Twasn't Lady Margaret."

I patted the back of the chair next to me. "Tell me."

The proprietress nodded to her, and the woman sat. "There's a young man in the village who wasn't born with all his wits. He followed Lady Margaret around, and she always had a puppy or kitten with her. She drowned one kitten herself, while carrying the creature when she was trying to climb into a boat. She slipped and nearly fell in herself. The young man was there and saw what happened."

She shook her head. "After that, her pets would be found drowned after a few weeks or a few months. No one understood why, and for a long time Lady Margaret was suspected, despite that she was upset at their deaths. It was finally discovered that the young man was to blame."

"Was there evidence against him?"

The woman nodded. "Caught in the act. However, Lady Margaret was fanciful, temperamental, spoiled. She was feared in the village because if something didn't go her way, someone would pay."

"Pay?" That didn't sound good.

"Outsiders would get sacked, but not without a good reference and a month's wages. Villagers would be warned to stay away for a few weeks or shifted to another post. This didn't happen as often as folks will tell you now that she's gone."

The woman stared at the fire for a moment and then continued. "Lady Margaret spent most of the little time she had with her family alone with the duke, and a duke has real power. Her idea of what was normal was warped. Especially after her mother's death. Until then, her mother was her whole world. After that, no one had the heart to say no to her."

"What happened to her mother?"

"You know the duke. Ask him."

I planned to as soon as I reached London.

TWO DAYS LATER, I arrived back home to find Sir Broderick had called a meeting of the Archivist Society for that night. Proclaiming that I couldn't face another hour with the grime and soot of travel on me, I left Frances Atterby helping Emma in the bookshop while I heated water in the gas geyser and poured myself a bath.

After four days of smoking railway engines, bouncing horse carts on dusty roads, crowded train cars, and lumpy beds, sinking into a tub of steaming hot water was glorious. While my body reveled in the twin pleasures of heat and soap, my mind studied what I'd learned on the trip. The locals appeared to suspect Lady Margaret of killing herself that night two years before and I was left wondering why. Did guilt drag her into the water?

And that led me back to Victoria Dutton-Cox's puzzling

death. I had no answers there. After letting my thoughts run in circles a few times, I picked up the sponge and rubbed down my skin.

If I'd found understanding Margaret's and Victoria's motives difficult, my parents' killer was a complete enigma. Why had he killed my parents? Why had I seen nothing of him for a dozen years? His face haunted my dreams. That was my first investigation and my one failure. I needed to find him.

After a good soak and a scrub, I felt human and ready to face anything. Even reasons beyond my understanding.

PHYLLIDA HAD ALREADY unpacked for me and laid out clean clothes. She gave me the welcome news that there'd been no domestic accidents and there were spring peas for dinner.

She helped me dress in a white shirtwaist and blue skirt, but instead of going to the shop, I put on my cloak, hat, and gloves and went to Hyde Park Place. At that time of day, the sidewalk was busy with well-dressed men and women heading home from shopping or visiting or meeting with their men of affairs. Traffic on the street was busy with hansom cabs and carriages traveling between the City or Regent Street and the wealthy residential area on this side of Hyde Park.

I walked slowly along a four-block stretch, looking at every top-hatted man around me before I turned and strolled in the opposite direction. After my second circuit, a bobby stared as if considering whether I was up to no good, but I gave him a big smile as I walked past and he appeared to ignore me after that.

Clouds were blocking the sun, bringing an early end to the day and speeding pedestrians along their way. I couldn't tarry much longer looking for my prey, when I heard, "I doubt you'll find Drake along here."

I swung around to find myself facing the Duke of Blackford, an umbrella replacing his usual walking stick. "No, I'm here on a different search entirely."

"I hadn't heard the Archivist Society handles more than one investigation at a time."

"We don't. This is a private matter."

He raised his eyebrows.

I was saved from answering as a fat raindrop hit my nose. The duke put up his umbrella instantly and held it over both of us. "There's a tea shop nearby on Oxford Street. Shall we have a cup of tea while we wait out the storm?"

"Thank you, Your Grace."

His smug smile made me think he'd offered to save me from a soaking for the pleasure of forcing me to call him "Your Grace." I had to hurry to keep up with him, although he didn't appear to be rushing. We arrived before we were dripping. The duke arranged for us to have a table by one of the windows to share a pot of tea and some biscuits.

"This is very kind of you."

"My father raised me to be a gentleman. And while he'd never approve of leaving a lady out in the rain, he would expect me to ask why she was walking slowly along a busy sidewalk for quite some time."

Our tea arrived and neither of us spoke until I'd served us both. "I told you, it's a private matter."

"Not so private that you can't tell me. Who are you looking for?"

"What makes you think I'm looking for someone?"

He glared at me. "Please, Miss Fenchurch, don't treat me like a mental defective. You were slowly walking down a major sidewalk staring at every passing man. I repeat, who are you looking for?"

"You'll laugh at me." Sir Broderick had told me it was hopeless.

"No. I won't. I can tell it's important to you." His expression showed genuine interest.

"I'm looking for the man who killed my parents."

"Why here? Why now? Didn't your parents die years ago?"

"Yes, they did. However, I recently saw their murderer walking down that sidewalk. I was on an omnibus, and by the time I climbed down, he was gone. I'm hoping he has a reason to be in this area and I'll see him again."

"Have you looked for him before?"

"Every day for the past dozen years. Not actively, but I'd walk down the sidewalk, see a top hat, and immediately glance at the man's face. The day I met you was the first time I'd seen him since the day my parents died."

"You're certain it was him?"

"Yes," I snapped. I held up my hands. "Sorry. You sound like Sir Broderick."

"Sir Broderick doubts you?"

"Yes."

"Has he ever spotted someone he thought was that man?"

"He couldn't. He wasn't there when my parents and I were taken hostage. When I escaped, I ran to him as my father's partner and as someone who knew how to take care of himself."

I shivered, knowing it wasn't from watching the rain fall. "When I pulled Sir Broderick out of the burning cottage after the beam fell on him, I saw our abductor standing nearby. Sir Broderick was unconscious at that point, or nearly so. And that was the last time I saw that horrible man. Until recently."

The duke stared at me for so long I began to wish he'd say something. He reached over and touched the bare back of my hand with his fingertip. His skin was warm against my flesh. I reveled in his gentleness and the intimacy of the contact. A touch that overcame the differences in our stations in life and shouted out our human connection. I could love a man who said so much with one small gesture.

"You pulled Sir Broderick, a much larger person, out of a burning building?"

"Yes."

"How?" He took a sip of tea while he waited for my answer.

"The cottage was being renovated. There was a lot of lumber around. I grabbed some boards and worked them under the fallen beam to raise it enough to drag Sir Broderick out."

"You did that alone?"

"Yes." Then I realized—"You don't believe me."

I started to rise, but the duke gestured with one hand for me to sit. "I believe you. What I find amazing is the amount of physical effort you put into your rescue."

Sitting again, I took a sip of tea to keep from crying. "I can't believe how badly I failed."

"You saved his life."

"His legs were crushed. And I couldn't get back in to help my parents. The roof collapsed. I did a very bad job of saving anyone."

"I find it amazing anyone survived. That two people did is a testament to your ingenuity." He tapped his fingertip on the back of my hand again. "Can you tell me where this cottage was?"

"I'm not likely to forget. Why?"

"Somebody owned it a dozen years ago. That might give you a hint to who your mystery man is." He ran one finger along my hand to my wrist. His touch felt like a warm breath and made my insides tremble.

I dragged my mind back to our conversation. "We tried that at the time. Neither the owner of the property nor the farm manager had anything to do with what happened. I met the farm manager, and the owner was in Egypt."

"Still, give me the location of this cottage. I may be able to learn something useful."

I was suspicious. "Why would you want to assist us in finding a man who's done nothing to you? Our interests are similar concerning Mr. Drake, and you don't want our help."

"Give me a chance to try to help find this killer to repay you for your help at the Arlingtons' ball. At worst, you'll know as much as you do now. Let me talk to some people for you."

I was grateful for his help. The duke had contacts I would never have. With his aid, I might finally find this elusive man.

I held out my hand to him across the tea table. "Thank you, Your Grace. I accept your offer."

CHAPTER EIGHTEEN

SHORTLY after we closed the bookshop that evening, Emma, Frances Atterby, and I ate fish, peas, and potatoes with Phyllida. After the terrible meals I'd had while traveling, I was grateful for Phyllida's artistry with herbs and seasonings.

After dinner, we walked to Sir Broderick's. Our conversation traveled from sales at the bookshop to the latest news in the neighborhood. I caught Emma's eye and she gave a small nod. Neither of us mentioned the stealthy footsteps following us to the meeting, but I saw Emma ready the knife in her grip. Each soft step felt like a tiny jab in my spine, and I wanted to run to the safety of Sir Broderick's front door.

Warmer spring weather had descended on London in my absence, but Sir Broderick's fire burned as hot as ever and he sat as close. I thought I would melt as I walked over to him.

"Was your trip successful?"

"It was certainly surprising. Are you ready for me to start?"

"Have a cup of tea first. We have a lot to go over tonight.

The ball is tomorrow. Hopefully your dresses will be delivered to Lady Westover's in the morning."

My stomach did a painful flip. "And if they're not?"

"It'll be hard to be the Fire Queen in your normal attire." He grinned and I looked down at the clothes I'd worn while having tea with the duke and then working in the bookshop. Blue skirt, white shirtwaist. Professional. Middle class. Ordinary. There was nothing extraordinary or regal about me. I needed the disguise of being wrapped in flame-colored material and rubies to act the part of a queen.

By the time we poured tea and Frances had two of Dominique's scones, Fogarty had arrived and Jacob came up to join our meeting. Sir Broderick looked around and said, "We have a great deal to cover tonight. I'm going to recap what you've told me previously, and then we'll learn what information is to be added."

He settled in his wheeled chair and began. "Nicholas Drake, a known thief and blackmailer, was the victim of an attempted abduction. He escaped to his home outside Hounslow, where an attempt was made on his life. A friend of his, Harry Conover, was killed in his place. Nicholas Drake has since gone to his home in the London suburbs, from which he hasn't strayed. We have someone watching the house day and night."

Because of my trip, I was four days behind. "Have we notified the police of who was killed in Hounslow and who the target really was?"

Sir Broderick gave me a wry smile. "We have. The police have been less than pleased with our help. Our choices for attacker include the dukes of Blackford and Merville; the Earl of Waxpool; and Lords Naylard, Dutton-Cox, and Hancock. And then we found we could add the current Lord Caphart."

I paused my teacup halfway to my mouth. "Lady Caphart was the one to sell Drake the cottage in Hounslow. Something new's come out?"

"It turns out after leaving his wife Anne in prison and arriving in London, Drake went to work as a footman for the dowager Lady Caphart. She had inherited a few properties from her family as well as many works of art. Shortly before her death, she gave Drake the property in Hounslow and a couple of Renaissance paintings. He sold the paintings and bought his house in town. He kept the house in the Hounslow countryside for himself while he rented out the adjoining acreage to a nearby farmer."

"And?" There was more. There had to be more.

"After Lady Caphart's death, the current Lord Caphart found out his mother had given expensive gifts to a footman she hadn't employed long and had a lawyer look into it. They lacked proof, but accusations of theft and forgery flew. Lord Caphart swore he'd get even, but he says he had nothing to do with the attacks on Drake."

"What do you think?"

"Lord Caphart has been at his country estate until the day before yesterday, confined to his bed with pneumonia for the past four weeks. I don't think his mind was on Drake."

"Another possibility gone bad. I wish someone would slip up." One day to go and we had no idea who was after Drake or why we were attending the ball. I felt the presence of a puppet master pulling everyone's strings, but finding him was like walking in a strange neighborhood during a thick fog. I was unlikely to do anything but get lost.

Especially since I kept coming back to one puzzling suspect, one I didn't want to consider. Blackford.

Sir Broderick started ticking our suspects off on his fingers. "Naylard doesn't care that his sister converted. Blackmail over. Waxpool sent his son away to France and ended any possible embezzlement and the blackmail in a single day. The Mervilles are still paying blackmail over a child they don't want society to know about, but Drake hasn't proven to be greedy. They can afford it. Dutton-Cox married off his problem, and his son-in-law refused to pay a farthing."

I remembered the scene when I learned about the Dutton-Coxes and felt my body overheat. Despite her large family, Lady Dutton-Cox seemed more alone than I was. She had everything but lacked what she wanted most. I pitied her.

"Georgia, you're very red. Are you all right?" Frances asked.

"Probably just fatigued from my travels." Then I recalled Viscountess Dalrymple's confession. "The son-in-law refused to find out who was being blackmailed in private and Drake wouldn't speak out in front of witnesses. Apparently, the viscount thinks what he doesn't know is better for his marriage and his peace of mind."

Jacob laughed. "It must be hard to blackmail someone when they don't want to find out what you're selling. Have we been able to confirm these stories?"

Sir Broderick said, "Some. We don't have independent testimony to prove Merville's willingness to continue to pay or whether Waxpool's son embezzled from the family. The viscount, Dutton-Cox's son-in-law, sent Drake packing from his club by ordering the doorman to throw Drake out bodily in front of a dozen witnesses. Naylard cheerfully admits to turning Drake down at his sister's insistence while wondering if he should have, since he and Drake are friends. That young peer is hopeless."

I waved at Sir Broderick as a thought struck me. "Have any of them been told Drake was killed or about his miraculous resurrection?"

"So far as we can tell, the only one who knows Drake might have been killed was the man who ordered his death."

"So we still have Hancock and Blackford as suspects. And Waxpool has been lying to us." I told them what I'd learned from Lady Julia Waxpool about her father's secret and Drake's blackmailing him with his incriminating love letters.

"Lady Julia is right," Fogarty said. "As long as her father stays in France, nothing can be done to him here. By the time Waxpool's son has to return, Drake may no longer have the letters or be in a position to use them."

"Time may be against them. I've heard Waxpool hasn't long to live," Sir Broderick said.

"A dying man can't chase after someone young and fit like Drake," Jacob pointed out.

"Waxpool has a manservant, Price, who the old man bragged to me about at Lady Westover's. Price will do anything Waxpool tells him to do. The earl may want to remove the threat of blackmail from the title before he dies, fearing his son will destroy the family fortune to save himself from prison." I shook my head. "Poor Lady Julia."

"Waxpool may also be worried about the family name. Consider him a suspect," Sir Broderick said. Ticking the names off on his fingers, he continued, "Hancock is in deep financial trouble, which makes him a good suspect but not a good candidate for blackmail. The market for his one big invention is drying up as new chemicals make it obsolete, and nothing he's worked on since has found a viable application. In fact, his inventions have a nasty habit of blowing up and injuring the people they are supposed to help."

Sir Broderick shifted in his chair before he continued. "Any unentailed land the family had here or at his country home was sold off long ago. No, blackmailing Hancock wouldn't have gained Drake anything, so I doubt he tried very hard."

"Hancock tried to sell an old book to me for ten times what it's worth," I told them.

"Did he seem desperate?" Sir Broderick asked.

"He seemed angry."

"The Duke of Blackford, however, is still a mystery." Sir Broderick stared at me as if daring me to refute his words. "Not any longer." I had to tell them. "Lady Margaret, Blackford's sister, died nearly two years ago from drowning near their country estate. She's buried in the churchyard under her own name, but the death was never reported to the authorities, so it doesn't appear in the books on the peerage. Anne Drake knew about the death from her mother."

"And presumably she told her husband," Emma said.

"What I don't understand is why Blackford, who would recognize Drake from when he was a footman for his family, didn't give him away when he met Drake out in polite society spending time with Blackford's fiancée. Drake pretended to be descended from French aristocracy, but Blackford knew his true lineage." Blackford was the only one in the group whose actions made no sense to me. Perhaps that was why I found him so fascinating.

"Do we know if Blackford is paying blackmail to Drake?" Fogarty asked.

"We don't know. Blackford did admit Emma and I are to be bait tomorrow night," I answered.

"Do we have any idea what's behind Blackford's plan for the masked ball?" Sir Broderick asked.

"No." I could feel tension mounting in the room. All signs were pointing toward Blackford, and, while he was up to something, I didn't want to believe he was the one who'd hired thugs to attack Nicholas Drake in his home. Remembering the way he'd looked at me, I couldn't believe he'd hire anyone to hurt me. And after meeting Sumner, there was no possibility I'd think Blackford would hire anyone so inept as to kill the wrong man.

I'd come to admire Blackford. I didn't want him to be guilty. "Do we know who followed Conover to Hounslow on the train that night?"

Fogarty shook his head. "Two strangers got off the ten o'clock train. One went into the Red Lion and the other disappeared into the town. We haven't been able to get a good description or find out when the second man returned to London."

"That's a dead end, then," Sir Broderick said. "Jacob, you're going to be one of the footmen for the ball tomorrow night. And you will be armed. Fogarty, we're going to have to find a way to get you into that house as well."

"I think Blackford deserves scrutiny," Fogarty said.

"Well, I don't." I sounded mutinous rather than sensible.

"Based on what, Georgia? He invited you to a ball and bought you a pretty dress?" Jacob asked.

"Based on a feeling. He wants Drake in his hands for reasons he won't share, but I don't think he'd hire thugs to find Drake. He's using us to do that job." I looked around the room. "Our fancy dresses will make us easy to find in the crush of the ball."

Part of Blackford's plan came to me in a rush. "What better place to hide than in plain sight in a costume? My guess is Blackford has set up a meeting with Drake that will take place at the ball. Blackford has probably told him about our eye-catching gowns."

"I hope you're right, Georgia," Sir Broderick said. "We'll keep an open mind. But you must be ready to act if Drake's attacker is Blackford."

"I will be. And I've thought of an addition to our costumes. Sir Broderick, don't you have a friend with a collection of ceremonial jeweled daggers?" I gave Emma a smile and she grinned in return.

Before we left the house, I sat down across from Sir Broderick. "I want you to know I've been looking for my parents' murderer in the area where I saw him from the omnibus."

His voice went soft. "I'm not surprised. Any luck?"

"No. But while I was searching this afternoon I ran into

the Duke of Blackford. He's going to see if he can learn anything about the cottage and its ownership."

"We both tried that. And failed."

"Do you mind if he tries?"

"No. But don't be upset if he's unsuccessful, and don't overlook him as a suspect in Drake's disappearance because he's offered to help you on another matter."

After all these years, I'd developed that much sense. I was about to object when Sir Broderick said, "I've made a small breakthrough in locating the killer."

I instantly forgave him for doubting my ability to separate the duke's assistance on one investigation from his role in another. "You found him."

"Baby steps, Georgia. This man covers his tracks well."

I was nearly jumping with anticipation. "What have you learned?"

"Do you know Weldon Parrish?"

"Bookshop owner, antiquarian collector, hates women who own shops." I'd once tried to broker a deal with him over an old copy of the Psalms. I didn't plan to do business with him again.

"He came here yesterday at my request. The sort of request Adam Fogarty and his friends can deliver."

Sir Broderick seldom used muscle, preferring persuasion. "Why did you—?"

"Parrish was the one spreading the Gutenberg Bible rumor."

"He has the copy my parents were killed for?" I'd kill him myself if he did.

"I don't think so. I told him I didn't care why, I just wanted the truth about the book. He was finally convinced to tell me he was acting for a South African collector who has decided to take his book off the market."

"And you think this South African—?" I was halfway out of my chair.

"No. Sit down. The man most interested in buying the book was tall and blond with a faint accent. He gave his name as Mr. Jones. Parrish said it's obviously fake, but his money is real. A fortune, apparently. His description of Mr. Jones matches yours of the killer."

"Does he have an address for Mr. Jones? How does Mr. Parrish get in contact with him?"

"Parrish claims he doesn't have any way to get in touch with him. The man seeks out Parrish. Parrish says he seems to know when he's heard back from the seller."

"I don't believe Mr. Parrish."

"Neither do I, but that's what I learned."

THE NEXT DAY, we closed the bookshop at noon so we could get cleaned up, put on our best corsets and shifts, and hide the jeweled daggers Jacob had brought us in our bags before we left for Lady Westover's.

We were shown into the parlor where Madame Leclerc and her assistant waited. "Oh, good. Try on the dresses, ladies. I can't wait to see you in them," Lady Westover said. Her eyes glowed with excitement.

Emma went first. In her dress, with her mask and the jewels the duke had sent over that morning, I wouldn't have recognized her. She was beyond regal. She was mesmerizing, icy, devastating, and she hadn't even done her hair yet.

Madame Leclerc looked her over and said, "There is one more detail." She brought out a sash in the same fabric and fastened it from one of Emma's shoulders to the other side of her waist, mimicking the sashes royalty wore.

I reached into her bag and pulled out the diamond-encrusted dagger. I handed it to Emma and said, "Think this will be a good addition to the sash?"

She smiled beneath her half mask. "Perfect."

"Daring," Madame Leclerc proclaimed and fitted it to the

sash by the fastener on the back of the dagger's sheath at Emma's waist.

"That is certainly unique, although not quite what I had in mind." Lady Westover glanced over at me and raised her eyebrows. I shrugged in reply, knowing she couldn't imagine the dangers we might face. I didn't like not knowing what we'd encounter. She turned toward Madame Leclerc and announced in a firm tone, "Now, let's get Emma out of her dress and get Georgia into hers."

I expected my appearance to be a disappointment after seeing beautiful Emma so exquisitely dressed. After helping me into my petticoat, Madame Leclerc and her assistant lifted my dress over my head and lowered it into place. They buttoned the back, fastened the sash, and put on my mask. Then they put the tiara on my messy hair and hooked the necklace so it lay cold against my chest.

Finally, they led me over to a full-length looking glass. The eyeholes in the mask were large enough that I could see most of my reflection. Once I got past the décolletage, what I saw amazed me.

The dress flickered and rustled like flames around me. Emma, wearing a wrap over her corset and stockings, brought the ruby-handled dagger to me, and Madame Leclerc hung it from my sash. I looked like a Renaissance queen or an avenging goddess in a fairy tale. Except for my hair, which needed taming, I didn't look like me.

I took a few steps away from the mirror and then returned. Emma and Lady Westover applauded. The skirt shimmered around me. The woman looking through the mask at me was no bookseller. She was a warrior, passionate and invincible.

"Yes, you will do very well." Madame Leclerc and her assistant reversed the process, and when they finished, one of Lady Westover's maids handed me a wrap to cover myself and keep me warm.

The dressmakers left to a round of thanks and then Lady

Westover invited us to a late tea of cakes and sandwiches to hold us over until the midnight supper at the ball. Our best corsets were never designed for a full meal in our stomachs, and I was too nervous to eat more than one sandwich.

"How are we traveling to Arlington House?" I asked.

"By unmarked carriage. The two of you will arrive alone, and when asked for your names so you can be announced, say, 'The Ice Queen and the Fire Queen.' You are to arrive precisely at ten while the ball is in progress."

"These are the Duke of Blackford's orders?" I asked.

"Yes. It would so help if we knew what he has in mind." Lady Westover wrung her hands. I'd only seen her do that once before, when her grandson disappeared in the course of an investigation.

I laid one of my hands on top of hers. "It'll be all right. I'm sure the duke wouldn't do anything to put us in danger."

"Are you coming to the ball tonight?" Emma asked.

"Dear me, no. Balls are for young people. Besides, I need my beauty sleep. Waxpool is coming over tomorrow for a full report."

I raised my eyebrows. "Do you two need a chaperone?"

She laughed. "No, just a full account after this affair ends."

The longest part of readying for the ball was Emma doing her hair and then attacking mine. She called Lady Westover's maid in for her assistance, holding strands of my hair while she pinned others. When they finished, an explosion wouldn't have upset my coiffure.

Only then did Lady Westover's lady's maid help us into our clothes, necklaces, and masks, while Lady Westover outfitted us with our tiaras. The clock downstairs struck the half hour as we finished.

"How do I look?" I asked.

"I wouldn't recognize you if I attended the ball tonight. And I'm certain there won't be another costume like yours."

I smiled at the dowager and started to leave the room.

"Oh. This won't do," she said behind me.

"What?"

"Long gloves. I almost forgot. Two pair, please," she said to her maid.

When the maid returned, Emma slid on her twenty-button gloves and only needed to work three buttons at the wrists like a pro. I fumbled mine at first and needed help with the buttons from elbows to wrists. "Where is the mirror?" I asked when we finished.

"Downstairs in the parlor."

My arms were bare from above the elbows to my flouncy little sleeves, but they were covered compared to my chest. When I looked in the mirror, the first thing that caught my eye was how much milky white breast appeared below the large ruby necklace. The part of my face not covered by the mask flamed in embarrassment. I felt as if I were flaunting myself.

"It's a role, Georgia. Relax," Emma said.

"Not one I've played often."

"Perhaps you should more often for our investigations. You have the body for it," she said and smiled.

"Thank you. And you look magnificent. As if you were born to play this part," I told her.

"Come, ladies. Your carriage awaits. And come back here after the ball. I want to hear every detail," Lady Westover said.

"Won't you be asleep?"

"My maid will wake me. After all this planning and secrecy, I can't wait to hear what happened. Especially since the duke has told the other blackmail victims that Drake will be at the ball."

"What? Why did he do that?" Was Blackford hoping the guilty party would show themselves? Or was he hoping someone else would kill Drake and save him the trouble? Whatever the reason, our job just became more dangerous.

"I have no idea why. He mentioned it this morning." Lady Westover hugged us each carefully so as not to wrinkle our dresses and walked us to the door. Her butler helped us into dark-colored evening cloaks. Now we looked the part on the outside. On the inside, I was a frightened little girl.

The carriage was spacious, clean, and unmarked. The footman who helped us in wore livery without markings. Before he climbed up to join the driver, he said, "We're to wait for you nearby until you need us."

"Who do you work for?" I asked.

"Someone who wishes you well," he replied and walked to the front of the carriage.

The carriage jerked into motion and my stomach lurched with it. Emma reached over and squeezed my hand. "This will be fun."

"I hope that's all it is."

The closer we moved to the Duke of Arlington's residence, the more crowded the streets became. It was a clear night and the gas lamps shone brightly as we sat in a jam of horses and carriages, all appearing to have one destination.

Sitting there, waiting to move closer to the house as our driver jockeyed his horses into position, I had time to think. And that was exactly what I didn't want to do. I was scared. Hornets flew around my insides, buzzing and hammering, while a voice said in my head, *You're a fraud.*

"Let's get out here and walk."

"No, Georgia. We're going to make an entrance like everyone else. I've waited my whole life for this. To enter one of these houses by the front door during a party."

Emma's job as a child in her East End gang was to sneak into the homes of the wealthy and let the adult members in or bring the valuables to them. I understood how hard she'd worked and how much she'd learned to make her entrance tonight.

I took as deep a breath as I could with my corset crushing my insides. "Then we wait."

After a moment, Emma said, "Have you ever been to a ball before?"

"No. They don't usually invite bookshop owners."

She smiled. "No, I meant for an Archivist Society investigation."

"No. Never."

"We go inside where there will be a cloakroom and retiring room for the ladies. We leave our cloaks and then proceed to the ballroom where we'll be announced. Phyllida has been telling me about the usual setup. There will be rooms set aside for supper and for cards, but I think the duke will expect us to be in the ballroom."

The duke. The stage manager for this evening. "I wonder what he has planned."

The carriage jerked forward, and Emma patted my hand. "We'll find out soon enough."

The driver didn't seem to be satisfied until he had us directly in front of the house. Only then did the footman jump down and open the door, helping first me and then Emma alight.

I could see the heads of the couples leaving the carriages in front and behind us turning our way. The shepherdesses, the Romans, the members of the French court of Marie Antoinette were all examining us with interest. We were new, different, unique.

Lady Westover had outdone herself in that regard.

"Smile," Emma hissed. "We're on show."

I glanced her way and grinned. "Are you ready?"

"Yes."

We lifted our chins in unison and swept up the stairs, where a liveried footman opened the door to us and gestured toward our left. We entered like queens.

CHAPTER NINETEEN

DIVESTED of our capes, we followed the crowd moving upstairs and then toward the back of the house. As we drew closer to the ball, we could clearly hear a waltz. Although I tried hard not to show it, I was as fascinated as Emma was by all I saw.

On one side of the red-carpeted hall was the dining room, with a table that could seat two dozen set up with delicacies on platters and wine goblets in rows. The chairs were placed around the outside of the room, leaving plenty of space to walk by the table. Emma leaned to the side to look around the footman guarding the door. "Everything is beautiful," she said to him. "You and the others must have worked very hard to bring everything to a shine. You are to be congratulated."

She must have blessed him with one of her dazzling smiles, because he grinned at her as if she were bestowing a treasure on him.

I looked into the parlor across the hall. The dark blues in the upholstery and wallpaper made the room appear chilly.

An elderly Greek goddess and an equally elderly Eleanor of Aquitaine sat by a warming fire in close conversation. Three tables had been set up and were already in use for card games by friars, medieval rulers, and two King Charles the Seconds.

I recognized the Louis XVI facing me without his mask. The Duke of Merville. He appeared engrossed in his cards, and a large number of silver coins scattered on the tables explained why no one looked up while I stared from the doorway.

The Duchess of Merville, dressed we had been told as Marie Antoinette, wasn't in the room. I'd have to look for her in the ballroom with the other chaperones, since their younger daughter was engaged, not married.

There was one highwayman, but he was pudgy and lacked the purpose and energy that poured out of the Duke of Blackford and affected everyone around him. More disappointed than I expected to be, I turned away.

Emma and I looked at each other through our masks and moved on. At the end of the hall, open double doors led to a flight of stairs. At the bottom was a huge, high-ceilinged ballroom with French doors on the far end, no doubt for access to the gardens. Intricate crystal chandeliers lit by gas lamps hung above the dancers.

As we started down the steps, I looked out over the glittering, masked throng milling about and moving to the music. The room was already crowded. Soon it would be a crush and the society matrons would declare it a success. How were we supposed to unmask a killer in this crowd?

We reached the landing halfway down the stairs where a footman said, "Names, please."

"The Ice Queen and the Fire Queen," I said.

"No, your real names."

I looked at him down my nose and in my haughtiest tone said, "Those are our real names. The Ice Queen and the Fire Queen."

He raised an eyebrow and then glared at the line backing up behind us. In a loud voice, he proclaimed, "The Ice Queen and the Fire Queen."

Once we set foot on the polished parquet floor, we were surrounded by gaudy costumes and jewels that sparkled beneath the bright lights. Dancers moved around the center of the room to the music of an orchestra tucked to one side of the stairs. Emma and I tried to make one circle of the room together to see if we recognized anyone, but we were soon separated in the crush of people who each wore a different flashy outfit and a different perfume. Without knowing who wore which costume, we found the half masks hid identities.

By the time I reached the stairs again, I'd received two indecent proposals. I hadn't expected *that* sort of party. I climbed up two steps, but I didn't see any sign of Emma or the Duke of Blackford in his highwayman disguise. All I saw was a sea of multicolored masks and costume hats.

I was frustrated as well as amazed and dazzled by the brilliance of so much wealth and power. I had to remind myself to ignore the overwhelming mix of inherited position and status as the crowd swirled and shifted around me. I couldn't afford to be impressed, not with so much at stake. Blackford would be wise to show up now and tell me what he wanted done, so we could take care of the problem and then enjoy this carnival mix of glamour and music. I found, with my identity hidden, I wanted to join the waltzing throng.

I stepped down from the staircase and wandered among the crowd watching the dancers. I felt as if I walked alone, swallowed up in a shiny, writhing rainbow. The only thing I wished for was that the highwayman would whisk me out on the floor for a waltz. No doubt the duke was a superb dancer. He did everything with grace.

Since that wouldn't happen, I'd settle for a cool breeze. Several hundred bodies pressed close together created a heat similar to that in Sir Broderick's study. Oppressive.

I bumped into Joan of Arc and said, "Excuse me." Then I looked more closely at the square chin and wide mouth and burst out laughing. "I didn't think I'd see you here, Lady Julia."

"Ssh. I can come in disguise to these parties and be sure at least half my dance partners have no idea who I am or how much I'm worth." She started to back her way through the crowd to get away from me.

I grabbed her arm to detain her. "Does the Earl of Wax-pool know you're here?"

"Grandpapa has no idea either my brother or I am here, but he'd be proud of us for finding a way to have fun without being valued like a racehorse."

"Then I'll add my congratulations on your brilliant idea."

"I have nothing more to say to you."

"It's not about—that subject." I hesitated a moment and Lady Julia looked at me sharply. "I need to ask you one question about the day Miss Victoria died."

She glanced around before she nodded. "Very well. One question."

"What do you remember about the flower arrangement in Lady Margaret's parlor?"

"Nothing. Why?"

"Nothing odd happened in connection with the flowers?"

"That's two questions."

"Please."

"I didn't see anything unusual happen with the flowers. When I first arrived, Victoria was saying something was a very strange custom, and one she didn't think was too hygienic. Margaret dismissed her with a wave of the hand and rose to greet me. I never found out what they were talking about."

"And you didn't see or hear any more about this strange custom?" I let go of Lady Julia's arm. I was certain she wouldn't leave now.

"No. It was never mentioned again."

"Not even when Victoria was taken ill? In the carriage or in her room?"

"No. I think whatever Margaret suggested, Victoria rejected. Victoria did say something later about not being a follower of silly peasant customs."

"But nothing else?"

"Nothing else. And nothing about flowers."

That was it, then. There was no evidence to either clear Margaret from suspicion or prove she killed Victoria. I looked at Lady Julia's eyes through the two sets of eyeholes in our masks. I could see defiance growing in hers.

"Margaret's my friend. I'm not going to help you hang her."

I held her gaze. "You think Margaret poisoned Victoria, don't you?"

"I don't think it was physically possible. I was with them almost the entire time they were together. What I remember most from that day was that Victoria was wretchedly unhappy."

"What?" Victoria was unhappy? That was news.

"Victoria didn't want to marry the duke. She couldn't stand him. She thought he was stuffy, dull. The duke and her father arranged the match. Her mother was thrilled. Victoria felt like a sacrificial lamb. And she planned to make everyone pay for her misery."

"She told you this?" We couldn't be talking about the same Duke of Blackford. He wasn't stuffy or dull. He was infuriating, helpful, riveting; and he deflected danger and unwanted questions with grace.

"Every time we were alone after the engagement was announced."

"Thank you for your honesty. And I'm sorry to hear about your grandfather." Would she be honest about this rumor, too?

Her eyes widened. "I didn't know you knew. I'm heartbroken. He has less than a month to live and I don't know what will happen with Papa and the title then." She grabbed my hand and squeezed it. "Please don't tell anyone."

I nodded, mouth slightly open, and then watched Lady Julia walk away. If Waxpool's impending death was the reason Drake was being hunted, then Waxpool's manservant, Price, would be somewhere in the crowd looking for the blackmailer. Blackford told his fellow victims that Drake would be here tonight, and I suspected our costumes were designed to be beacons for the search.

Now I'd heard both Victoria and Margaret were unhappy women. What role had it played in their deaths? I doubted I'd get an answer to that question, but I still had to ask it, if only to myself.

I pressed through the crowd looking for Emma. I thought I saw her and her shimmering blue mask near the French doors and worked a path in that direction, only to lose her again in the crowd.

Then I spotted her on the dance floor, whirling around in a waltz with a slim, trim Henry VIII with blond hair and a neatly trimmed beard. They made a handsome couple. I hoped Emma wouldn't lose her head. A man in a wizard costume watched them closely from the edge of the floor. I suspected he'd be Emma's next dance partner.

The crowd parted slightly for a tall figure in a black hooded robe, a scythe gleaming in one hand. Who had come to the party dressed as the angel of death? His full mask and his hood hid his face, but his head swiveled between watching Emma and looking at me.

I slipped back to the chaperones' section with its scattering of chairs and found the Marie Antoinette I wanted carrying a bow-covered green parasol. I recognized the parasol from my visit to Portman Square. "Your Highness," I began, "or should I say Your Grace?"

"You recognized me?"

"You wear the same costume every year." I hoped what I'd been told was correct.

She nodded. "Do I know you?"

"Archivist Society."

"Oh, yes. Your costume is quite unique."

"Just the effect I was hoping for. What is your daughter wearing?"

"A shepherdess. I wish she weren't. She looks so lifeless next to Daisy Hancock."

I glanced in the direction the duchess was staring and saw two shepherdesses standing in conversation. Daisy Hancock's blondness and animation were hard to overlook, especially next to the demure, dark-haired girl she was talking to. A man came up and took the laughing Daisy away for more dancing. The duchess's daughter slipped away into the rainbow-hued crowd.

"Your daughter will keep her looks and her warm disposition much longer than Miss Daisy," I said. I hoped I was right. The duchess's daughter had my build and pale complexion. "Where is Miss Daisy's chaperone?"

"Hancock? Who knows who he has minding her this season. And I wouldn't be surprised if he didn't attend. In fact, I'm certain he's not here. If he were, he'd be boring the guests with how they should invest in his latest creation. Merville positively runs when he sees the man coming."

"He has a reputation for that?"

"At every event he attends. And it's been worse lately. Merville says the rumor around the City is he's completely broke, and you know how expensive a season is." She looked at me down her long nose. "Well, I guess you don't."

I did know how much Miss Daisy wanted another two seasons. Poor Hancock. He couldn't be blackmailed by Drake, not if he didn't have any money and his niece was demanding more frocks for parties.

Voices nearby nearly made me miss her next words. "I'm sorry?"

"He's going to miss Waxpool. The earl is dying."

I glanced in the direction Lady Merville was looking. "Is that Price dressed as the angel of death?"

"His manservant. Yes. It suits him, don't you think?"

"How do you know him?"

"He's been with Waxpool for a generation, and these days has to travel with that frail old man everywhere. Tonight I saw him without his mask outside when we arrived. Quite a clever costume."

I thought it was creepy, especially since Waxpool was supposedly close to death. "What will happen to the title when Waxpool dies?"

Lady Merville pursed her lips. "The son won't receive a Writ of Summons from the queen to take his seat in the House of Lords if a warrant is issued for his arrest. Of course, no one in our class will say a word against him." She sniffed. "But you never know what persons of the lower orders might do with the right evidence. If word gets out, it'll be a juicy scandal and the queen will be forced to ignore him. In older times, the monarch took away titles from nobles he didn't like, but that was usually for insurrection."

The servant's scythe glittered with reflected light as he disappeared into the crowd. "Why is Price here?"

The lady shook her bewigged head gently.

I moved on, uneasy since I guessed Price was there to find Drake. Waxpool couldn't act on his own, but I could imagine the orders he might have given his manservant. I glanced around, hoping to see Blackford or Drake and warn them.

Emma was dancing again, this time with a dandy dressed like Voltaire. How the man waltzed while balancing a flowing powdered wig and with a half mask blocking his vision, I couldn't guess. They made a graceful pair, and I noticed the wizard and Henry VIII watching them as closely as I. I was surprised the wizard hadn't asked her to dance yet. Maybe the Frenchman had beaten him to Emma's side. Her beauty was difficult to ignore.

I continued my circuit of the room. The music changed, and I saw Emma dancing with Henry VIII again. When I stopped and looked around, I heard a smooth male voice in my ear. "Let's go out into the garden, Miss Fenchurch."

I spun around and found myself facing a black half mask and a tall, white wig. Looking down, I saw pale blue knee breeches and black shoes with silver buckles. There were a half dozen identical costumes at this ball. "Who are you, and what have you done with Marie Antoinette?"

"Unlike her, I'm trying not to lose my head. Nicholas Drake, at your service." He gave me as much of a bow as he could manage with bodies squishing us from all directions and his wig threatening to topple off his head.

"How did you know it was me?"

"I'd like to say it was a brilliant deduction, but the Duke of Blackford told me what you would wear. I wanted you here to assure my safety."

I'd never been in a situation where I was less able to assure his well-being. All I had was a ceremonial dagger, and we were being pushed on from every direction. "Why have you come here? There must be safer places for you to hide."

"I received a tempting proposition from the Duke of Blackford. This seemed the safest place for us to negotiate. He arranged for my invitation." Even with his mouth next to my ear, I had to guess at every other word.

My suspicions of the duke intensified. "What proposition?" I found I was nearly bellowing in Drake's ear to be heard.

"We can't talk in here. Let's go out in the garden."

I trusted Drake almost as much as I trusted the Duke of Blackford. Putting a hand over my dagger, I nodded and followed him outside.

The veranda near the doors was well lit with gas lamps. The music and the laughter from inside poured over us. The garden beyond was a mass of shadows cast by hanging lanterns and thick bushes. While this dark area would be a great place for a tryst, it wouldn't be good for a business meeting. Or preventing an attack.

Drake nodded his head toward the garden. "That way. It's too loud and public here."

"And much safer."

He laughed, a seductive sound if I were to fancy him. I didn't, but I could understand why the young debutantes flocked around him. "I didn't take you for a coward. Come on. I won't hurt you."

No, he wouldn't. That was why I wore a dagger.

We walked a little way into the garden and looked around to make certain we wouldn't be overheard. "We had your house under watch. You were safe there. Why come here tonight?"

"No place is safer than in the middle of a crowd."

He might sound foolhardy, but I saw how his eyes glanced all around him. He was scared. "What is the duke's proposition?" I whispered.

"All of my blackmail material in exchange for a sizable sum of money and two first-class passages to Canada."

"It sounds like a good deal. You should take it."

He shook his head and glanced around, making certain no one was approaching. "I want assurances."

"What kind of assurances?"

"The kind that doesn't have me handing over the letters only to get a knife in the back."

"I think if the Duke of Blackford wanted to double-cross you, you would already be dead."

"Are you positive he isn't the one who's sent his thugs to kill me?" Despite the shadows, I saw him raise an eyebrow.

I considered my answer. "Yes. He's done everything to

make himself look guilty, including lying to the Archivist Society and planning whatever is supposed to happen here tonight. But I'm certain he's not the person threatening your safety. He doesn't threaten. He just acts without warning or explanation."

"Thank you for that robust defense of my honor." I peered into the thick shadows away from the house where the deep, ironic voice came from. Then a highwayman stepped out of the darkness. Black half mask, black tricorn hat, a pistol tucked into the black sash at his waist. Straight black hair gleaming in the light of a hanging lantern. The only white was his shirt. I suspected there was a knife strapped to his forearm under the loose sleeves.

The air fairly hummed with danger, and I could have sworn I smelled gunpowder mixed in with the scent of spring flowers.

I glanced from Drake to the duke. There was no comparison. The duke raised my heart rate. Drake annoyed me.

Wanting answers to the mysteries he left in his wake, I took a step toward him. "We need to talk, Your Grace."

"No time for that now. Stand guard while Mr. Drake and I negotiate."

Drake took a couple of steps into the darkness and I stood next to a tall bush, keeping an eye out for anyone entering or leaving the veranda. I rubbed my hands up and down my bare upper arms as I grew chilled standing outside. The overwarm, overbright ballroom looked more appealing by the moment.

I could hear the two men talking behind me in low, strident tones. There were no other sounds of footsteps or voices nearby, and the only time I could hear the music was when someone opened the French doors. It was peaceful out there. Unfortunately, I was only aware of being cold and bored.

To fend off boredom and, I admit, to satisfy my curiosity,

I tried to hear what the two men had to say to each other. I thought I heard a large sum of money mentioned and decided that couldn't be right. A couple, a Harlequin and an Elizabeth I, started in my direction and I moved a little. They must have wanted privacy because they turned toward the far side of the garden.

Between the gasps and giggles at a distance and Drake and the Duke of Blackford muttering figures closer at hand, the evening was less boring but still chilly. I tried counting stars but the sky was too cloudy. I resisted the growing urge to tell the two men to make up their minds before the ball ended.

Just as I ran out of patience, they approached me. "Miss Fenchurch, if you'd come with us," Drake said. "For a sum of money that the duke is going to remove from the bank tonight, I'm going to hand over all my . . . incriminating papers. I'd like you along to assure fair dealing."

"How do you plan to get into a bank at this hour?"

"Sir Izzy Fairweather is in the card room. I'll ask him to join us," the duke said.

"And the papers?"

"Are in a safe box in his bank," Drake said.

The duke laughed. "Wise man."

Amazing how the letters Drake held and the duke's money were both in the bank owned by a guest at the ball. Some people would call that a coincidence. Knowing how much the Duke of Blackford had interfered, I suspected he'd somehow learned where the papers were and made certain the money and the banker were available tonight.

We'd reached the French doors. "I need to tell Emma all is well and to enjoy the ball without me."

"No need. Sumner is here watching out for her, and I'm sure you have guards here, too. We'll bring you back as soon as our business is finished."

Sir Izzy Fairweather, dressed as a portly Lord High Justice

in judicial wig and gown, appeared overjoyed to see us and rose from the card table immediately. As I collected my cloak, I heard him grumble to Blackford, "You'll drop me off at home after we stop by the bank? I've had enough of Arlington's kind regards for everyone in my family. The man must want something, and it's difficult to say no to your host."

The duke gallantly swung my cloak over my shoulders, one hand tenderly grazing my neck. For an instant, I felt as if I belonged in this dress, in these jewels, with these men.

As soon as I stepped outside, Fogarty approached me, reminding me of my place in society. "It's all right," I told him. "Emma is still inside. Watch out for her. I should be back shortly. If I'm not, question Blackford."

I entered the carriage with the Duke of Blackford, Sir Izzy, and Drake. In the hours between the beginning and the end of a ball, the roads to the City appeared empty compared to the workday. We were soon at the bank, where the night guard recognized Sir Izzy and let us in.

All I was required to do was stand nearby and make sure all the papers from the safety box came into Blackford's possession and a stack of banknotes from Blackford's account was handed to Drake. The whole business took two minutes, and then we left the bank to the visible relief of the guard.

Blackford summoned a hansom cab for me and said, "Go back to the ball. I'll take the papers to Sir Broderick after I drop off Sir Izzy and then I'll join you there. I look forward to claiming a waltz."

I stopped him with a hand on his sleeve before he sent the cabbie on his way. "I would love to waltz with you, Your Grace. But first, I must know. Why are you giving blackmail material you paid so much for to Sir Broderick?"

"There are only a few letters I'm interested in. It's best if Sir Broderick is in charge of the rest. He's famous for his discretion." He gave my hand a squeeze and signaled the driver to take me back to the Arlingtons' ball.

I returned and handed my cloak to a servant. By the time I reached the top of the stairs, I could hear a lively dance tune from the orchestra. I walked past the card room, down the stairs, and into the ballroom, picturing myself at the center of the dance floor with the duke.

I didn't see Emma. Brightly costumed revelers filled my view in every direction, but I couldn't find the shimmering blue fabric.

Jacob, dressed in a formal footman's uniform now splattered with goo, frantically waved to me from a doorway in the corner of the room. I bolted toward him around chairs filled with wallflowers and chaperones.

"Georgia. Thank God. Emma was carried out of here not five minutes ago. She's been abducted."

CHAPTER TWENTY

I grabbed Jacob's flailing arms. "What happened? Who carried Emma out?"

"I don't know. She looked fine the last time I saw her, dancing with a man in a wizard costume. Then I saw that same man carrying her down the servants' hallway. I ran after them, but the wizard knocked over two maids carrying trays of ices and strawberries along the back way to the dining room. In all the slipping and sliding, I lost the man carrying Emma. He escaped the house through the side door. And Emma was limp."

The wizard. Not Price dressed as the angel of death. "Oh, good heavens. Where were they going?"

"I don't know."

"Show me the route he took." I held up my skirt to follow Jacob as fast as he ran. My feet skidded on the liquid left on the wooden floor. Once out the service door, we were on a dark, narrow path that led in two directions, to the garden or the street.

"Which way?" Jacob asked.

A glimmer close to the street caught my eye. I rushed forward and pointed, since my corset wouldn't allow me to bend enough to pick up the jewels.

Jacob reached down and swept up Emma's tiara. Her very expensive tiara. "No common thief would leave this behind," he said, pocketing the crown.

A bulky shadow in worn clothing and a battered hat came up to us. "Georgia, Emma's been snatched. I couldn't stop him."

"Oh, no, Fogarty. Did you see where Emma was taken?"

"I heard," the ex-policeman said. "He told the driver Chelling Meadows. I couldn't get a good shot at the man in the funny robes without hitting Emma."

"That's all right," I said. "We'll save Emma."

Fogarty was pacing in front of me. "I told your driver to come around front and I told the bobby on this beat to get word to Scotland Yard."

"Chelling Meadows used to be Hancock's home," I told them. "I don't know who lives there now. It's past Holland Park. We'll have to go there at once." Why had the villain taken Emma to Hancock's former home? Then I remembered Emma telling me Hancock still worked in his laboratory there. I was embarrassed by my failure to realize who Drake's enemy was and ready to rip Hancock apart.

"I saw that ugly brute that works for Blackford jump on the back of the carriage. He must have had orders to follow if either of you were abducted from the ball. They should have reached Chelling Meadows by now." Fogarty helped me into the unmarked carriage that had brought us here.

"That must be Sumner you saw. Was Hancock's niece with them?"

"No. I noticed the man in a wizard costume talking to a young, blond shepherdess shortly before he asked Emma to dance. The shepherdess could have been his niece. Whatever he said, she shook her head no and went off to dance with someone in a knight costume," Jacob said as he and Fogarty piled in behind me and our driver started to pick his way around the other carriages.

"The wizard was alone when I spotted him carrying Emma. She appeared to be unconscious," Fogarty said. "I think she was still alive."

My heart squeezed tight. I had to save Emma. We finally broke free of the tangle of carriages and rode out past Kensington Palace and Holland Park.

"Why does it have to be out in the country?" I asked. Traffic had been heavy through town and our trip was slow. I could have run faster. It was all Fogarty could do to keep me from bolting from the carriage.

"This isn't the country anymore," Fogarty told me. "He still owns the house and grounds, but the estate has been sold off and built up. Part of the London suburbs now."

"Are we ever going to get there?" Tears were filling my eyes.

"If he drove the horses any faster, we'd tip over on a curve," Fogarty said. "Jacob, are you armed?"

"I've got my knife."

"I have a dagger," I added.

"Can you throw it?" Fogarty asked me.

"No, but I'll have no problem stabbing him in the heart. Poor Emma. She's so young. What did he do to her?" I started to pull the weapon out of its sheath, but Fogarty put out a hand to stop me.

"Leave it where it is until we know there's no other way."

Fogarty stopped the driver on the road in front of Chelling Meadows and told him to wait for us. Then we climbed down and entered the grounds past a tall wrought-iron fence. None of us spoke as we stepped through knee-high weeds and around a dry fountain, Fogarty leading the way with a lantern from the carriage.

The house loomed before us, an old three-story structure

with a two-story wing on one side and the crumbling remains of a conservatory on the other. Every window was dark.

Fogarty turned the knob on the front door and it opened with a creak. We walked inside the empty front hall, expecting to be challenged by a thug at any moment. The only footsteps and breaths we heard were our own.

Holding the lantern ahead of us, Fogarty was the first to see the wire across the doorway in front of us. He held up his hand, and we stopped. He stuck his head into the space beyond and looked around. Then he dropped to his hands and knees and crawled into the next room, pushing the lantern ahead of him.

When Fogarty was through, he stood up and gestured to the side. I stuck my head over the wire and saw it went to the stopper of a glass vial perched on top of a barrel of whitish powder. Hancock was an inventor of weapons. I guessed this was one of his creations.

Fogarty carefully unhooked the wire from the loops on either side of the doorway and pushed it to the side. Now no one could accidently trigger the fire or explosion or whatever Lord Hancock had planned. We walked on, smelling wood rot and stale air, until we reached the back of the house, where we found a door with light showing underneath.

Fogarty set down his lantern and pulled out his pistol. Then, with a nod, he pushed open the door and the three of us spilled into the room.

I had never seen a room like it before. Once it had been a small ballroom, but now it was covered with tables holding glass vials in metal stands with gas jets underneath, glass tubes running from glass jar to glass jar, and clear containers of different-colored powders and liquids. In one corner, barrels were stacked up. The air smelled of sulfur and coal fires and spices.

In the very center in the crossroads of two aisles, Emma

sat bound to a large wooden chair with thick ropes. Her head drooped forward. There was blood on her skirt. I reached for my dagger.

Fogarty put out a hand to stop me.

"I'm glad someone in your group has some sense." Lord Hancock, in a heavy canvas coat like the one Lady Westover wore for gardening, stood facing us a few feet away from Emma. He stood behind a table three rows back, measuring an orange powder into a beaker.

Emma looked up then, and I saw relief in her eyes. She tried to squirm, but she was tied too tightly to move more than a shiver. Then she glanced upward.

That was when I noticed the beaker of clear liquid poised over Emma's head. It was held in place by a rope and pulley that ran through a glass dish containing a reddish jelly. The dish was on a metal stand. A few inches beneath the dish sat an upright tubular gas jet, and Lord Hancock stood near the gas jet. He set down the beaker and picked up a friction match.

"Would you like a demonstration of how this works? I'd love to show you, but I don't think your friend would like the outcome. Acid causes such frightful burns."

I thought for a moment I'd throw up. Emma was so incredibly beautiful, inside and out. I'd never once regretted my decision years before to take her in. She was my sister in all but name, and at that moment she depended on me to save her. "Why did you abduct her from the ball?"

"You were the only two not announced by name. The Ice Queen and the Fire Queen? Really? I was certain you were from the interfering Archivist Society. If it weren't for you and the rest of your nosy group, I'd have Nicholas Drake and my papers. I'd be free to continue my work."

I had to find a way to stop this madman. Taking a deep breath to steady my heartbeat, I said, "But why abduct Emma?"

"To use her for a trade, of course. Her life for Nicholas Drake and his papers."

As long as he was talking, he wouldn't strike the match and Emma would be safe for the moment. "Why use Emma for a trade? Wouldn't anyone do?"

"She's part of the Archivist Society. The society found Nicholas Drake. I want him. Turn him over to me. Now." He waved the gas jet to his left. "And make this man disappear."

Glancing in the direction he pointed, I saw Sumner standing with his weight on the balls of his feet and a knife poised in his hand. He and Fogarty seemed to have reached some sort of agreement with the slightest of moves.

Hoping I'd make a good distraction, I took two steps forward but I wasn't nearly close enough to pull Emma free. How long did we have until Hancock decided to act? The man was insane. "Why did you bring Emma here? I thought you'd moved out."

"It's being stolen from me by my creditors. I used it to get loans to continue my research, but I've not been able to sell any of my ideas and couldn't repay the loans. They've been trying to take this away from me since last summer. My laboratory!"

"Why bring Emma here when you never let anyone in?"

"Because I knew you couldn't resist coming here to search for her. And I have the advantage of knowing every inch of my laboratory and what each chemical will do."

I tried again. "Why are you doing all this?"

His sneer said he didn't think I was too bright. "Ultimately? Recognition in my field. My inventions in use by the British army. Respect. Drake stands in my way. He and those damnable papers will ruin me. I should have destroyed them long ago, but I didn't know about the one until recently when Drake told me what he'd stolen from Daisy. And I kept the other locked safely in here where only I would see it. That letter's a memento of my cleverness. That is, until Drake broke in here and stole my prize from me."

"It wasn't very clever to let Drake gain the upper hand." Seeing his eyes narrow and his grip on the gas jet tighten, I knew I'd erred badly. I held up my hands, palms out. "We're not experts in your field. And Drake knows nothing about weapons. He's not in a position to order your inventions. What do you want with him?"

"I don't want him. I want what he has. His blackmail papers." Lord Hancock struck the match.

"What's in Drake's papers that you want?" Desperation clogged my voice. I knew Lord Hancock could hear it. I certainly could.

"That's none of your business." He moved the match toward the gas jet as he turned it on.

"Wait! If it's a document or letter, Drake doesn't have it any longer."

He turned off the gas and blew out the match. "What do you mean, 'any longer'?"

"He sold all his papers. He handed them over to a buyer tonight. You don't have to worry about Nicholas Drake any longer."

"Who did he sell them to?"

"The Duke of Blackford."

"Bloody hell. He's worse to negotiate with than Drake. Where is he now?"

"I don't know. All I know is the duke said he's giving the papers to someone else. All of the papers."

"Who?"

"Someone who would never harm you." My voice rattled from my shivers.

"Who?" Louder this time.

"The head of the Archivist Society. Sir Broderick duVene."

He stared at me for a moment before speaking, and I

exhaled with exhaustion. I hadn't realized how stiffly I was holding myself in my terror over Emma's plight.

"He's giving all the blackmail letters to the head of the Archivist Society? After he paid good money for them? Why would he do that?"

I had captured Hancock's attention for the moment. I hoped I could hold it until someone thought of a way to stop him or to free Emma. "Blackford only wanted a few of them that belonged to him. He doesn't care about the rest of the letters."

"It doesn't matter whether it's Blackford or Sir Broderick who reads them. Once those letters are read, I'm a dead man." He began a crooning wail as he twisted his whole body from side to side.

"You're a dead man? Why? What could be so terrible?" Anything to keep him talking.

"Army headquarters rejected my latest invention today. The official said not to worry. Perhaps some other time." He gave a hysterical laugh. "And the chair of the Royal Society told me they'll reconsider my application for full membership in the autumn. Said he was sorry. Nothing he could do. I need two useful inventions, not just one, to become a full member."

His laugh turned into a sob. "I won't have another chance. My creditors will seize my laboratory. I'll hang. Anything that's left will go to either my creditors or a distant cousin as the next Lord Hancock. I'll miss out on the accolades and the successes that should have been mine. Mine! All my life I've had to take second place to someone else. My perfect older brother. Other scientists. Well, no more." He held a match against the friction paper.

I had to say something to stop him. "Surely you haven't done anything so terrible. And what about your niece, Daisy? Who will take care of her?"

"Who cares about Daisy? All she cares about is money

and parties. I never guessed she'd kept her last letters from her parents. Stupid chit. Or that her father would write her about his discovery. She should have died with her parents."

What a terrible man. I looked at him, furiously trying to think of something to calm him down while my own blood boiled. I tried to sound serene. "Perhaps if you talk to Sir Broderick—"

Jacob was inching his way to the left when Hancock looked at him and said, "No. Sir Broderick can do more damage than Drake. He'll recognize the importance of those papers. He'll give them to the police. It's finished. All I can do now is as much damage as I can to the Archivist Society and Drake and Blackford. That'll give me a chance to escape the country. I'll either escape or hang, and I won't hang." He lit the gas and stepped away.

I dove straight down the middle of the room. Fogarty and Sumner both took the right side, after Hancock, and Jacob the left. The rope seemed to weaken almost immediately as the jelly in the saucer began to liquefy from the heat.

There was no time to cut Emma's bonds and set her free. I ran for the chair and shoved it in front of me until we smashed into a heavy table on the far side of the room. I heard glass break and something sizzle behind me.

I stepped to the side and looked back. A puddle of glass melted into liquid steaming and bubbling on the wooden floor. I checked my skirt and shoes. Apparently I'd moved far enough away not to be splattered by the breakage.

Jacob ran down an aisle between beakers and gas jets, knocking things over in his rush to reach us. He pulled out his knife and cut Emma free as I removed her gag. She choked and coughed, but she managed to gasp out, "He covered my face with something noxious. The next thing I knew, I was tied up here."

I looked Emma over for signs of injury. Her face and arms

were bruised and she had small cuts on her hands. "Are you all right?"

"Where did he go?" she cried out frantically, whipping her head from side to side.

I glanced around. Lord Hancock, Fogarty, and Sumner had all vanished. I didn't see any door or stairs to exit. "I don't—oh, dear Lord. Let's get out of here." A fire had broken out on one of the worktables and was spreading from beaker to vial as glass shattered and acrid smoke rose.

The room was rapidly filling with a noxious fog, hiding any escape. I could hear Jacob coughing and something nearby sizzling. Breathing burned my lungs. The air smelled like a sewer. We were trapped.

For one terrible moment, I stood paralyzed. To my right, flames shot toward the ceiling. My parents' voices cried out to me from the fire, telling me to save myself. The way they had shouted to me the night they died.

Not this time. This time I would save my friends.

I grabbed Emma's arm and lifted. She rose stiffly and then Jacob pulled her along. I pushed her, following in the trail of their coughs as the smoke grew denser. Then I heard breaking glass in front of me.

The smoke cleared enough for me to see Jacob had smashed a metal stand through a window. Smoke slid out the gaping hole in the glass, but iron bars kept us in.

"We've got—to get out," Emma managed between coughs.

"This way. Through the house." Fear paralyzed every thought but one. I was determined not to fail again. I grabbed her hand and led her along the wall until we reached a corner. Perhaps ten strides more and we'd be at the door leading into the house. And freedom.

A popping, swishing sound came from in front of me. A bright band of fire raced for the barrels in the corner. I had no idea what was in them, but it couldn't be good. "Run."

I pulled Emma behind me as I rushed for the door. I wouldn't leave her behind. Yanking it open, I hurdled through the doorway and ran, tripping over my skirt. Emma collided with me and Jacob brushed our sides as we fell. He jerked Emma up by the grip he kept on her arm.

"Get out!" I yelled at the top of my lungs, not certain if anyone else remained in the building. Pulling myself up by clutching a door frame, I held my torn skirt up with one hand and raced after the other two Archivists.

I was in the front doorway when a great wind and a huge boom blew me forward. I crashed into Jacob. We both fell into the tall grass and weeds as fire arched over our heads. I kept my face down as searing heat scorched my back and objects pummeled me.

Just when I thought I couldn't stand the pain any longer, the wind died away. I looked behind me to see fire in every window of the house. Smoke glowed pale in the night sky above my head. Jacob and Emma lay sprawled on the grass in front of me. We were alive. I rose, my hairdo slipping into my eyes and hanging to my shoulders, and looked for Fogarty, Sumner, and Lord Hancock.

They were nowhere to be seen.

CHAPTER TWENTY-ONE

A tall, antique carriage rumbled up the street behind matching black horses and stopped behind our borrowed conveyance. I walked to the edge of the road, putting one foot wearily in front of the other. Now that Emma was safe, now that Lord Hancock and the others were missing, I lacked the energy to speak, much less walk. This night, with its glamorous ball, had been horrible.

The duke leaped down from the ancient carriage, his high-wayman costume ridiculously appropriate in this setting. He plucked the tiara off the side of my head where it had come to rest. "You're a wreck."

I glared in reply. "You're very kind. What papers did Drake have of Hancock's?"

I could hear the fire wagons racing toward us and a bobby blowing an alarm on his whistle. A series of coughs left me unable to catch my breath. The smoke from the house made my lungs burn.

The duke put a protective arm around me. "You need to sit down. I'll help you into the carriage."

"Not until I find out what Drake stole from Lord Hancock and where Hancock, Fogarty, and Sumner are now."

I shivered and the duke pulled me closer, supporting my weight. His breath warmed my ear as he said, "Daisy invited Drake to a large gathering here last season. During the party, Drake pinched a letter from Daisy's room. A letter written to her by her father, the late Lord Hancock, dated shortly before his death while she was visiting her mother's family in the country. It contained his formula for the amylnitrohydrated sulfate."

"Hancock's one big success." I tried to remember what I'd learned about the formula.

"Published by Hancock a few months after his brother's death. Whatever honors he received in the world of chemistry came from stealing a formula from a dead man."

I shook my head. "No wonder everything he's done since then has been a failure."

The duke stared at the burning house. "Or been too unstable for practical use."

I coughed again. Breathing was coming easier now and it made me light-headed in relief. "I don't think he meant to blow up the house. I think we might have done that saving Emma. Beakers seemed to break and set off the next glass dish and so on to barrels stacked in one corner of the laboratory. But he did say he wanted to destroy you and Drake and the Archivist Society before he escapes or hangs."

Firemen raced past us dragging a hose. Water sprayed onto the house in a stream, but it was too late to save anything. The roof rose and sank in rumbling waves before another hose could pour more water into the building from another direction.

With a shout, the firemen drove everyone back as the roof fell into the house with a mighty crash of sparks and thunder.

The sight was an all too familiar one and I shivered at the memory of that day twelve years before. The day I made the choice to rescue Sir Broderick first.

I turned away from the house, sickened by my memories.

A bobby came up to us. "Is there anyone inside?"

"I don't think so," I told him and discovered I was crying.

"Are you the homeowner?" he asked the duke.

"No." He looked at me. "Where is Lord Hancock?"

I bit back my sobs and swallowed. "Fogarty and Sumner chased him out of the lab while we got Emma out. I didn't see or hear any servants."

"The house has stood empty for months," the bobby said. "It's been an eyesore for the neighborhood and a target of young boys with their catapults and stones. Few in this neighborhood will be sorry to see it burn down."

More hoses were dragged across the scraggly lawn and pointed at the fire. The water began to dampen the fire, or perhaps it was burning itself out.

A figure trudged toward us out of the darkness into the blazing light encircling the fiery building. When he reached us, Fogarty said, "I lost him," and dropped to a sitting position among the weeds, breathing hard.

If I'd had more energy, I'd have found a way to hug him. "I'm glad you're safe," I said, patting his shoulder.

"Not the ending we expected," Fogarty replied, his chest heaving as he pulled in air.

Emma reached us, supported on one side by Jacob. He jostled her and she shook him off. "That's enough. Georgia, are you all right?"

I realized I was still hanging on to the duke for support. I straightened and jumped forward guiltily, feeling the loss of all the warmth and security that had enveloped me. "Yes. The smoke took my breath away."

Embarrassed, I turned to Adam Fogarty. "Where did you lose Lord Hancock?"

"A few blocks away. He might have doubled back, but I couldn't find him anywhere."

"Any idea where he intends to go?"

"None."

"Where's Sumner?" Emma asked.

"Here." Sumner stumbled into the light. Dark liquid puddled between his fingers where he clutched his arm. Sweat beaded along his hairline, and he was missing his hat.

"Oh, no." Emma ran and put an arm around him.

I covered my face with my fingers. "I'm so sorry. What happened?"

Sumner gave Emma a grimace and turned to the duke. "Stupid mistake. He was waiting in the branches of a tree. Jumped down on me. I got stabbed by my own knife. Lost him."

The fire was dying down and under the control of the fire brigade. The police didn't need us any longer. Jacob handed over Emma's tiara and then he and Fogarty departed in the unmarked carriage that had been lent to us by the duke. Sir Broderick would be waiting for details of the night's misadventure and could use help sorting through the letters purchased from Drake.

After traveling to the duke's home to drop off Sumner for medical care and the jewels for safekeeping, Emma and I were escorted to Lady Westover's by the Duke of Blackford in his ancient carriage. We were silent the entire trip, and Emma kept twisting her fingers.

Although she met us wearing a dressing wrap over her nightgown, I suspected Lady Westover had not gone to bed. She appeared wide awake when we arrived, ordering her sleepy-looking servants to fix tea while her lady's maid helped us out of our ruined gowns and into our everyday shirtwaists and skirts.

As I looked at the burns and tears in the Fire Queen costume, I felt my eyes dampen and my throat tighten at the loss. I hadn't expected to wear that dress again. I wasn't born to be a queen. But my dream of waltzing with the duke and being admired by men and women alike was not to be.

I caught Emma hiding a yawn, which started me yawning. Lady Westover came in and frowned at my wide-open mouth.

"Come along. The sooner you tell my grandson and me what happened, the sooner you can get to your beds."

We found the Duke of Blackford and Detective Inspector Grantham waiting in the parlor, brandy glasses in their hands.

"Do you want tea or would you rather have brandy?" Lady Westover asked.

"Tea. I can barely stay awake now," I told her. "How much have you heard, Inspector?"

"I've learned about the letter Mr. Drake stole from Miss Daisy and how Lord Hancock couldn't allow anyone to know his late brother created the formula. How any evidence that his brother created the compound would have been in the laboratory Hancock never let anyone into, and that has now burned down. The surviving Hancock made the fortune he subsequently lost and his reputation from his brother's formula. I take it this is why Drake was attacked and then disappeared. Blackmail is a dangerous game," Grantham said.

"Drake swears he never tried to blackmail Hancock," Blackford said.

"Then he was the only person in your club he didn't try to blackmail," I said in a peevish tone. It was late, I was tired, and I had run out of patience for circling the truth.

"Drake is a known blackmailer?" Inspector Grantham asked, looking at Emma and me.

"Yes," I said.

"No," Blackford said. When I glared at him, he said, "Not provably. None of his victims will admit to it, in part because most of them have managed to extricate themselves."

"Are you telling me there's no sense starting an investigation?" the inspector asked.

"There's no proof of a crime," Blackford said.

"What about the letters and papers Drake sold to you tonight?" I asked.

"They're not proof of a crime unless someone wants to

come forward and press charges." Blackford gave me a cold smile over his brandy snifter.

"And no one will press charges for blackmail against the wishes of a duke." I gave him a hard stare.

"Georgia," Lady Westover began in her *remember where you are* voice, "you must be overwrought from the dangers you faced tonight. Your ball gowns were all sooty and torn. Surely you'll feel better after a good night's sleep."

"Sir Broderick and I plan to return all of the letters to their rightful owners, or burn them if the owners are dead," Blackford murmured.

I nearly jumped to my feet, and then remembered where I was. "You did all this—the dresses, the jewels, the invitations—to buy back letters you had no intention of keeping?"

"Yes."

"Why? Do you want sainthood? Or just the power to make people leap at your every command? I don't think a good night's sleep will help this, Lady Westover."

"Miss Fenchurch," the duke began.

I'd had enough of the Duke of Blackford pulling the strings while the Archivist Society danced. I rose and stormed from the room, not knowing if I was angrier at him or at myself. I wanted to believe his goal was the same as ours. Instead, he was circumventing justice.

He caught up to me in the hall. "Georgia, listen to me."

I spun around and glared at him. "While you subvert the course of justice? No. And it's 'Miss Fenchurch,' Your Grace."

"Miss Fenchurch, I am not subverting justice. I am giving a bright young man and his very loyal wife a chance to start over without having to resort to crime to fund their lifestyle. I think Canada will be a good place for them to begin again. And Mrs. Drake has a sister there."

I had forgotten about Edith, whose name Anne had borrowed. Staring into his eyes, I said, "Be truthful with me. Now that you have the letters, be truthful with me for a change. Why did you hide your sister's death?"

He gazed at a spot over my head, but I knew he wasn't studying the coffered ceiling. "You went to Blackford and saw her grave. Didn't you?"

I nodded and he continued. "You're resourceful, I'll grant you that. I didn't plan to keep it a secret forever. Only until I took her letters, her embarrassing letters, back from Drake. He made me pay for his silence. He wouldn't give them to me because he knew I let her die."

I grabbed hold of his arm. "You didn't let her die. You weren't there."

"He holds me responsible for her death, just as I do. Her letters spell out how Drake was going to help her escape my control, how I was unfairly imprisoning her, how I sided with Victoria, everything. Drake gave me copies of them. He held those letters to remind me how wrong I'd been about Margaret, how I'd failed her, and how I'd forced her to make her daring escape."

He leaned forward, scowling so close to my face I was forced to bend backward to keep him in focus. His clothes had captured the smoke from the fire and he smelled of brimstone. His straight hair now ended in a few curls at the nape of his neck. I could have sworn his hair was rigidly straight when we arrived at Lady Westover's.

"I wasn't there, but I should have been. From her letters, from the reports I was getting from the castle, I thought Margaret was getting better. I learned later she was hiding things from me. She believed Drake could give her the freedom I wouldn't, while I kept thinking Drake was a good influence on her. If I'd been there, I could have stopped Margaret before she reached the river. I could have saved her."

Tears filled my eyes. How many times had I said similar words to myself? "No. You couldn't have. I was right there, and I couldn't save my family."

Puzzlement, followed by dawning understanding and then sympathy crossed his face. "That's why you work with the Archivist Society? To help others so they don't suffer like you have?"

Thinking of the murderer hardened my expression and I crossed my arms protectively over my chest. "Someday I'll find the man who killed my parents and stop him from killing ever again."

He nodded. "I'm certain you will." He studied the ceiling again. "Tomorrow I'll have my solicitor correct the records concerning Margaret's death. I've given up blaming Drake for encouraging her to escape. It's time to let her rest in peace."

He sounded so mournful for his sister. Had he shown as much grief for his fiancée? "If she can. Did she kill Victoria?"

He stared at the floor. "Mrs. Potter told me about your questions. Did you learn anything more than I did?"

"Lady Margaret ordered lilies of the valley for a floral arrangement that day. Lilies are highly poisonous, even the leaves Sally saw her cutting up into pieces. If Margaret had somehow put them into the tea, anyone who drank it would have died of symptoms similar to Miss Victoria's."

"That's pure speculation, and certainly nothing that can be proven years later."

My voice rose in fury as I confronted him. "What I find distressing is that you suspected what she'd done, and you did nothing about it. She may have murdered the woman you were supposed to spend the rest of your life with. You were supposed to love and protect Victoria, and instead, you protected her killer."

"I sent Margaret away. Locked her up. I imprisoned my half sister on a suspicion that she might have killed my fiancée. *Might* have. If she didn't, my lack of trust could well have been what sent Margaret to such despair that she deliberately went into the water. And if anyone was guilty of Victoria's death, it was Victoria and me."

He glared into my eyes as the twin scents of brandy and smoke enveloped us. His face became a mask of rage, but I couldn't tell if he was about to strangle me or burst into flame. "Victoria rode her hard and I stood by and let her do it. Victoria said I coddled her too much, and I believed her. Don't women know more about raising younger half sisters than men?"

"I don't know."

"Neither do I. And Victoria seemed so certain. That was the one thing I liked about her. Our marriage was to be a dynastic union. She told me so from the start. She'd give me an heir, but not her heart. I didn't realize until too late she didn't have one to give."

If that was Victoria Dutton-Cox's epitaph, I felt very sorry for her.

The duke must have been overtired, or I doubted he'd have been so open with me. "I was relieved when Victoria died. By then, I'd realized the marriage would be a mistake. She was too rough on Margaret and too disinterested in anything about me but my title. I was so embarrassed when Victoria died, because all I could feel was thankful.

"The way everyone, including me, watched her after Victoria died made Margaret snap. I thought she was doing better, but after that day she lost what little connection she had to reality. I had no choice but to take her back to Castle Blackford."

"Are you saying Margaret was insane when she killed Victoria? Her plan was very clever. She nearly escaped detection." I'd hoped to get the truth, but what I heard was as inconclusive as everything else.

"As Margaret grew older, she'd lose the threads that tied her to reality for periods of time. She told me shortly before Victoria died that she'd been thinking a lot about her mother. That should have warned me. We have never had insanity in the Ranleigh bloodline. Margaret's mother was the first to bring it into our family. She loved Margaret, but not enough to stop her from killing herself in front of the child."

I realized my mouth was hanging open over this revelation, and I snapped it shut.

He shook his head. "Margaret's mother suffered from the same . . . confusion as Margaret did. In the grip of madness, she threw herself off the castle walls onto the rocks below. Margaret was a young girl, but old enough to understand what she saw. She was too afraid to ever go near the castle walls again.

"As Margaret grew older, the same malady showed up in her. I didn't want to believe it, but I had to make certain Margaret never married and passed on this curse."

"How awful. I'm sorry."

He didn't seem to notice as he continued. "As soon as the wedding was over, I planned to take my sister back to Blackford Castle under the guise of showing my bride her new home. I felt if I kept Margaret there, she and Victoria would both be easier to live with." He let out a deep sigh. "Events overtook my plans."

A throat cleared behind us. "Grandmama thought you might be in need of a chaperone. I thought you might prefer it not be her."

Blackford gave him a sad smile. "I've heard the police can be very tight-lipped."

Inspector Grantham nodded in reply.

"I was just assuring Miss Fenchurch that Scotland Yard will find Lord Hancock. He's still free to cause trouble, and I'm afraid after tonight's events he's gone completely mad."

"Do you know where Mr. Drake is?" Grantham asked.

There was a slight pause before Blackford said, "He went home to pack. He and his wife will be leaving England tomorrow from Southampton."

"I'll have a guard posted at his house until he leaves. If Lord Hancock goes after him again, we'll catch him." The inspector said his good-byes and went back into the parlor.

I started to follow, but the duke reached out and caught my arm at the elbow. "You won't tell anyone?"

"No. It's not my story to tell." The Archivist Society seemed to be in possession of more secrets than our government intelligence services.

Blackford smiled. "Drake insisted you be present at the ball while we negotiated the price of the papers he held. He didn't trust me to act fairly with him, but he trusts you. I arranged for your invitation and costume so he could find you easily, and Miss Keyes's so you'd have a chaperone. I thought you'd want to know."

I didn't return his smile, still angry about the danger he'd put Drake in. "I also know why Hancock and Waxpool's man Price were both at the ball tonight. They knew Drake would be there. And you were the one who told them."

"Yes." I must have looked ready to create havoc, because he continued, "The best way to catch whoever was after Drake was to tell them where he'd be."

"No wonder Drake doesn't trust you to act fairly with him."

"If I had known my actions would put you or Miss Keyes in danger, I wouldn't have told a soul." He cupped my cheek in the palm of his hand and gazed into my eyes. "I'm sorry."

I stared back at him, amazed to hear an apology from a duke, especially this one. "Are you really sorry?"

"Yes. I'd never deliberately do anything to hurt you or Miss Keyes." He stared at my mouth, then shook his head and stepped back. "Now, I think it's time that I take you both home. I want you to know I'll see Sir Broderick in the morning to properly thank him for the help of the Archivist Society." And then the most extraordinary thing happened. He bowed to me. A duke bowed to me.

Drawing on the regal persona I had worn with my Fire Queen costume, I smiled and gave him a nod such as our queen might bestow on her subjects.

CHAPTER TWENTY-TWO

THE duke and I gathered Emma on our way out, thanked Lady Westover for her hospitality, and went out into the early morning darkness to climb into the towering carriage. I stopped and looked up, hoping to see the stars. I wanted to see something clean and pure outside of my narrow boundaries. Grayish clouds blocked the sky and wisps of fog swirled around still-burning street lamps and trickled down basement stairs. The street smelled of sulfur. The world matched my mood.

The ride home was quick, since we'd found the time after the partygoers and theater enthusiasts traveled home and before the tradesmen and market stallholders went to work. The clip-clop of horse hooves on pavement was the only sound until Emma said, "Please let me know how Mr. Sumner recovers from his wounds. He was a great help at Lord Hancock's until the Archivist Society arrived."

"He's a brave man," the duke said.

"Yes, and a thoughtful one. His actions ensured I stayed alive until you came to rescue me, Georgia."

"What—?" I began, but she shook her head. I was too tired to ask anything more.

I was falling asleep on my feet by the time we reached the door to the flat and the duke made his escape, but Phyllida wanted to hear about the ball. As soon as we mentioned Emma's abduction, she pulled Emma tightly to her breast and cried out, "Thank God you're safe. That you're both safe. Georgia, you take too many risks."

"I had a job to do. And Emma was dancing with Henry the Eighth."

"And you know what happened to his wives."

I blinked as a smile crossed Phyllida's face. It was late, and I was too tired to think of a reply.

After a moment, Emma rose, kissed Phyllida on the cheek, and said it was time that we all got to sleep.

I couldn't have agreed more.

EVEN IF JACOB and Fogarty had already given Sir Broderick a full accounting, both Emma and I wanted to tell him our thoughts on the events of the previous night. Rising early after a very late night followed by little sleep, we turned down Phyllida's offer of breakfast and headed out into the busy London streets.

Every bakery and kitchen window we passed gave off luscious smells that reminded us we'd not eaten since our early dinner at Lady Westover's the day before. We'd only have enough time to talk to Sir Broderick and hopefully be offered some of Dominique's biscuits before it would be time to open the bookshop.

We hadn't bothered with our cloaks, since the day was sunny and the cool air would help to wake us up. I hoped my sleepy brain would be able to make change in the shop, since I wasn't awake enough to see the brewer's cart barreling down on us until Emma pulled me out of the way.

We cut through the park in Bloomsbury Square and hurried to Sir Broderick's door, pulled on the bell, and waited. And waited.

"Maybe Jacob is busy getting Sir Broderick dressed and didn't hear the bell." I rang again.

When Jacob still didn't appear, Emma grumbled, "I'm hungry," and grabbed the doorknob. It turned in her hand and the door silently opened.

No one locked their front doors when there were always servants around to answer any summons, so we walked in. I was surprised not to see someone hurrying in our direction. We were halfway up the stairs to the study before I thought to call out, "Hello?"

"Now is not a good time," Sir Broderick replied. Something in his voice made me hesitate, but Emma pushed around me on the stairs and kept going.

"Sir Broderick, you wouldn't believe what—" Her voice died away as she hesitated in the doorway.

"Come in, young lady. Have a seat over here, next to the cook."

Lord Hancock's voice. Why was he here? Where was Drake?

Emma stood rooted in place.

"Come in. I insist. Or I'll shoot Sir Broderick right now."

Emma moved slowly into the room. I crept back down the stairs, keeping my feet close to the wall so there was less chance of a board squeaking. My heart thumped in my ears. If Hancock didn't hear me, I could get out of here and summon help.

Each step was a gamble and the staircase went on forever. When it finally ended, I still had to cross the endless entry hall. So far, none of the wooden boards had creaked and given me away. How much longer would my luck last?

My breath caught in my throat as my foot hesitated before taking the first step.

"What did you do to him?" I heard Emma say loudly. "He's bleeding." I took two quick steps while her voice covered my movements.

"He'll be fine as long as you follow directions." Hancock used a quieter voice, but the menace was unmistakable. I balanced on my toes, ready to move again when there was more noise upstairs.

"Oh, this is terrible. You must stop this at once. I insist. He needs medical attention," Emma shouted again. This time, the volume of her voice hid my steps across the entry hall and opening the door.

I slipped out and eased the door shut behind me. Then I looked up and down the street in a panic. No sign of a bobby. I decided my best chance was toward New Oxford Street and rushed in that direction. People might have stared. I didn't care.

I'd run two blocks before I found a policeman. Relieved, I let my feet slow as I tried to pull air into my aching lungs. When I reached the bobby, I gasped out, "You must get a message to Inspector Grantham at Scotland Yard immediately. He's after a killer named Hancock. The man is in Sir Broderick duVene's house, holding him and others hostage. Inspector Grantham must come at once."

"I'll come with you, miss," the bobby said, sounding doubtful.

I grabbed his arm by his scratchy wool sleeve and stared into his eyes. "Not until you get a message to Inspector Grantham to come at once."

The bobby slowly pulled out his notebook and a pencil, and I let go of his arm.

"Inspector Grantham, Scotland Yard," I repeated. "Hancock has taken prisoners at Sir Broderick duVene's house. First-floor study. Come at once."

He laboriously printed every word. "And how would you know this?"

"I escaped from there."

His pencil hovered in midair. "How did you do that?"

"He didn't realize I was in the house. I sneaked out the front door. Hurry. We must get that note to Inspector Grantham immediately. He'll know what to do." I raised my voice, hoping futilely it would speed up his writing.

The constable flipped over to the next page in his notebook and continued printing. "And your name is . . . ?"

"Miss Georgia Fenchurch." My fingers itched to grab the pencil and write the message myself.

More printing, onto the third page. "And this Sir Broderick duVene. What's his address?"

"The inspector knows. That's why you need to see this message gets to him immediately."

A tall, antique carriage rounded the corner. I began to wave my arms frantically. "That's the Duke of Blackford. He'll help. We'll get this message passed on to Scotland Yard now," I shouted.

The duke, looking spotless and wearing perfect creases, without an errant curl in his precisely combed hair, climbed down from his carriage and set his top hat on his head. "Miss Fenchurch, what's wrong?"

I grabbed his arm, wrinkling the soft fabric of his coat sleeve. "Thank heavens you're here. Lord Hancock is holding Sir Broderick and Emma hostage in Sir Broderick's study at gunpoint."

"At gunpoint?" The bobby's pencil scratched faster across his notebook.

"Bloody hell, man. Get that message to Detective Inspector Grantham at Scotland Yard immediately," the duke said in his most commanding ducal tones. Then he called up to the carriage driver, "Take this police officer to Scotland Yard and wait for his return with Inspector Grantham. Sumner, come with us."

Sumner jumped down from the carriage, and the bobby

backed up at the first sight of his scarred face. With an evil-looking grin, Sumner said, "Need a hand up?"

The bobby darted past him and clambered inside.

The carriage took off, and Sumner and the duke rushed up the sidewalk with me. Sumner growled "He has Emma?" in his raspy voice.

"Yes."

Heat flashed in the man's eyes, and I suddenly felt almost sorry for Hancock. "How is your wounded arm, Mr. Sumner?"

"It won't slow me down."

The duke broke in with rapid-fire questions. "How long has he been there? Does he have any of his chemicals with him? What kind of a gun does he have?"

"I don't know. Emma went ahead of me, so she was the only one Hancock saw. I never reached the study. I left the house and went looking for help." I sounded like a coward to my ears, but it was the only plan I'd had at that moment. All I could do now was dash back into the house and pray none of my friends were hurt.

"Does he know you were in there?"

"He didn't seem to when I left."

"Sumner, are you armed?" the duke asked.

"Always."

"If you get a clear opening, take it. Don't wait for my permission once we enter the study."

Sumner nodded once.

We reached the house. "The door's unlocked and doesn't squeak. The study is upstairs and on the right," I whispered.

"Wait outside," the duke said.

"No. He won't be alarmed to see me. I can get in first and signal you as to where everyone is." I looked into both men's eyes. "You know it's the only way." I didn't see agreement, but I didn't care. Archivist Society members were in danger. I couldn't stand aside and leave them in peril.

I turned the knob and marched briskly and noisily across the hall and up the stairs, the duke in step with me at my back. "Sir Broderick?"

"This isn't a good time for a social call," he said loudly. I hoped Hancock hadn't learned I'd been here earlier with Emma.

"Anytime is a good time for a social call." I stomped up the rest of the stairs and stopped in the doorway to the study as if I'd hit a wall. I tried to speak but no words came out.

Jacob was tied up on the floor, his head bloody, his body limp. Emma and Dominique were tied back to back, their arms bound behind them. Both of them were gagged. The ropes binding one woman's legs wrapped around the other's throat. If either moved, the other died of strangulation. Sir Broderick sat in his wheeled chair, his hands pinned to the chair's arms, and his eyes looked past me to the door.

Lord Hancock was gone.

"Who did this?" I cried as I ran first to the two women. As my fingers fumbled with a knot, the Duke of Blackford reached around me with a knife and sliced the rope wrapped around Emma's throat.

I pulled the gag out of her mouth and she whispered, "Behind you."

I whirled around, air leaking from my lungs with a gasping sound. Lord Hancock had pushed the door half-closed so he could come out from the corner where he'd hidden. The barrel of the gun in his hand looked large enough to bring down an elephant.

The duke had already freed Dominique's neck by the time Hancock said, "So the duke arrived with Miss Fenchurch. Good. Now, who has my letters? Sir Broderick says you didn't give them to him last night. Miss Fenchurch told me you would."

Blackford sounded completely relaxed when he said, "I don't have your papers with me. I only planned to call on Sir Broderick this morning and discuss a transfer."

"Once again, I move against people to get back my papers, only to learn they don't have them. Blackford, you're no better than Drake."

"What do you mean, 'once again'?" I asked before I considered the wisdom of my words.

"I sent a fool with a bottle of phosphorus and other chemicals to burn down that house outside of Hounslow and get rid of Drake and the letters in one move. It wasn't until later I learned he got the wrong man and the letters weren't there. You can't imagine my disappointment." He sounded annoyed at the man's incompetence rather than sickened by the murder. Lord Hancock had to be mad, and I knew that didn't help our chances of getting out alive.

"Why do you want a copy of your old formula? You must know it by heart," Blackford asked.

"I want my brother's letter to Daisy because of what it proves. And don't try to hide your knife. Set it down on the rug. Good. Now kick it over here."

The duke did as he was told with an air of complete indifference. "What does the letter prove?"

Hancock kicked the knife to the corner of the room without taking his eyes off us. "You know very well what it proves. That my brother developed the formula before he died. And that I killed him and his wife."

"Why would you kill your own brother? Just for the formula or for the title?" I asked. I needed to keep him talking. Sumner had to be nearby, ready to rescue us.

"The title is useless. It didn't come with anything but debts. I sold off everything I could, but it wasn't enough. The formula gained me money and fame for a while, but now I need to come up with another invention as successful as the first. Another chemical compound that will bring me lots of money and full membership in the Royal Society."

"But your laboratory was destroyed."

"All the fault of that clumsy young man there. If he hadn't

knocked over those beakers, the fire wouldn't have traveled to the explosives. I kept them safely tucked away in the corner so nothing would happen to them. One reason why I didn't want people marching through my laboratory." Watching us all the time, he walked over to where Jacob lay and kicked him in the stomach.

I couldn't let him abuse Jacob. I took two steps toward him. "Where are you going to find another laboratory?"

"After I finish with all of you, I'll have to escape back to Africa. There I'll study the effects of plants on humans. I have experience in the field. I'll regain my fame. I just need to find the right plant."

"Going to practice on yourself?" Blackford asked, his arms crossed over his chest.

"Of course not. There are plenty of natives I can use."

"They may not like it," I suggested. What was taking Sumner so long? Then I realized. Hancock was staying to the side of the doorway. Sumner would have to show himself before he could find Hancock to kill him, and by then, Sumner would be dead.

"That's of small importance."

"Tell me about poisoning your brother," Blackford said.

"You know how I killed him? Oh, yes, you've read the other letter." He kept the gun trained on me. I kept my chin up to mask my trembling and watched him. "It was Daisy's birthday. My brother and his wife were having a family dinner with their wretched daughter. I'd already said I had a previous engagement. One of my brother's favorite dishes was cooked with spinach fresh from the garden. It was easy to mix a quantity of leaves from the foxglove growing in the flower garden into the basket and remove some of the spinach. The effect of foxglove isn't diminished by cooking." His chest seemed to swell and his smile reminded me of the expression "licked his chops."

"But Daisy survived," I said.

"You can't imagine how disappointed I was to be saddled with that self-important little minx. It turned out she didn't like spinach, so her parents allowed her to decline the dish. Can you imagine? A child telling her parents what she will or will not eat? Preposterous."

"But why kill them for the formula?" I asked.

"I knew he had discovered something clever. Something that would make money. And more importantly, something that would garner praise from the Royal Society. Though how he could come up with a brilliant formula when all he did was dabble, while I devoted my life to scientific research, was something I don't understand. Of course, he had that wonderful laboratory. I wanted that, too." Lord Hancock frowned at Blackford and raised his pistol to aim straight at the duke's heart.

He nodded toward a coil of rope on the floor. "Tie Miss Fenchurch up in that chair," he instructed the duke.

I began to walk toward the chair, encouraged by Hancock now pointing the gun at me. "You mentioned a letter?"

"Didn't the duke tell you? Daisy insisted on hosting a large party while we were still living at Chelling Meadows, during which Drake broke into my laboratory. He found the letter the cook wrote to her sister a few months after my brother's death, spelling out her suspicions.

"The cook'd been looking at me in an odd way. When she sneaked out of the house the night she was supposedly killed by a thief, she was going to mail the letter. At the time, the shortest way to the postbox was by the laboratory. I saw her and followed her. She never mailed the letter." He smiled and turned his head toward Blackford. "Tie her up."

Blackford had worked his way to the side wall. "You tie her up."

Hancock's finger moved on the trigger as he aimed at me. "Then she won't be tied up. I'll just shoot her."

CHAPTER TWENTY-THREE

"WAIT." I was certain Hancock was about to shoot me. He was crazy, and I had to stop the madman from killing me. Talking seemed to be my only weapon. "I don't understand why you didn't burn the letter. It's not proof of anything, but it seems dangerous to keep it."

"Why? It was in my laboratory. Mine. No one was ever allowed in. I could sit in my room, surrounded by my equipment, and look at the letter that showed how clever I'd been in removing the people who were in my way. Just as I'll remove the people who now put me in danger." Hancock aimed at my head and cocked the trigger.

I sat down hard in the chair as my knees gave out under me. The duke stalked toward him.

Hancock's hand shook as he swung around, backed up, and aimed at Blackford. He raised his voice to proclaim, "You may be a high and mighty duke, but I hold the gun."

"And I'm the only one who can get you your letters. You need me." The duke advanced. Hancock continued backward until he was clearly visible in the doorway.

"Hancock," a gravelly voice said.

Hancock wheeled around and fired as he tumbled onto his back, a knife handle protruding from his chest and the gun still in his grip. The noise in the small area shook the walls and left my heart pounding at a gallop. The room smelled of gunpowder like a Guy Fawkes Night celebration. Blackford stepped forward and grabbed the pistol. I could see there was no need to hurry. Hancock's hand was already lifeless.

I swung around to discover if Sumner was hurt. He appeared uninjured as he faced Blackford and pointed upward. There was a hole in the plastered ceiling near the doorway, with spidery cracks leading away in all directions and plaster dust sifting into a coating on the faded carpet.

After that, everything became a commotion. Inspector Grantham and several uniformed constables arrived in a clatter. Sir Broderick, Emma, Dominique, and Jacob were freed of their bonds. The police carried Jacob to his bed and sent for a doctor to examine him. Inspector Grantham examined the room before Hancock's body could be taken away for the police medical officer to examine. Blackford and Sumner followed Inspector Grantham as he pushed Sir Broderick in his wheeled chair into another room to hold a conference.

I sat on the sofa between Emma and Dominique, one arm around each of them as they spilled out their tears and their tale of Lord Hancock's rambling complaints. I listened to them and dried their tears, but my gaze kept returning to the closed door across the hall where the men were deciding Sumner's fate.

I was glad I didn't have to play a part in that conversation. My nerves were still on edge from facing that horrible pistol.

The doctor went into the other room and then left the house. We continued to sit. My fright changed to surprise as I looked at the ornately painted mantel clock and realized on any other day I'd be greeting customers in my bookshop.

My ordinary customers in my ordinary bookshop on my ordinary street. I hugged Emma tighter and blinked back my tears. She was still alive to work side by side with me.

Emma leaned her head on my shoulder. "Aunt Phyllida is going to be angry with me when she hears I was tied up twice by the same madman."

I could hear the gray-haired spinster lecturing us and began to laugh. Emma joined in until neither of us knew if our tears were from fright or hilarity.

We'd calmed down and dried our eyes by the time the men finally ended their conference. Grantham left with the bobbies. Sir Broderick talked to Emma and Dominique. Sumner stood brooding in a corner. And Blackford came to me.

"Georgia. Er, Miss Fenchurch, I'm going to Waterloo Station to see the Drakes off. If you and Miss Keyes would care to join me, I'll take you to your bookshop afterward."

I probably hadn't missed too many customers. And I did want to see this investigation finished. Perhaps I just wanted to make certain Drake left the country if he wasn't going to be prosecuted for his crimes. Spending a little more time with the duke was a bonus I hadn't planned on. "Yes, thank you, Your Grace. And you may call me Georgia."

"Call me Blackford." The hair at the nape of his neck seemed to be curling in a most beguiling fashion. I'd taken my gloves off to comfort Emma and Dominique, and without thinking I reached out to touch his curls and discover if they were as soft as they looked. They were wringing wet. His collar was soaked. Blackford may have appeared indifferent while we'd faced Hancock, but he'd broken out in a sweat. No doubt he was as frightened as I was.

He pulled away with a shocked look. When I continued to study his face, he gave me a fleeting smile before setting his expression into one of ducal disdain.

I shoved my surprise away and focused on the problem at

hand. "All right, Blackford. I don't understand why you didn't tell society Drake had been your stable boy and why you're letting him leave the country. His blackmail has had terrible consequences."

The duke's eyes proclaimed his honesty as he said, "I gave him my word as part of the deal to obtain his blackmail material, all his blackmail material, that I'd help him start a new life. I don't go back on my word."

"That was a terrible promise, Your Grace."

"It was his condition for exchanging his blackmail papers for pounds, and he made me promise, knowing I don't go back on my word."

We gathered Emma and Sumner and climbed into the duke's carriage. This time I was slightly more graceful about it. I decided I was getting too much practice.

Emma spent the ride fixing her hair, which had been mussed while she was tied up. Sumner sat across from her, staring with naked devotion in his eyes. I looked from him to the duke, caught Blackford's eye, and grinned as I nodded toward the other couple. He nodded solemnly.

We rode to Waterloo Station and easily found the Drakes. They were outside the station watching a porter load their luggage onto a cart to move it to the train. We climbed down to join them.

Immediately, Lord Naylard and his sister arrived, followed by Inspector Grantham with the finely dressed young Viscount Dalrymple and his wife. All of them appeared angry, and Viscount Dalrymple, standing beside the inspector, looked as if he would strike Drake. I stared at the group, trying to puzzle out why all these people were there to see off their blackmailer and his wife.

Sumner and the duke shifted slightly to fence the Drakes in on one side while a couple of constables took up positions behind them.

Drake forced a smile and said, "What is this?"

"Is this the man?" Inspector Grantham asked.

"Yes," Miss Lucinda Naylard said.

"That's the cur," the viscount responded, his hands in fists.

"Nicholas Drake," Grantham began, "I am arresting you on suspicion of blackmail."

"What?" Drake swung toward Blackford. "You promised."

"I promised I wouldn't press charges. But these honest citizens, once they received their stolen papers, have elected to press charges. The Earl of Waxpool has pressed charges in writing, since his health doesn't permit him to point you out to the law in person." Blackford smiled broadly.

"What? You can't!" Drake shouted as two bobbies fitted him with handcuffs. "I'll tell. I'll tell the papers!" he bellowed as he struggled against the policemen leading him away to a police carriage with bars and locks on the double doors on the back. "You'll be sorry, Blackford."

Anne Drake broke down and sobbed.

Blackford moved next to her. "You can go to Canada without him. You can go back to Blackford village. Or you can stay in his house in London and wait for him. Let me know when you make up your mind and I'll assist you. In the meantime, you have the money I gave him last night in exchange for the letters he stole."

She looked at him, tears streaming down her face, and nodded. He squeezed her hand and then turned away to assist me into the carriage.

The four of us took the same seats as before and the driver took off at Blackford's signal.

"You need to answer some questions, Your Grace," I said.

"And those are?"

"When did you find out about Viscount Dalrymple? He's not a member of your club, is he?"

"Yes, he is. Before they married, his wife, Elizabeth, wrote

Drake some foolish letters. Her parents, the Dutton-Coxes, paid Drake off, but her husband refused. Until last night, the viscount had avoided a private meeting with Drake so he was saved from knowing his wife was the one who wrote the letters Drake held. Once he read them, he was pleased to receive the letters in return for pressing charges. I don't believe Elizabeth was as happy to have those letters in her husband's hands."

My hand jerked up to cover my mouth. I knew how much Elizabeth didn't want her husband to see her childish correspondence. "When did the viscount get the letters?"

"All of the blackmail material was returned in the early hours of this morning. Three of the victims agreed to press charges."

"You must have been up all night." I was impressed with the duke's determination, but less so with his choice of recipients.

He yawned. "I can sleep all day. You have to work."

This was going to be a very long day in the bookshop. "I hope we can count on your help, and Sumner's, if the Archivist Society has need of you again." My smile must have told him how much I hoped I'd work with him again.

He nodded. "And I'll be sure to bring this carriage. You really believed I'd use a carriage given to my family by the Duke of Wellington to abduct a man?"

"Not once I got to know you. And the carriage."

He smiled at that.

We had almost reached the bookshop. "One more thing, Your Grace. Why didn't you give Drake away two years ago when you first saw him out in society? You knew he wasn't related to French royalty."

"Because he was my half sibling, the same as Margaret. His father was the old duke. He's family, even if he was born on the wrong side of the blanket, as they say. His mother was a parlor maid who had a long and loving affair with my father. My mother hated her and made her life hell. After the maid died in childbirth, my mother transferred her hatred to Nicholas. My mother died and was replaced by Margaret's mother, who was kind to the boy. Out of gratitude to her mother, Drake was always loyal to Margaret."

He looked out the carriage window and shook his head before he continued. "Drake was present at the first ball Margaret attended. At first, moving to London had improved my sister's state of mind, but by the time of the first ball, she was slipping badly into old habits. Sudden fits of temper, claiming to hear things that weren't there, making up preposterous tales. Something small set her off at the ball. Before I could reach her, Drake was there. He managed her beautifully. There was no scene to blot our family name, and she was fine the rest of the night."

"You were grateful to him." I knew I would have been if I were the duke.

His gaze stayed focused on the passing traffic. "That night, Margaret made me promise not to tell anyone about Drake's true parentage. Perhaps that was her greatest problem. I refused Margaret nothing. Drake kept warning me I was driving Margaret away by being too strict with her, and then giving her whatever she wanted. She confided in Drake." And then he added in a whisper, "She trusted him."

"Drake found out about Margaret's death almost immediately. He showed me copies of her letters and demanded my silence about his parentage in return for his not telling anyone about Margaret's death or her insanity. I took the easy way out and went along with his request. Until very recently, I didn't know he was doing anyone harm."

Staring into my eyes, he said, "As soon as I heard Drake was blackmailing others, I moved to get all his material returned to its rightful owners. It was my fault and my responsibility to correct."

"You're an honorable man, Your Grace." If an idiot for giving Dalrymple his wife's letters and letting Margaret's feud with Victoria get so far out of hand. He was a brilliant man, but not too bright.

"No. An honorable man wouldn't have encouraged others to press charges. But I'm a fair man. I'll see his wife gets a new start if she wants it."

"And the man I want to find?" The duke's help could prove invaluable.

"I'll look into the matter and see what I can learn."

The carriage came to a halt and a footman opened the door to help Emma and me descend to the crowded sidewalk. Emma headed not for the bookshop, but for the flat. No doubt she needed to tell Phyllida about her adventure and bury herself in the older woman's concern.

Door key in hand, I took our first mail delivery from the passing postman before I turned to face the open carriage window. "Thank you, Your Grace," I called up to him.

"No, Miss Fenchurch, thank you. Until next time." The carriage waited to pull into traffic while I glanced at the three letters in my hand. The top one was addressed to me in a firm, tight script and marked *Private.*

I ripped open the envelope and pulled out a single sheet of expensive paper without a letterhead.

I'm sorry we won't have a chance to meet during my current trip to London, Miss Fenchurch, but business calls me away. You appear to have done well for yourself, moving both your home and your bookshop to better locations in the past few years. I'm sure your parents would be proud of you.

Your move without finding the Gutenberg Bible tells me your father didn't hide my property for Mr. Lupton. While I realize you blame me for your parents' death, it was not my fault. I was simply seeking the return of my property. Instead, blame those who have separated me from my prize possession.

I hope you enjoyed the Duke of Arlington's ball. Perhaps you will tell me about it on my next trip to London.

No. The letter was unsigned, but my racing heartbeat told me I knew.

He couldn't leave. Not now. Not when I finally had a chance to find him. To capture him. And all this time he'd been following me.

London's busyness and traffic faded. I looked around, expecting to see the remembered face as a winter's chill invaded my body. I backed up, putting my shoulders against the glass window of my shop for the feeblest of protection. I felt vulnerable in the midst of the swarm of people along the street.

I looked for the duke's carriage, but it had disappeared into the traffic on Charing Cross Road.

Quickly unlocking the door to the bookshop, I slipped in and flipped over the sign to *Open*. It was time to attempt getting back to normal. To the day before the duke entered my life and the murderer reappeared before me.

I refolded the letter and hid it under the counter, but I couldn't get rid of my desire to look over my shoulder. I knew someday both the Duke of Blackford and the killer would return.

I planned to be ready.